I0789480

K.A. KNIGHT
WRITING THE MONSTERS YOU LOVE TO HATE.

THE NATIONS

THEIR CHAMPION BOOK FOUR

K.A. KNIGHT

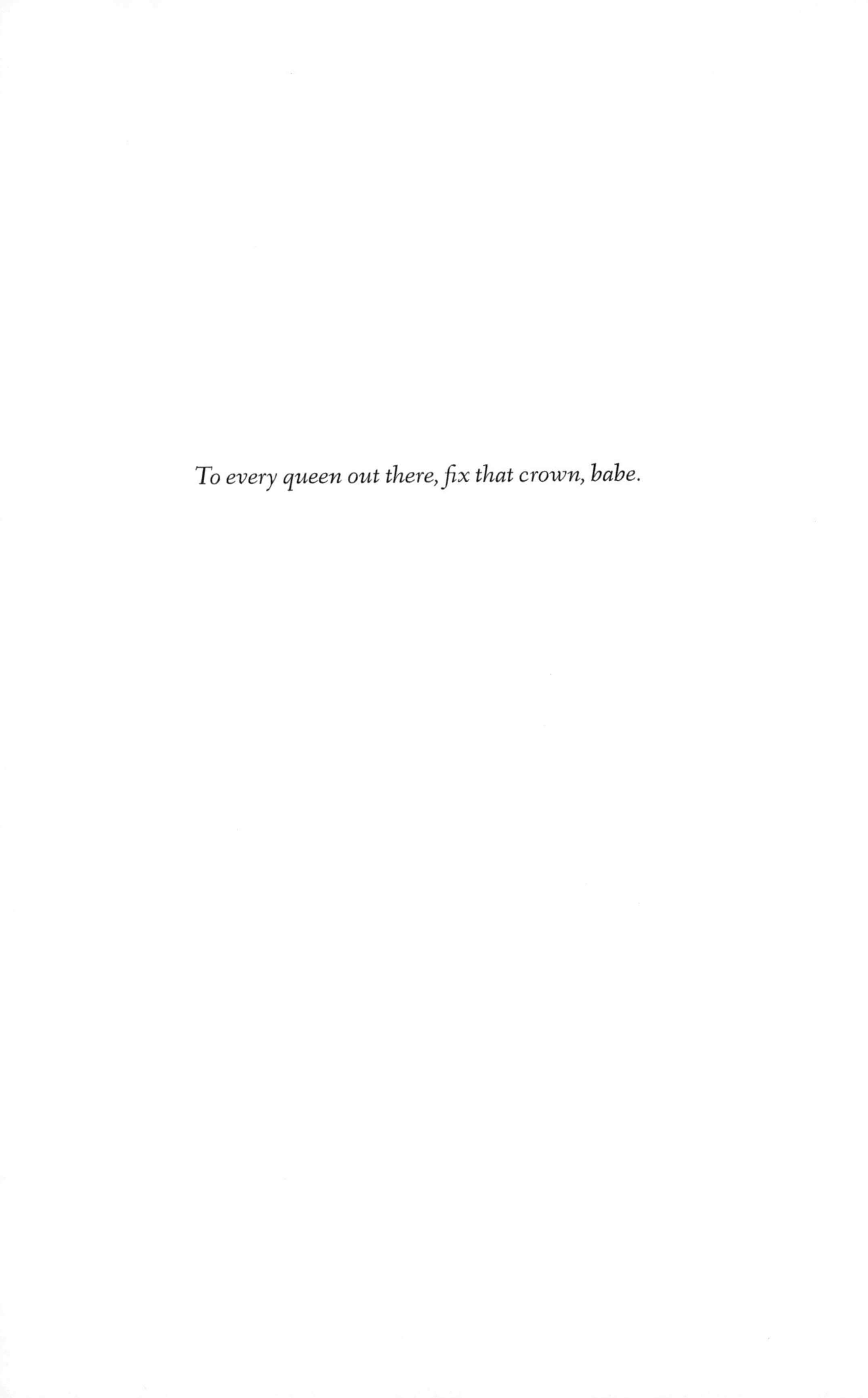

To every queen out there, fix that crown, babe.

"Being deeply loved by someone gives you strength, while loving someone deeply gives you courage."

– Lao Tzu

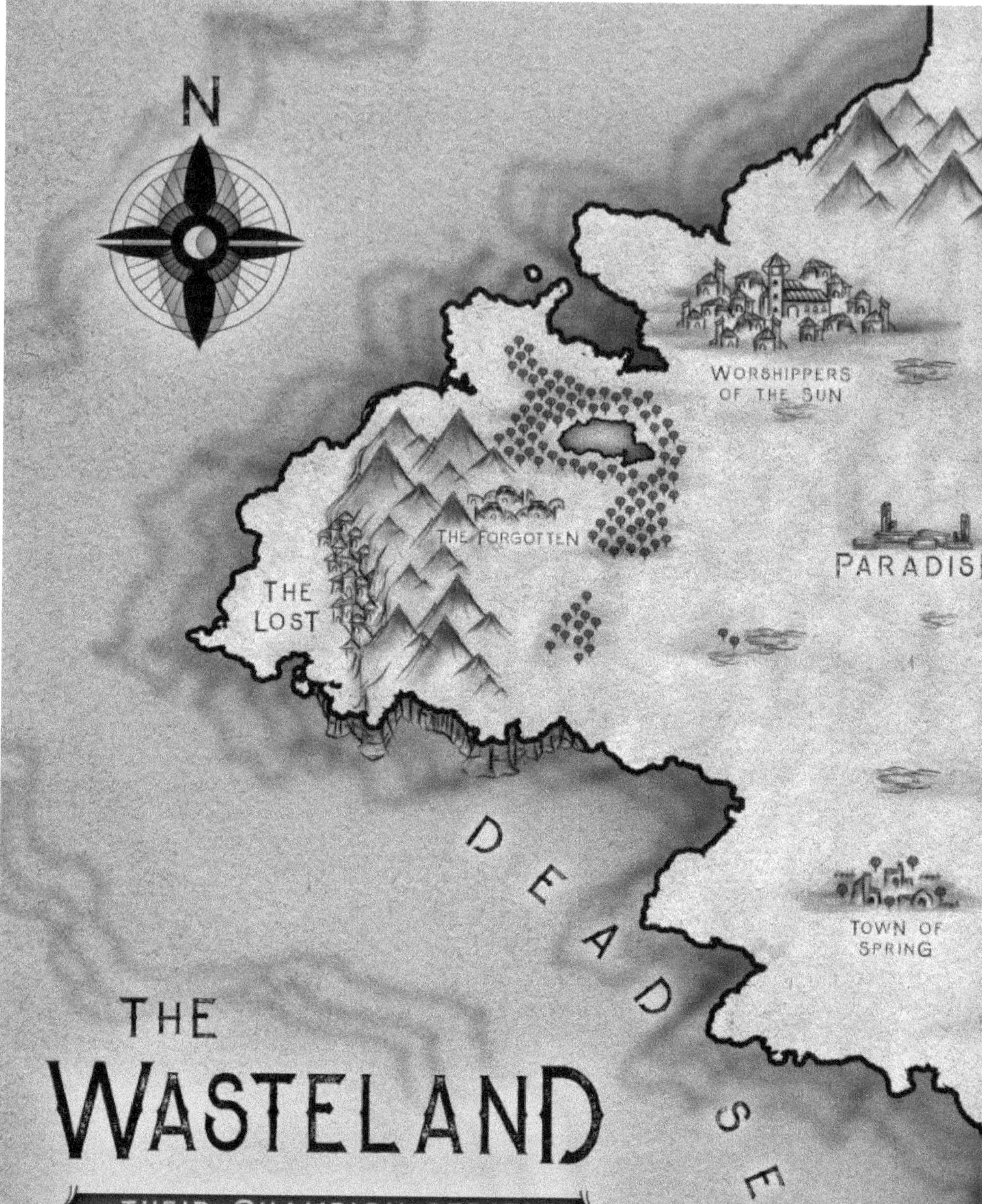

N
WORSHIPPERS
OF THE SUN
THE FORGOTTEN
THE LOST
PARADISE
TOWN OF
SPRING
DEAD SEA
THE
WASTELAND
THEIR CHAMPION SERIES

E BERSERKERS
THE RING
THE SEEKERS
REEVES
THE RIM
THE CITIES
DEAD
SEA

PROLOGUE

The smashing of the hammer against the wooden cross is loud amidst the crowd of gathered warriors. People have come from all four corners of The Wastes for the funeral.

Berserkers.

Seekers.

Worshippers.

Scavs.

Roadies. Paradise. Lost...

All in one place, all brought here by one person.

No one talks, their heads bowed in reverence and respect. Arms remain crossed before them as warriors chant and sing the songs of goodbye to honour the dead.

Five men stand apart, their eyes sad and bodies hard. War wounds cover them, healing but still there. They bear fresh scars, both emotionally and physically.

Smash.

The swing of the hammer comes again as the cross is forced into the ground, a perfect place to be laid to rest. Here in the sands, under the sun, and below the tree carved with markings.

Finally at peace, after all the battles and uncertainty.

The body is lowered into the ground, the dirt and sand clouding as it's thrown back atop it.

The end... A goodbye.

CHAPTER ONE

THE WAR

Blood sprays as people fall, the sand covered in corpses and the dying. Our war cry echoes across the dead land, stretching to The Cities' soldiers. I see them hesitate for a moment, fear filling their faces as they take in the horde of savages, scavs, warriors, and ruthless killers.

They called us savages, beasts, and now it's time we show them that is exactly what we are.

They brought this on.

They came to The North, they poked the beast. We fight now, or we die on our knees at their feet. I have spent enough years on my knees, so I don't plan to find myself there ever again.

I am who my past made me. A slave, a champion, a queen.

A queen never surrenders, a queen never second-guesses. A queen leads her people into battle with only one thought—to win. Live or die, my people will be free.

I have seen how they treat their citizens, how they look after them. That won't be us, not now or ever. We survived this dead world on our own, and we will continue to thrive.

"Now!" I scream, my hair flying behind me as I turn to see Piper waiting at the edge of the line for my order. She nods, and the first explosion rocks the earth. The ground rolls beneath our feet as I turn, watching trucks explode in flames as they cross the line. More explosions sound, again and again, as bits of people, trucks, and fire soar into the dusty air.

The line of warriors cheers behind me as smoke billows into the sky, blocking our vision. It grows silent, our breathing the only sound to be heard, until suddenly, from the smoke, comes more trucks.

Their guns are aimed at our front line.

They roar towards us, powering through the carcasses of the exploded vehicles. We took some down, but not enough. They are still approaching, and the death toll will be unimaginable.

Fear fills me.

Not for me, but for my men. For Piper and Nan. For my friends. But I have lost too many to give up now. Everything has led me to this point where I have to choose.

To run and let The North fall, or stand, even while facing death. I know my choice—to fight, always.

"For The North!" I scream, as I rev my bike.

The sentiment is echoed as our death call fills the air, our war drums beating in our hearts as we face the oncoming trucks. My focus narrows to this—the fight before me. I have experienced a shitload in my life, nothing ever as important as this, but the rules remain the same.

Focus on yourself, look for weaknesses. Exploit them. Kill them.

I search the trucks for vulnerabilities as I shoot straight towards the line. *Weakness. Come on, Worth, fucking think!*

Then I see it. Their trucks are struggling to manoeuvre over the hard, uneven ground from the explosions, unlike our bikes. Turning my head, I spot a particularly large verge on three sides up ahead, obviously opened and unveiled by the explosions. It's the perfect place. I wave my finger in a circle and spin, heading straight there.

I feel blasts rock beneath us as more trucks are destroyed. Their guns fire, and I hear them hit the people following me, their cries of pain filling the air as they fall, but I keep my focus on that wide battleground.

Because that is what it is.

The trucks turn with us, and as I ride into the battlefield, I spot a fucking rocket launcher being placed on a roof, aimed right at us. I don't have any way to stop it.

We are sitting fucking ducks.

But then, just when I think all is lost, the truck explodes, as does five others. I stop my bike on the edge of the clearing and look to see Piper cheering. I throw her a wink and climb from my bike, pull my sword, and wait.

The trucks blow up, flipping into the air and creating a barrier of sorts around the battleground, which means the others can't get through. The engines are loud as we finally see them step from behind the metal. Their guns and weapons are drawn as they weave through the ruined vehicles and create a line before them.

My own reforms behind me, and I raise my chin and wait. With a cry, they rush us, but it is neither coordinated nor clear who is leading. They are fighting and ready to die, but with no leader. I search the area behind them for one and find her.

Regina.

She's standing next to a fucking tank way up above us on a sand dune overlooking the battlefield, watching the show. Regina is not even wading in to give her troops orders.

She would watch them die without remorse.

That's the difference between her and me. I would never ask them to die for me without being willing to die for them. It will be her downfall.

I don't have time to stare at her because her troops are here. The guns fire, taking down rows and rows of my men, while I rush into the barrage of bullets. I have to get too close for them to hit me, knowing they have to reload sometime, so I can take advantage and kill them.

My men follow me with a cry as we charge their masses.

The world doesn't slow down, no, it speeds up as our two factions clash in a snarl of grinding metal, blood, and death.

I lose my people, keeping my eyes on the enemy while protecting my back. I feel my men close, but they are fighting too. It's hard to tell who is friend or foe as I raise my sword and take down two Cities boys.

Cries and screams of agony fill the air. Blood splatters the sand, and bodies dot the landscape as they start to fall. Guns still fire from both sides, but I can't see who is winning, so I stop trying.

And instead, I do what I do best. Fight.

My sword clashes with a soldier's gun, his snarling face turning red as he tries to best me. With a snarl of my own, I jerk my head forward and headbutt him. He howls as he falls back, giving me the opening I need. Ripping the gun away, I toss it aside as I run him through with my sword.

I yank it free before he collapses and spin to find the next dead man walking. I am fast, I am brutal. I am a fucking champion. I slice and cut, stab and spin, fighting with everything I have. I slip through arms and grabbing hands. I use their own guns against them.

Two men circle me, and I turn my head to keep them in view, noticing Maxen a few feet away fighting five men. He roars in anger, his expression feral and wild, his brown hair loose around his face, and his chest bare and covered in blood. He swings an axe around, slicing at people and knocking them back, throwing them like bowling pins.

I glance back at the two men surrounding me and swing my swords. I smirk at them. "Should have stayed home, boys," I taunt as I sprint at one of them, taking him by surprise. He tries to get off a shot, his arm extended to aim, but I'm already there, arcing down with my sword.

His hand falls to the sand, still twitching and holding the gun as he screams and falls to his knees, eyes wide and fastened on the now bloody stump. I hear a whistle behind me and turn in time to clash my sword against a downward swinging machete.

The soldier grins at me through our locked weapons, so I blow him a kiss and kick out, hitting him right in the cock. He staggers back with a groan, and before he can move, my sword is at his neck, slicing through the soft flesh. With all my force, I swing back and hack off his head, watching it tumble to the ground and roll. Flicking my braid over my shoulder, I turn back to the other man, who's still staring at his lost hand in pale-faced shock. Grabbing his gun, I press it to his head and pull the trigger. The kick stings my wrist, so I toss it away.

I fucking hate guns.

I don't have time to rest though, because four more men take their place. Cracking my neck from side to side, I grin at them, knowing what I must look like. I can feel the blood dripping down my face and chest. My scars, tattoos, and brands are on full display. My hair is in braids, my face snarling.

I am a fucking Berserker.

I can almost smell their fear and see the sweat on their foreheads as the sun glares down on our battle. They aren't used to the sands and heat out here, but we are. We know how to live and die in it, they don't. Their boots are too heavy and clean, causing them to stumble in the sand.

I lunge forward as one looks down at the body he tripped over and, with a quick swipe of my arm, I slice his belly and throat before spinning around his back to the man next to him, impaling him on my sword before I duck a shot and look at the other two.

"Should have brought more men," I pant out with a laugh.

They share a look and charge me, so I meet them head-on, swinging my sword in a wide arc with a strength from years of battle —a strength they don't have. As the blade comes towards them, they duck, making a deadly mistake. They take their eyes from the weapon to recoil and don't see the other one coming for them. I slice their thighs with my other sword, and as they scream and look down, I spin behind one, grab his head, and yank it back, slitting his throat before tossing him forward. The other man tries to run, so I grab a knife from my side and toss it. It flies through the air before embedding in his back.

He stumbles forward before falling to the sand, his fingers clawing into the gritty, blood-stained granules as he tries to drag himself away from me.

Stepping up next to him, I place my boot on his back, stopping his progress before lifting my sword and stabbing downwards. He screams and jerks before going quiet, and only then do I withdraw my sword with a distinctive squelch. I ignore the blood coating the blade and turn to see how we are doing.

Men and women lie dead and dying. There are too many to count.

I spot Drax and Jax fighting side by side like madmen. Their blond hair glows in the light, and their eyes are hard as Drax fires at the incoming men with his bow. Jax throws himself at the others, swinging and hacking.

I search the surging crowd and find Thorn. He got a flamethrower from somewhere, and he is laughing as he uses it, the smell of burnt flesh reaching me even here.

"Soulmate!" Dray yells, and I look over my shoulder to see him ripping someone's heart out before lifting it up to me. "For you!"

I laugh but turn away when I hear somebody running towards me. There is no time for breaks, even as sweat covers me from the hot sun and exertion of battle, even as my arms ache from swinging my sword. Bodies pile around me, their blood coating every inch of my skin, and it's still not enough.

More and more soldiers pour onto the battle ground, pushing us back, and I see our people start to fall. Our is line breaking.

We are losing. Their guns are too big, their trucks are too hard to penetrate, and even our explosives haven't stopped them, just simply slowed them down.

We are losing.

I watch Reeves take a bullet. I watch Nan scream in pain and anger, her shotgun firing repeatedly into the soldiers surrounding her.

I see Priest walking through his fallen angels, ready to deliver vengeance.

My Berserkers fight to their dying breaths. My men are scattered to the sands, battling with everything they have to win this war.

For me.

But it's still not enough. We are going to lose.

Chapter Two

Winning Means Sacrifice

We can't lose.

Not now, we have come too far!

Think, Worth, fucking think.

Ivar. Of course! When I killed him, his people fell. Without a leader, a warrior is nothing and these...these soldiers follow one person—Regina. The prime minister. She's sitting pretty on her fucking hill in the shade as her men die and suffer in a bloodbath down here. For her and her Cities.

I know by now Strand will have taken it over, they have nothing to go back to. But she won't be going back. Kill her, and the others will fall. I know it. I'm not merely a warrior anymore, I'm a queen, and it's time I thought like one. Fighting down here helps, but thinking two steps ahead? That is how we win.

I think that was what Major tried to teach me. It's a shame I'm only understanding now.

Dispatching the last soldier around me, I look to my men, but they're all busy. This is on me. They are fighting back the surge and trying to stay on their feet. I'm alone.

But I've been alone since I was a fucking kid. While they protect my—*our* people, I will kill the prime minister and stop this war. Once and for all.

I start battling my way through the throng, but it's slow going. We are almost fighting back to back, and I have to stop to kill a soldier every now and again. I hear a shout and look around, spotting Bern. I wave and point to Regina. He follows my gesture and nods as he rips someone apart. Stomping my way, he begins to clear a path with brute strength. He takes a few hits, so I rush behind him and clear those trying to sneak up on him.

When we break out on the other side, he looks down at me. "Good luck, ma queen." Then he turns, and with a roar, draws the gazes of the soldiers to himself and off of me. "For the queen!" He races into their masses as I face Regina.

Rushing up the sand dunes, I head her way. She must spot me, though, because the soldiers who have stayed back to protect her step into my path, and about fifty meters away, I realise my mistake.

They have an archer.

He takes aim and fires. I don't have time to avoid it as it soars through the air. I duck swiftly to the left, stopping it from entering my heart, and it instead hits my shoulder. I feel my arm twitch and start to go numb as pain explodes through me.

But I'm used to pain.

I know how to fight through it. To use it, to let it fuel me.

Pushing back my uncertainty, anger, and agony, I snap off the arrow with a cry and sprint towards them. I throw myself at the archer who stands before them and stab the jagged shaft into his eye. Blood drips from my shoulder and the wounds sustained from battle, but I get to my feet regardless, steady and sure as I stare down the five men she hides behind.

I step onto a flat piece of sand and swing my swords, ignoring the pain in my shoulder. "I'm coming for you, and your men won't be able to stop me."

She laughs from behind them as I smirk at the soldiers. "I've killed more men than you could imagine, you should be scared," I warn, as I widen my stance. "I eat fuckers like you before breakfast."

"You're just one woman," one of them spits.

"This one woman is about to slaughter you, so show some respect, boy, because I'm a fucking queen!" I roar and, done with talking, I make the first step. I catch them off guard by throwing a knife. I don't look, but I know it hits one.

The other four are big, but one is bigger and stronger. I take him first. Lunging at him, I knock him to the sand, and while he's fumbling with his weapon, I slice his throat. Rolling to the side to avoid the man behind me, I come up swinging, cutting through both arteries on his thighs. Blood spurts as he stumbles before dropping to the sand.

Two left.

I leap to my feet, grinning at them. "Don't say I didn't fucking warn you!"

They both rush me, our weapons clanging as we clash. I parry and duck, slice and cut, stand and spin. It's second nature to me, the dance of swords. I've been training my whole life for this moment.

They will not win.

One stumbles from a cut, and before he knows it, I have him impaled on my blade. I leave it in his chest as he falls and dies as I turn to the other, holding my remaining sword with both hands as I smirk at him.

"And then there was one," I murmur.

He glances to Regina and shakes his head. "Fuck, she isn't worth this." Yet he still stands there, knowing he should leave, but his duty doesn't allow it. I can respect that.

"I offer you a quick death," I declare and step towards him. I stab my sword into his gut before grabbing my knife and slicing his throat. I keep my eyes on his as he sputters, his blood spraying across me as he starts to fall. I grab my sword, letting his momentum pull it free, before turning and pulling the other from the dead soldier with a grunt of pain.

Swinging them, I look back at Regina, her protectors dead around me. Her people are dying down there for her, yet she does not care for their lives, only hers.

"Please, we can make a deal!" she begs, backing away with her hands up.

I snort. "We don't negotiate with pale faces," I mock, using her words from before while twirling my blades as I advance on her.

Suddenly, her pale, scared face transforms into that cold calculating one from before, and she smiles. "So confident, it will be your death."

I hear the person too late, she was distracting me. I was so caught up in being so close to her, I didn't pay attention to my surroundings

—a stupid fucking error. One that might cost me my life.

She waves and begins sauntering towards the truck. I know she is running away. I can't let that happen. It's a split-second decision. I can feel the man advancing on me from behind, intent on my death, but it's either her or him.

I can't do both.

One decision saves me, the other my people...

So, with a war cry, I swing my sword and catch her mid-turn. She screams as I pull it free and swipe again, bringing it down on her head. The blade gets caught there as she drops to her knees, and I turn, my other sword ready, but I already know it's too late.

He's there.

The pain registers first as his smirking, sweaty face looms above mine from inches away. His eyes are blue, a dirty shade, his hair is thinning and grey, and he's bulky like a warrior.

A soldier.

I follow his gaze to the blade protruding from my stomach and the blood seeping around it. It's bad. I know it. It's almost a numb thought as all sounds disappear. I can't look away, even as he pulls the blade free, the metal coated with my blood.

I stumble back, my body sluggish as blood pumps from the wound. My arm finally goes numb, and I almost drop my sword, but he's coming at me again to finish me off. I hear my name screamed and the pounding of feet as they race towards me.

My men.

Did it work? Did I stop the battle? It's almost quiet now, no guns. I raise my eyes to the soldier who is grinning, his blade arcing down for the killing blow. With the last of my strength, I channel it all into a yell as I raise my sword and throw myself forward. We fall to the sand, and I blink, staring down at my blade buried in his chest. His eyes turn empty underneath me. Rolling from his body, I feel my back hit the solid sand, my blood pooling on it.

My hands fall to my sides, I can't keep them up anymore. I dig my fingers into the granules, feeling my sticky blood coating them as I try to hang on. My weapons are gone, but it doesn't matter, I couldn't lift them now anyway.

Darkness edges my vision, and the pain is excruciating as it flows through me. At least I killed her. Turning my head slowly, I blink and look at the battle. The soldiers are trying to retreat, but my people are there to kill them. They circle them and take them down efficiently.

I see my men running towards me, Piper too, with Doc and her men. I swallow hard, knowing they will be too late. Between one blink and the next, they are closer. I am losing time. Their faces are contorted in agony and horror. They know it too.

I'm going to die.

Here in the sands where I belong.

I look back up at the sky, knowing the sun is heating my body, but I can't even feel it. I'm cold now. Too cold. I never thought I would miss the heat, but I do. After all the fights, all the pain I have endured and survived, this is where it ends.

But at least I'm not alone. At least I will die for something, a cause. Not just my freedom, but everyone's in The North. *Not bad for a slave girl*, I think dazedly. I just wish Major was here to see me.

"*I've got you kid, I've got you*," he whispers, as my eyes start to close.

I'm sorry.

"Death comes to everyone eventually. All you can ask for is that you go out on your own terms and in your own way." Vass' words echo through my head as the world goes dark, and even at the end, they are with me. I see all those who were lost in the fight to get here waiting for me on the other side, wearing smiles on their faces. Vass has a baby in his arms and a woman at his side. Major's hand is clasped in Cara's, his other reaching for me. Noah is there too.

Von is calling my name.

My mother is there. I feel my lips curve into a smile as I extend my hand and reach for them.

This is on my own terms.

Bringing safety to my people and loves.

My one regret? Never having the life I always dreamed of with my men.

The pain is gone, not just today's, but all of it. The pain of living, of surviving, of the scars covering me, and the blood on my hands. I've fought for so long, never stopping, but now...now it's over.

"Come home, baby girl, it's time," my mother calls.

It's time.

Chapter Three

Death Is Easy, Living Is Harder

Fire flows through me, pulling me from the abyss. Agony soon follows until I'm screaming, my mind and body breaking apart before the sensation disappears as soon as it comes, and I fall back into that waiting darkness.

I float there, warm and happy.

But the tugging comes again, a sharp pain ensuing until I can almost feel my body, but the darkness swallows it once again.

Voices surround me in the murky gloom, calling to me. Begging me.

Pleading.

The pain in their voices brings tears to my eyes. They sound so hopeless, so lost and distraught, I want to hold them.

But then they are gone too. There is nothing.

No one.

Just the pitch-black.

"It's not your time yet, kid, they need you."

I push the voice away, wanting to stay in the comfort of the dark, but it comes again, louder, nagging, and familiar. It sends a pang of pain through me for some reason. The words flow through me with aching familiarity and loss.

"Did you know butterflies are strong? They have beauty and are covered in marks from life, but they still keep flying."

I turn away, and another voice comes. "Little queen, fight."

No! Pain resurfaces at that voice, so much pain. I'm tired of the pain… I'm tired.

"You can do it, pain is temporary. Fucking fight!" comes the roar. "Fight, kid!"

Fight…

But how can I fight what I can't see? I am swallowed once again.

"She's still here! She's fighting it!" comes a frantic voice.

"Come on, soulmate! Don't you dare fucking leave me!" demands a deep tone.

"Angel! Please!"

Pain registers as hands press against me, making me bow and scream. "That's it, baby girl. Fight for us, we are right here."

"Come on, babe! Please." Their voices are choked and frantic. "*Mi Alma*, you can do this. Do not fucking die on me!"

But the darkness is back again. It promises peace, and as hard as I fight to stay, knowing those voices and the hearts they belong to…it drags me back, kicking and screaming.

I'm warm.

Really warm.

It starts slowly, the floating blackness heating up until it becomes unbearable. Noises and words filter through, but they make no sense, and then the pain comes.

Flames.

The dancing flames... Ivar? No, no, Ivar is dead.

Am I dead?

Why does it hurt? Why am I so hot?

"Fuck! She's going to get an infection!" comes a snarl. "Pip, pass me—"

I bury my head again, whimpering at the flames. *Please, no more.*

A soothing, guttural voice wraps around me like an embrace. The lyrics flowing through me are familiar, reminding me of dark cells, but that can't be a happy memory, can it?

"Little queen, you can find happiness anywhere if you remember to look," comes a whisper before the lyrics start up again.

Vas?

It's a song about a woman and her lover, and the fight they endure to be together, but at the end, she dies... It's sad.

"It is, but death isn't the end. The only true end is if you give up fighting. You are not a coward, nor are you weak, kid, so don't start to be now. Pain awaits you back there, so much pain. But you can handle it. Only you, Tazanna. They need you, and we will be here waiting when it is finally your time."

I love you.

I don't know if I scream it or whisper it, but I need that person to know. It's a gut feeling.

"I love you too, kid." He laughs, the sound covering me like a blanket and reminding me of home, like a father... Major? Can it be?

"But they love you too, so go. Your fight isn't over."

I close my eyes, only to find more blackness, and focus past that voice to the pain circling and waiting to be let back in. With a cry, I throw open that door to the hurt that awaits there.

He is right.

My fight isn't over.

Agony surges through me, and my eyes snap open with a scream.

Chapter Four

Never Say Goodbye

"Oi, you stubborn bitch, can you hear me?" The voice is insistent, making me groan.

"Fuck off, Doc," I slur, and I hear him laugh. It's a bark and almost choked.

"Baby girl?"

"Angel!"

"Babe!"

"Soulmate!"

"Ma queen!"

It all comes at once, and I groan at the onslaught. It's suddenly quiet as I just breathe, trying to figure out what happened. I smell copper, blood. I'm used to that scent, but there is a sweet odour as well. It's warm, like always, and I'm lying on something soft.

The last thing I remember was killing Regina and then— Fuck, I was stabbed.

My eyes open again, and I blink away the blurriness to see faces crowded above me. "That was fun," I croak, my voice rough, and Dray laughs as the others watch me worriedly. "Did we win?"

"*Mi Alma*," Maxen starts, but I narrow my eyes and he grins.

"We won. When you killed Regina, it turned the tide, and once we started winning again, they stood down."

I nod but groan when it causes pain. "So I didn't die?"

"Oh, you did for almost five minutes, and it's been touch-and-go ever since," Doc answers next to me. I try to lift my head, but it's heavy. Then Jax is there, his grey eyes haunted and his lips thin as he helps raise me slowly so I can look down at my own body. He's silent, which is not a huge change from normal, but I can feel the tremor in his hands. It makes sense if they almost lost me. In fact, Dray looks surprisingly calm, considering I died.

I blink down at the bandage covering my stomach. "You'll have a scar." Doc shrugs. "I did the best I could to stitch you up and stop the bleeding, but you will be weak for a while and need to stay in bed and recover."

"Yeah, fuck that, I have shit to do," I snap, making him chuckle as he presses another bit of tape to the bandage.

"I figured, which is why I've taped it a lot to keep it still as you move." He snorts and stands, looking at the men around me. We appear to be in a tent of some kind. "No sex, not unless you want her to bleed to death, and try to keep her in bed if you can."

"Without using sex?" Drax laughs. "Hard to do." He winks over at me, and I grin, wincing when pain flows through me, making him sober.

"Babe, what can I do?" he begs.

"I'm fine." I wave it away. "Tell me everything."

Maxen slips behind me, propping me up and restraining me like he knew I was going to try and stand to head out and sort things. "*Mi Alma*, we almost lost you."

The atmosphere of the tent becomes somber as they all stare at me with various stages of anger and hurt. "I'm sorry. I had to, okay?"

"We know, baby girl," Thorn whispers. "But we will never forgive ourselves for not being there to watch your back."

"No, no regrets. We've had enough of them for a lifetime, and I'm here, I'm fine," I order.

"But you weren't, soulmate," Dray snarls, and when I look over, his cold eyes are locked on me. His chest is still covered in blood, but it's dried. How long was I asleep? I need to ask, but we need to get all this out of the way first. They are hurting and angry and need to reassure themselves I'm still here.

"Surprised you didn't lose it." I laugh and then wince when it pulls on the wound, making me hiss out a breath.

He presses closer, uncaring about Maxen, and rests his forehead against mine, his cold, predatory eyes holding mine. There is a gleam there of anger, hurt, and love. The usual Dray.

His hand covers the bandage, leaving a bloody handprint as he presses on it slightly, making me whimper. "Oh, I did. They surrendered, but I killed them all. Every single fucking one, and I carved your name into their chests and sent them back to The Cities in pieces."

"How romantic," I grumble, and he smirks as he presses harder. "You try and leave me again, and I will kill everyone, friend or foe. Understood, soulmate?" he snaps.

I lean into him and kiss him. "Understood," I murmur. "Seriously, he isn't joking. We thought we were going to have to

knock him out. It took Bern, Archel, Erik, and us to restrain him," Maxen murmurs in my ear, making me grin wider.

That's my crazy man.

I drop a kiss on the brand on his chest above his heart just as I hear a noise. I turn my head to the front of the tent to see Bern there.

Bern ducks as he enters, and when he sees me, he grins. He has a black eye, though, and a busted lip. I narrow my eyes on Dray, but he just winks at me, the crazy bastard. Bern crouches at the entrance. "Ma queen, good to see you awake."

"Thanks. Death count?"

"Over a thousand, both sides."

I nod, even as my heart drops. "Who did we lose?"

He winces and glances briefly outside. "Reeves took a bullet to the chest for Nan. Henry is also dead, among a few others you knew."

"Henry...fuck and shit, Reeves?" I groan as I try to stand. I remember seeing it now, fuck. "How's Nan?"

"Erm...she's currently yelling at some mountain man, he looks terrified," he offers, and then sobers. "We are getting ready to bury the dead."

"Yeah, we need to before they rot in the sun. Help me up," I demand, and Maxen sighs. I turn my head and meet his gaze. "I have to be there. These people died for me, with me, I need to help them."

The burden of those deaths already weighs heavily on me. I can't be in here lying around when those who fought for me are out there burying their friends. I can't. He searches my eyes before nodding, and the others help me stand. I have to lean against Thorn. He keeps his arm wrapped around me, especially when agony rips through my stomach, making me grit my teeth.

The pain reminds me I'm alive, but sands below, what I wouldn't do for some booze right now.

CHAPTER FIVE

THE GRIEF CRIES

Thorn helps me walk out of the tent, and when I do, the heat hits and instantly makes me groan. Grinding my teeth, I walk slowly past the tents, and once we break out into the clearing where the battle took place, I freeze. There are so many bodies.

The people left behind limp around, their arms, legs, and torsos covered in bandages. Their eyes are wide and grief-filled as they move corpses and dig graves. Sweat pours off them from the sun pounding down on us. The scent of death and blood fills the air, almost making me gag.

So much fucking death.

Each body I see weighs me down further. They died for me, for us, The North. But I led them into it. I will never wash my hands free of that blood, and I refuse to let them die in vain or go without respect. We will bury them all. I will remember every single fucking face and name.

I will learn who sacrificed their lives for us. Who died for us.

A murmur goes up, and they all turn, some shielding their eyes as they look up at me. It's silent for a moment, and I feel the heaviness of their stares and judgement, making me stand taller and pull away from Thorn. I am a leader, I am a fucking queen. They are looking at me for leadership in their grief.

But then, suddenly, a cheer goes up, causing me to blink in shock.

They chant my name, pumping their fists into the air. All clans join in, mixed together as one. "Champion! Berserker Queen!"

I can't do anything but gape as I feel my men spread out behind me. Why are they cheering? "Look at your people, Angel."

"*Mi Alma*, you gave them a reason to fight and you won. You did what no other could do. Look at your people, because they are looking to you now more than ever...but we are here. Remember, you don't need to be strong with us," Maxen murmurs, and I turn my head to see him next to me. He offers me his hand, and I gladly take it, accepting his strength.

He's right.

We won, but that was only the beginning. The rest is up to us now, and they are waiting to see how I will respond. I refuse to ignore our dead, however, since this isn't a case of you lose some, you win some. These people lived and they died, they deserve respect. They deserve grief.

They had lovers. Family. Children.

Whole lives were snuffed away. Now isn't a time for celebration, so I lift my hand. They slowly grow quiet, their expectant eyes on me. I search the gathered people, noting they are looking for the same—the right to grieve.

"I've never been good with words, but I want you to know how fucking grateful I am for all of you. For continuing on, even injured and broken. We won the war, The North is ours." I shake my head. "But now isn't the time to celebrate, that will come. Now is the time to bury our dead and mourn the loss of life. We all knew it was a possibility we would die today, but that doesn't fucking make their loss any easier. I see them, the men and women who died for me... No, not me. Us. For The North, for our freedom. Today, we bury them and fill the sands with the songs of their lives and sacrifice, and tomorrow—tomorrow we celebrate and plan our future, but today? Today, we mourn." I look to Dray. "Shovel."

He nods and grabs one from a passerby before handing it to me, his fingers stroking along mine. "My queen," he murmurs respectfully, which is odd for Dray, but then I realise he's a leader. His people lie dead down there, and there's one thing I know for certain about Dray—he might be crazy, he might be rough and insane, but he loves his people. He is grieving, he just doesn't know how. He's never been allowed that luxury, none of us have. It is deemed a weakness, but caring for others so much that you embrace your pain and honour their memory when they are gone isn't a weakness.

It's the ultimate strength, because even though you knew they could hurt you, you loved them anyway.

I turn back to the onlookers, somber and grieving now that they know it is okay. "We bury our dead. We don't leave them like The Cities does! We bury them, and we mourn! You have every right to be mad, to be fucking angry and sad. I wish I could change our people lying out on the sand, but I can't. I will, however, feel this with you. Your pain, our pain.

"This might be our beginning, but it's their end, and without them, we wouldn't have this chance. Let's never fucking forget that!" I lower my head and press my fist to my chest.

When I peek up, everyone is doing the same, paying our respects to the fallen.

After a minute or two, I lift my head and slowly start towards the closest body. Each step sparks agony through my body, and it fills me like fire, but the pain keeps me on my feet, even as my head spins and sweat covers me for a different reason. I refuse to be weak right now, I refuse to lie in a tent and lick my wounds while my people are out here.

A queen has many responsibilities, but I won't be one ruling from afar. Leading is about sacrifice, it is about pain, and even when it seems dark, you keep going, because if you don't, they won't.

A great queen knows how to lead, a great queen knows when to surrender.

I am not a great queen, I'm a fucking excellent queen, and we will never surrender. We will never stop. We are the fucking champions of The Wastes, and even as blood covers us and our dead lie scattered between us, we know.

This is the start of the rest of our lives.

The sand crunches under my boots, and I feel blood dripping slowly from my wound, but I ignore it. I stop above the body of a young woman. I didn't know her, but she was beautiful and strong. Her body was a weapon. Her eyes are open and unseeing, blood covers her, and her stomach is ripped open. Her skin is pale and flies hover around her. Leaning down, I close her eyes and bow my head.

"Thank you for your sacrifice," I murmur before standing. I stumble slightly before I find my balance, the weakness threatening to pull me under.

Pressing the shovel into the ground, I feel my arm protest, probably from the arrow, so I have to use my boot and dig it in. I groan when I throw the sand away, and I feel more blood running from my wounds, but it only makes me dig faster, anger filling me.

I can feel my men wanting to protest, but they know better, so instead, they grab a shovel and help. I hunch my shoulders as I dig, tears blurring my eyes that I will never let fall.

So much death. Everywhere I look, blood is baked into the sand. This place will forever be touched by it. I can't think about the victory or the future right now, all I can think about is honouring those who gave their lives.

I bury her and move onto the next, thanking them again before burying them. Each cold, empty face fills my head. They are dead on my orders. I want to cry and scream, but eyes are still on me.

They died for us, and I refuse to dishonour that with my own issues, so I keep digging, pouring all of my emotions into the task. Looking around after I finish burying an older Berserker, I spot Nan attempting to dig a few feet away, so I head over, wincing when I see Reeves on the ground.

His eyes are closed, there's a slash mark across his mottled face, and his chest has a huge, gaping hole in it, coated in blood and displaying bone as flies settle into the wound. I look to Nan then. She is staring at the ground and has stopped digging.

She loved this man, I know that, but Nan is like me. Words won't help her, not yet, so I start digging, working side by side with her, and when it's deep and wide enough, I step back to her side and stare down at him.

"He was a good man," I murmur.

"He wa a fookin' drunk and a bastard," she snaps, then laughs. "But a good fookin' man, girlie. He would be glad ta ave die in battle." She kneels, and I kneel at his head, both of us lifting with a grunt and managing to move him into the hole with great effort.

Nan looks worse for wear too, her grey hair wild, her face covered in sand and blood, and her cardigan is gone, as are her pearls. She looks like a fucking badass, a warrior. She kneels at the edge of the grave, and I kneel next to her as we stare down at him.

With him gone, there is a void in place for his people, but none of that matters right now.

She reaches over and clasps my hands. "I loved him, girlie. I didn't tell him enough."

"He knew," I assure her.

She laughs. "Fookin' cocky bastard did." She looks up at me then, tears swimming in her eyes. "When I die, girlie, bury me next to him, let us be together in tha next life like we could never in this un, you hear me?"

"Nan—" I start, but her eyes narrow.

"You fookin' promise me, right here!" she demands.

I swallow and smile. "I promise, you old bitch."

She grins then. "Fookin' respect ya elders." "Sure thing, old lady."

She reaches over and smacks me, her eyes running down my body. "Ya okay?"

I hold my chest in mock shock. "Oh my God, is that...concern I hear? I knew you loved me," I tease.

"Fookin' dick," she snaps as she stands, but her hand reaches down and she helps me up. "Just wanted ta make sure you weren't going to keel over, ya insane man would murder me." We both turn to see Dray not two feet away, his eyes locked on me, his hands covered in blood, just staring.

Okay...

"He's seriously fookin' nuts, that one," she murmurs, making me smile widely.

"He really fucking is," I say almost dreamily. "I heard he went insane when I died."

"Insane? Girlie, I thought the fookin' wrath of hell had come to earth again. One moment, he was just a bloody man, then the next, he was a goddamn monster. Remind me to never piss him off again, I know why they follow him nah." She snorts.

"Liar, you will still piss him off just for fun."

She winks at me. "And you don't?"

"Ah, but the difference is it leads to orgasms for me, for you it usually leads him to nearly murder you."

"Which ain't different from ya sex from what I've heard." She snorts. I know she is stalling covering Reeves, but I let her, knowing she needs this lightness in the face of such darkness and death.

Sometimes, you just need someone by your side when life gets hard to share a smile with, to hold your hand. Nothing they say or do can make it easier, but being there for you? It helps.

"I'm tired," I admit to her, "of burying my friends."

"I know, girlie. Ya lost so much, but look where you are and what you have done. The time for death is past, now you decide the future. Ya won't ever forget them, but it will get easier every day, and one day, tha will be stories and songs of the people who helped save The North."

"Goddamn, you old bitch, why you gotta be so smart?" I grouse, even as I clear my throat. "Go back to being a cranky old cunt, suits you more."

"Let's cover the old bastard. He would love this, two women staring at him, tha pig."

I laugh and help her bury him, patting the sand down and watching as Nan places her pearls across the top. I blink, wondering where she hid them, but now doesn't seem like the time to ask. "Bye, ya old bastard, love you."

I leave her to say her goodbyes and head to Dray. His arms circle around me as soon as I get there, but I don't care, I lean into him. My feet are almost dragging, I'm that weak and exhausted. Dying really takes it out of you.

His head drops to mine as he holds me up. "I knew the moment I saw you that you were something special, soulmate. It was the determination in your eyes, but even now, I see that same determination. Your journey isn't done, this is just a blip, so don't let the pain and anger consume you and blind you again."

I nod and pull back, staring into those cold eyes as his lips quirk up.

"And don't ever die again, or there won't be a force on this planet that can stop me from killing everyone and joining you."

"Crazy man."

"You know it, wife." He winks. "Now, let's finish up, then you need to rest. I like the blood on your skin, but I need you more than half dead for what I have planned for you."

"Oh, going to make it hurt?" I whisper.

"Always. Just a little reminder of what happens when you try to leave me," he murmurs.

Leaning up, I kiss him. "I can't wait, my king."

CHAPTER SIX

A SEEKER GAME

Drax and Jax head my way as I stumble over the sand. Jax instantly circles behind me and helps me lean back against him, taking all of my weight as Drax almost presses to my front, his eyes searching my face and body to make sure I am okay.

"Sweet cheeks, you falling for me again?" he jokes.

Winking, I lean further back into Jax, who holds my weight effortlessly, his hands on my hips as he trails his lips down my neck, making me shiver. We didn't get a lot of time together in The Cities with everything going on. I can't wait to just be with my men, but right now isn't the time, even though I wish it was, but I'm going to steal some moments, because I need them.

I need their strength right now.

When I'm racked with guilt, pain, and the pressure of leading so many people, they are the only ones who can help, who always have my back.

"Angel," Jax murmurs. "Have you had anything to drink?"

I close my eyes for a moment and sigh when Drax closes that last inch between our bodies and cups my cheeks, stroking my face as they support me. "No."

Drax laughs. "Figures. Always looking after everyone else first, babe, and putting yourself last. It's a good job you always come first with us."

Grinning, I open my eyes to see he is holding up some water for me. His blond hair is slicked back from the heat, and it's a bit longer than when I met him, almost to his shoulders now. It looks good. I reach out and finger a strand. "Your hair is long."

He winks at me. "Yeah? Knew you liked it, so I've been growing it out for you."

"I like it, huh?" I tease, as I take a swig of water. I'm so used to being thirsty, I don't even feel it anymore.

"More to grab onto when you're fucking me," he murmurs, his eyes heating as they drop to my lips hungrily.

Jax chuckles behind me, nipping at my neck, so I reach back, grab a fistful of his hair, wincing when it pulls on my stomach, and yank his head away hard enough that he moans. My silent demon loves the pain I offer. "You're right," I whisper to Drax, whose mouth parts on a moan as he watches me.

Our little bubble bursts, though, when the cry of a dying man reaches me, and I pull away from them, feeling even worse for laughing and joking while there are corpses all around us and people dying from their wounds. Infections are setting in, and blood loss is killing them, despite Evan's best attempts. I can see him working in the distance, even though he's exhausted, trying to save as many as he can.

Piper is at his side, helping when she is able, and when I catch her eye, she tilts her head and whispers to Evan before jogging over. A huge man is at her back. I don't even spot Archel, but just as suddenly, he is there, leaning against a bike near us.

Sneaky fucking assassin.

"You okay?" she asks, genuinely worried, her goggles perched on her head and her hair pulled back in braids. Her brown eyes are tilted up, and her lips are quirked in a smile. Across her face and chest is what looks like war paint. We used to wear the same in the ring. It looks good on her. She has a cut on her cheek and a deeper gouge across her shoulder, parting her leather jacket, but other than that, she looks okay.

She has blood under her nails and on her hands. "I should be asking you that," I retort. "I saw you out there, you were a badass."

She perks up under the praise. "Really? I mean, yeah, I totally was." She nods, making me laugh. "So were you—I mean, apart from the almost dying part, that sucked, but damn, watching you fight was amazing. You were incredible, like this feral ninja. I bet you made them piss themselves in fear. I mean, my knickers were wet, but mainly from sweat, and okay, yeah, I got a little turned on watching you. I have a serious woman crush on you—"

Archel laughs and appears next to her, covering her mouth as her eyes widen. She turns her head to him and winces when he grins down at her. "Stop talking, Princess."

She nods, and he removes his hand, laughing. "Did you lick me?"

"No?" She blinks innocently and then looks over at me. "Sorry, how's your wound?"

I look down at the bandages that have blood seeping through them. "Doc did really well, I owe him. It's sure as shit a lot better than when I used to sew myself up after fights."

Her mouth forms an 'O' as she watches me. "That's so fucking hardcore. Marry me?"

Archel sighs and wraps an arm around her. "Princess, I told you, if you're marrying anyone, it's me."

The huge mountain man steps forward. "And me."

She giggles as I shake my head and raise my hands to show her the rings. "Sorry, already taken."

Archel turns and gawks at me before he looks at Dray not too far away—he's basically lingering around me, even though he is pretending to help clean up. With a kiss on Piper's lips, Archel races across the sand and tackles him. We all watch as he tries to pin Dray, but within a second, Dray has flipped them and he has a knife at Archel's throat.

"You got married?" Archel laughs, face stretched with a grin, even though Dray almost slices his throat.

Men.

"Sure did." Dray grins. "Had to make sure she couldn't run away after the war."

Archel laughs harder. "Well shit, man, congrats! Gotta say, I thought you would have to tie her up to make it happen, but I'm happy for you!"

Dray stands and helps him up, and they both embrace, laughing at the idea of me saying yes. I turn away and stare at Piper. "Men, seriously, stick to your four, five is way too many." I raise my voice. "You hear me? Five is too many! I might have to kill one of you!"

Dray turns and winks at me. "You could try, soulmate, we both know I would get off on it."

"He really is insane." Piper laughs.

"Yup." I shake my head. "I love that about him."

I look back at her then, sobering once more. "How's Doc?"

She sighs and scrubs her face. "Hasn't slept or eaten. He's been working non-stop. He takes each person he loses personally. I'm trying to help him, but—"

"But it's hard." I nod. "He's doing his job. I can't thank him enough, but he's not going to let me order him to rest. Find a way to make him. I can't lose him as well, he's the only one I can tolerate."

"Apart from me, right?" she asks.

"Apart from you," I agree, making her grin.

"I'll use my boobs to distract him, like the piper of men, leading them to their beds to sleep. Tatas to the rescue." She nods solemnly and turns, and with her shoulders back, she marches over to Doc.

She sure is a strange one, but I'm happy having her at my back. She is an incredible warrior, and she is so young, she's going to grow into an even better leader.

"Let's finish burying the dead, then I need to speak to the other leaders. This isn't the end, merely the beginning."

The Nations

After the bodies are buried, we are all exhausted. My wound opened up again, but I refused to stop until the job was done. Each person I buried is a scar on my heart, a life snuffed out too soon.

I stand where she did, Regina, and stare out at the numerous graves. This area will forever be known as the place where we won our freedom, where we stood up for our homes, despite the odds.

Where we fought. Where we died. Where we grieved. Where we begin again.

I watch the people mingling below—Seekers helping Berserkers, and Paradise helping Lost. All the clans are interwoven, healing and bonding, bringing an idea to my head. No more division, no more infighting.

One north. One nation. Could it work?

As I observe them, I realise it might. For way too long, The Wastes have been divided, with different rules for each clan and too many people falling through the cracks.

Scavs, roadies, Seekers, and Berserkers, we are each our own people, but if this war has shown us anything, it's that we can work together. And maybe we need to in order to protect our world, our lands, to keep our people safe.

"Baby girl?" Thorn rumbles behind me, making me turn to look at him. He smiles, flashing those pearly whites, and I notice his hair is slightly longer too, no longer cropped to his head. The scar on his face stands out starkly. "They are ready."

I nod and look back before turning and taking his hand, letting him help me across the sand, my stomach rolling at the pain. I need to lie down soon before I pass out. That wouldn't be a good thing to do in front of everyone, it's a sure sign of weakness.

We head to one of the bigger tents, and when I duck inside, I see the leaders gathered. Nan, Priest, Dray, Piper...and a young man I don't recognise, obviously for Reeves. He nods as he stands.

"My name is Jon, I'm Reeves's second in command. I guess that makes me...the leader now." He sighs. He's a big guy, really big, with tattoos covering every inch of his body. He has blood covering one side of his face, and his eye is ballooned shut, but he stands tall.

I look to Nan, and she nods. "He's a good en, girlie, ma hu—Reeves was training him for years ta take over, the old cunt."

Jon's lips tip up at that. "Or trying to get me to. I always thought he should stay in charge. The stubborn bastard would have led until he died on his bike."

I smile and pick my way through the tent to the cushions piled up towards the back. Maxen, Drax, and Jax duck in, and Maxen instantly sits behind the cushions and helps me down, though he makes it look like he is simply touching me while I struggle to sit and lean back into him. I thank him mentally for supporting me.

I ignore the dizziness and sip some water as I look around. We are all worse for wear, all lost people. "Well, that was a shitshow," I start, making them all laugh as I smile. "But we won, and that's what counts. They won't be fucking with us again in the near future, but now we have some hard decisions to make. I want to meet you all at The Ring in a few days, once you have had a chance to mourn and celebrate with your people. Tonight, we will be having a feast to honour our warriors. You are all welcome to stay or leave. Thank you for fighting at my side."

Nan pulls a bottle from her shirt and takes a sip, winking at me. "I already started celebrating, lass." She passes it to me, and with a laugh, I take a swig before handing it to Dray. He leans down and kisses my hand before taking the bottle and, eyes on me, places his lips around the rim and drains some, his throat working. I shake my head of my dirty thoughts and clear my throat, looking around again. "I will meet with the new Cities leader I put in place, and make sure they respect our boundaries. I also have some ideas on how to strengthen our people, but it can wait for now. We are all tired and hungry and need some time to process what happened."

"Those who no longer walk with us will wait for us as angels. We have fulfilled the great prophecy," Priest intones, making me blink.

Piper shifts closer. "Does he always talk like that?"

Leaning into her, I conceal my mouth with my hand. "Always, but he's a scary motherfucker, don't cross him." I smile at him. "Great."

Dray grabs my legs and places them on his lap so I'm spread out between them. It's not very dignified, but when he starts massaging my calves, I can't find the energy to care. "Shall we say three days and meet at The Ring?"

"Make it four, lass, ya need to heal." Nan looks at my bleeding wound pointedly, the bandages more red than white at this point. Doc is going to flip.

"Fuck, fine, four days. Now...how many did you each lose?" I ask.

It's a hard question, but I need to know.

"Forty of my angels." Priest sighs. "Good believers, our church won't be the same."

"Around fifty or so," Jon adds, swigging the bottle. Nan plucks it from his fingers and downs the rest while we watch, wiping her mouth on her hand and letting out a loud burp.

"Too fucking many, but it was all worth it, girlie. Now, stop stressing. Ya don't need to act all queenie today, we won. Fucking celebrate! Screw your harem of men and drink too much. Tomorrow, ya can go back to never letting ya hair down." She pulls another bottle and tosses it to me. Drax catches it on my behalf as I shake my head.

She stands and glares at the others. "Come on, you bastards, I'll let ya buy me a drink."

Priest stands, as does Jon, and Piper winks as she gets up. Nan points in her face. "Not you, ya look like a lightweight. I don't do puke."

I watch them go, and when they leave, my men surround me again, and I just relax back into them. The bottle gets passed around, but I can't concentrate, my mind on everything to come.

There is still so much to do before I can relax.

Who knew the woman who used to drink herself to death every night and fight to feel something would be the one passing on the drink? I guess it's the burden of leadership, or maybe I have grown up and finally healed from my past.

Ivar still haunts my memories, and my body is covered in reminders, but I am so much more now than that slave girl. I'm a queen. Nan was wrong, a queen doesn't get a night off, not ever, but in the shelter of my men's arms, I can relax enough to let my body heal.

For a night at least.

"Soulmate, look at me," Dray demands.

Blinking, I turn my head and meet those cold eyes.

"I have led my people for a long time. They don't need you to stay apart from them and never relax to know you care. Go, join them, show you are still one of them, still the champion who stole the heart of a Seeker King and killed a Berserker King. The woman who saved The Wastes. Enjoy it, you deserve it, and we will be at your side."

"He's right, sweet cheeks. Killing yourself over those who died and what is to come won't help them. Your people love you because you are there with them."

"Sing their songs with them, drink with them, eat with them, and hear their grief and stories," Jax murmurs.

"You've got this, *Mi Alma*." Are they right?

I never saw myself as above anyone out there, how could I? I came from bloodshed and anger, a creature formed from the ashes of darkness and pain. I might be a queen in name now, but I am still the Champion, the one who rode The Wastes. Who hunted and captured.

Who joked and battled.

I am still her, and maybe they need to see that. Maybe I do too. I grab the bottle, drain it, and wipe my mouth. "You're fucking right, but if I get too drunk, someone needs to make sure Dray doesn't kill everyone."

They laugh, even Dray, who leans closer and bites my lip. "Soulmate, you would be right next to me, helping."

Too fucking true.

Sands below, I love these men.

They help me to my feet, and we head outside as the sun is setting. The fires are burning, and meat is already cooking, while bottles are being passed around. There are men arm wrestling, some playing drinking games.

It's rowdy, and laughter and song fill the air. It feels like home, it feels like being back at The Rim, but this time, the five men are at my back.

It relaxes that last part of me, and I pluck a bottle from Bern's hands as he lounges near one of the fires with a leg of an animal in one hand. Downing some of it, I hold it in the air as I look around. "Let's fucking celebrate!" I yell.

A cheer goes up when they finally realise it's not disrespectful. I head over to Archel and Piper, who are staring each other down over a makeshift table. I lean into Dray, wondering what they are doing, when suddenly, Piper blinks and lets out a curse, slamming her hand onto the table.

"Cock sucking dogs. Don't you ever blink?"

Snorting, I watch as they stand and two men take their places, their arms bare and facing up. I smile, knowing exactly what they are playing.

"Soulmate, want to play?" Dray murmurs into my ear as he steps around, pushes one of them off the barrel chair he was sitting on, and takes his place, straddling it. His cold eyes watch me. "I promise not to make you bleed...too much."

I can almost hear Evan scolding me, so I smirk, watching as the other man quickly moves and takes the other seat, facing him. "What we playing?"

"A Seeker game," he coos as he grabs a knife and places it on the cricket table between us. "Usually, we would do stabbing, but you have lost too much blood, so we will change up the rules. You spin the knife, and the person it lands on has to cut the place of the opponent, first to die or pass out loses." He leans in and almost presses his lips to mine. "I'm hard imagining you cutting me right now."

I smirk and push him back. "You always are when it comes to knives."

"What can I say, a woman with a blade gets me hard as hell." He grins.

Did he say woman...or women? Narrowing my eyes, I grab the blade and press it to his throat. "Women?" I murmur as he smirks and leans into the blade.

"Only one, soulmate. You, always you. Even when you hated me, even when I could taste the blood on your lips and see the ghosts in your eyes. There has only ever been you. Feel it." He grabs my other hand and drags it over his heart right in the middle of everyone. "It beats for you. Taste the truth on my lips."

Well, shit.

He sits back, and I try to slow my racing heart. "Ladies first." I grin.

He smirks as he grabs the knife and spins it. I watch it glide in a circle before slowing down. The crowd around us is huge now, the Berserker Queen versus the Seeker King. I know they are all excited, especially with the booze flowing.

When the knife finally slows, it's almost on me, but it slowly moves until it is pointing at him. "Fuck yes," he mutters, dragging his eyes across me. "Better cut me, soulmate, and make it deep."

I'm pretty sure this is foreplay for him right now, just with a crowd, but I can't back down. It's not in my nature, even if I love the crazy bastard. Though I bet by the end of this, he will be coming in his jeans while in pain and viewing our blood.

"Worth!" I hear my name chanted as I watch him with a smirk, making him wait. "Berserkers always win!" comes a yell, and I hear a scuffle, no doubt a fight starting.

I grab the knife and lean forward, pressing the sharp tip to his skin, right above his heart and his brand. His eyes are heating quickly, his tongue tracing his lips as he waits. With a harsh downward strike, I carve the blade around the brand, cutting a heart into his skin, the red of his blood bright as it starts to drip. Happy with it, I sit back as he looks down, a groan leaving his throat. "Fuck, I almost came."

Yeah, I don't fucking doubt that.

I have to shift as well, the sight of his blood making me wet. When Dray bleeds, it usually leads to hot as hell sex, and my pussy is well aware of that, even if I'm too injured to really do anything about it.

Dray leans forward and spins the knife as a bottle is plopped down next to me. Nodding my thanks, I take a swig as I watch it rotate before landing on Dray again. Laughing, I grab the knife and lean over, slicing across his arm quickly before sitting back.

He groans, his eyes closing for a moment. "How are you so perfect?" he murmurs, low enough for only me to hear.

Not answering, I spin the knife again, and this time, it lands on me. I brace for the pain and blood as he picks up the knife. Watching me, he leans closer. I keep my eyes on him, not flinching when he grabs my arm and slams it onto the table. He strokes along my flesh before the blade is suddenly there. Tracing where his fingers did, he makes a deep cut. I feel the blood fill it and drip instantly as he relaxes back and, eyes still locked on me, he licks the blade clean.

Holy fuck.

Looking down, I watch the blood trickle across my skin, just another scar to add to the collection. At this point, nearly all of my skin is covered, and anyone who is offended by that can fuck off.

Scars are a sign of strength, a big fuck you sign to those who tried to take you down. Kill you. Hurt you. Destroy you. They show the world that no matter what, you never give up.

I used to be ashamed of them, used to hide them and my brands. Now I let everyone see what I have survived. I'm a fucking queen. If a slave girl can become one, anything is possible. They need to know that.

We play for a bit longer, until cuts and blood cover both of our bodies. I even slice Dray's lip, which I swear he came over, making everyone laugh. The booze flows, and it loosens my inhibitions enough to relax.

Once, I was dependent on it. I used it to forget the pain, to black out the memories until I could function and sleep. Now it's the taste of victory, it's a shared celebration between my people and my loves. It brings us together where I was once alone.

I stand and stumble from a mixture of blood loss and booze, making those around us laugh. My other men are there, watching and waiting. I wink at them to let them know I'm okay when I hear someone grumbling and pushing closer.

"God fucking dammit!" Evan yells as he comes up on us. "I'm not stitching that up too, you crazy bitch!"

It goes silent as everyone waits for my reaction. Looking at Doc, I wink and laugh. The sound is taken up by the crowd as I clap him on the shoulder, grabbing the bottle from his hands and knocking some back before lifting it into the air.

"To The North!"

Chapter Seven

The Journey

Leaning back into Thorn's arms, I let the fire warm me as my eyes almost close. I stopped drinking a few hours ago and had something to eat on Doc's request... It was more like an order, but when Dray threatened to cut off his balls, it changed to a request.

Now we are all sitting, talking, eating, and drinking and telling stories of the day, of the fight, and I join in. I laugh when someone recounts how Jon tore the arm off a soldier and beat another with it.

Doc also cleaned my arm and patched me back up after I ripped some of my stitches, and then with a threat to stop hurting myself, he went and found Piper. I can hear her giggling from here, sitting in her mountain man's lap. I smile as I watch her. She deserves happiness, and I am so glad she has found it. I just hope she is strong enough to keep it, but knowing that girl, if anyone can, it's her.

She is a force to be reckoned with, just with a strange, rambling mouth.

Drax lies down, resting his head on my thigh. He's mirroring Jax, whose head is on my other thigh, my hand brushing through his hair. I drop my other hand to Drax's head and brush his hair, too, as

Maxen watches me from close by with a loving look in his eye. Dray is lying between my legs, stroking the cut I made on his chest almost lovingly.

I am so lucky to have them. Today, I nearly died. I know they are struggling with that, and so am I, if I'm honest. I was never scared to die before them. Now, dying means leaving them, and we haven't really lived yet. Now, we have a chance to, a chance to start a proper life with no Cities hanging over us. It won't be easy, there is still a lot to do, but I'm hopeful.

We can handle anything. We have survived torture, death, war, and separation. Everything else will be easy.

As my men speak and my friends join the fray, I close my eyes and just breathe in the warmth and laughter. It makes almost dying and all the pain worth it, this makes it all okay. When the sun rose today, the future looked bleak, but now it's filled with a bright sky.

The future is what we make it.

With my men and people at my back, we will change this world for the better. We can make it safer for people like us. People who have suffered, who were young and defenceless, who were controlled by evil persons.

We can make it a better nation.

Maxen carries me back to my tent when I am too tired to move. Usually, I would fight that, but I'm feeling weak. Exhaustion is settling in, which Drax points out is probably from blood loss, saying I need to rest and heal.

We leave the fires and laughter behind, letting the others carry on the celebration as we close our tent door. Jax helps me out my clothes, and Dray supports me as I lower down to the blankets and pillows. Peering across the space, I spot the blood-soaked bandage at my shoulder and wince. I can feel the one on my stomach bleeding again as well. Doc is going to kill me.

Maxen leans down and kisses it better. "We came so close to losing you. Never again, *Mi Alma.*"

I nod, holding back a yawn as he scoots in next to me and wraps his arm across my chest, careful of my stomach. The others scatter around me as I stare at the tent ceiling.

"Baby girl, rest, we will keep watch. Stop obsessing over everything that happened."

Shit, Thorn always knows.

I close my eyes, a smile curling my lips as I feel them shuffle closer.

"Soulmate, sleep, or I will knock you out myself."

"Crazy bastard," I mutter, even as I start to drop into that black void.

I wake with my heart pounding, sweat covering my body, and my mind caught in my nightmares. I dreamed of my men dying in the battle while I was held back, fighting to get to them, but always too late.

I watched them die over and over again, helpless to stop it.

Sands below, more nightmares to add to the mix. At this rate, I will never sleep. Even feeling their hands and bodies against me can't fight it off, so I slip from their grasps, wincing at the pain in my stiff body as I grab my shirt, jeans, and boots. Stepping out of the tent, I dress outside, noticing the world is quiet but filled with the snores of passed out warriors.

It's early morning, I can feel it, the freshness of a new day, as I manoeuvre around the tents and over the bodies. I sit on the sand, looking down at the battlefield, and just let myself feel.

All the emotions I fought back during and after—the fear, the anger

—I let it fill me, knowing repressing it will only lead to more issues. What happened was horrifying, terrifying, and blocking it out won't help.

I need to function, but I also need to be human and stop trying to be so perfect. I'm a warrior, a champion, but I'm also a living, breathing person who almost died, who lost friends, and now that the war is over, the adrenaline and stubbornness that keep me going is gone.

Nothing is left but regrets and grief.

I wish Major, Von, and Vas were here to see this. They deserve it. They sacrificed so much for me, and now that I have done what needed to be done, I wonder if it was all worth it.

They were all in so much pain, and they had such darkness in them, but that doesn't mean they wanted death, they were warriors. They were my friends. I can't forget them or what they did for me, because that's how they live on.

In our memories, even when it hurts.

"Mind the company?" comes a familiar, tired voice.

I swallow but nod as Piper sits next to me, staring out at the battlefield, for once not making smart remarks or rambling. She just reaches out and grabs my hand, holding it. "I'm here. I can't comprehend the magnitude of what you're going through, but I'm here for you, whatever you need. Worth, you are the strongest person I know, you can do this."

"What if I can't? I just keep thinking of everyone who died, all my friends and warriors, I don't want it to be for nothing," I admit, needing to let it out.

"Then don't let it. You know more than anyone what this world needs. You have seen the darkness it's capable of, the death and destruction, but also the love, determination, and strength. The North is scarred, just like you. But you can make it better. Do that for women like us. For those men and friends who died."

I swallow, unsure what to say. She is smart for her age, and for once, I don't feel the need to be strong. I need a friend, and right now, Piper is one.

"I look up to you, you know? I've heard the stories about you, I know what happened, yet here you are, fighting every day. Fighting for what you believe in. You let nothing stop you. But weakness is okay too, to heal, to remember. What you do...no one else can do it. You're the Champion, Worth. That is more than just a word. It means something. Everything you do means something, because you show us what it truly means to be alive, to be a warrior. You are allowed to make mistakes, to regret and grieve, but don't let it stop you now, or it's all for nothing. And we will be right here behind you the whole way, Queen. Archel told me once he saw your first fight, he saw this little slave girl who didn't stay down. After every hit, she got back up, stronger than before... Do that now, get back up stronger than before. Be the fighter we all know you are, and when you need to be weak? Be it. A great leader needs both."

I turn, meeting those brown eyes. "You're a leader now too, Pascha," I tease, and she smiles.

"Don't tell anyone, I'm winging it," she jokes. "Me too, me fucking too."

We both look back out to the sand, and together, our two broken souls heal a little bit more. That's what love does, and love comes in more shapes than soulmates and lovers, but in friends and family, in those who stay, even when it's hard.

"Piper?" I murmur.

"Yeah?" she asks, leaning her head onto my shoulder as the sun starts to rise.

"Is your hand on my ass?" I laugh.

She giggles. "Woops, I had to know. Gotta admit, cocks do it for me, sorry."

Laughing, I lean my head onto hers and watch the sunrise—a new day, a new dawn, filled with possibilities. Piper is right, it's time to get back up.

Stronger than before.

My fight isn't over, not yet. I will remember the fallen and do better in the future, knowing they laid down their lives for that. I will always miss them, but I can't live with one foot in the past when the future is filled with so much potential.

Sometimes, you have to let go, and now, I do. Letting that float into the sun, I stop blaming myself for what happened, and as it crests over the horizon, I feel the others wake up, and I smile.

The journey is never easy, but sometimes, you find yourself in a moment that lets you know it's all worth it, and with the brilliance of the sun shining down on me and the endless possibilities of our future laid out on the sand...I know.

This is worth everything.

CHAPTER EIGHT

TIME TO HEAL

After eating breakfast, everyone starts to pack up. I'm debating how to handle this. Doc says I need to rest, which I plan on doing back at The Ring while planning for the meeting in a few days, but then I hear the yells.

Cars are approaching on the horizon.

Everyone scrambles into defence mode as I peer out, but as I watch the sand kicking up around the tires, I realise who they are—Vert, it has to be. So I lean back against my bike and wait while others rush around me. I don't want to look weak, and today, my legs are shaking, so leaning back might look like I don't have a care in the world, but honestly, it's to keep me upright.

My men and people are spread out behind me, but I raise my hand to stop them from firing. The cars stop a few meters away, the sand slowly settling around them as their engines idle. I wait, a bead of sweat dripping down my spine as a car door slowly opens. I keep my hands loose and near my swords, ready just in case.

But I was right, it is Vert. I guess now is as good a time as any. He looks the same as the last time I saw him. His bright blue eyes are hidden by his sunglasses, his chin and cheeks are covered in stubble, and his brown hair shines bright in the sun. His body is encased in a three-piece suit with a few holes here and there, but he's very put together compared to me. I don't let him see how that affects me, instead, I tilt my head back like the queen I am. He stops between his car and my bike, leaving space between us with his hands out peacefully to the sides. "Worth." He nods.

I nod back, not giving a shit about the pleasantries. "How are The Cities?"

He smirks then before pulling down his sunglasses and wiping them on his shirt. "Like you predicted, it's under my rule now, and I will ensure our people stop starving and dying. The soldiers have been killed or run out."

I nod as he puts them back on. "Do I need to worry about you?" I ask.

He shakes his head as he looks behind me. "I don't want The North, and I wouldn't be able to take it anyway. It's yours. We will stay in our Cities, and you will stay in your Wastes. I would like a truce between us. One day, we could even start trading if that would be okay?"

"A truce," I agree, as murmurs go through the crowd. "But know this, you remember who put you on that throne. This is our land. Ours. You break this truce, and we will destroy you like we did the people before you and the people before that."

He grins. "Understood, and warning received. I'm going to head back now, lots to do, as I'm sure you understand. There is still corruption in the government I need to wipe out. I imagine you have a lot to do as well. I will send a messenger once I am sure it is safe, and we can discuss terms."

He turns away and begins walking back to his car, but then he pauses. "Oh, and Worth?" When he looks back, he grins. "Congratulations on your victory, Queen of The North."

He gets back in his car, and the engines rev as they pull away, spraying sand and dirt up behind them. I watch as the vehicles fade into the distance, racing towards The Cities. It's done. I don't think we will have any issues with them now. I relax, almost slumping into the bike. I worried he would turn on us after, but he seems like a businessman. Smart and calculating, he knows he needs us, so he will stay there, and like he said...we have a truce. It could work well for both of us.

Priest and Nan step up next to me. Jon follows behind them, as if unsure of his welcome. "We are heading back home for now. Shit to do. See you soon," he offers, and then turns to leave.

Priest nods at me, his usual black wavy hair frizzy from the heat. Unlike the first time I saw him, it's unstyled and a bit wild. His face has stubble growing across it, but his cold eyes are still the same. He's wearing his priest robes again, and his power makes me shiver as he stares. I never understood this man, but I respect his leadership skills and the fear he creates. He might be insane, he might run a cult, but he's a good ally to have. "Until the angels cry and the sinners beg."

Yep, just as batshit.

He leaves, and Nan and I watch him go. "He's short one too many screws." She laughs, and I smile. "Go home, kid, and get some rest. Let those strapping young men wait on you hand and foot. I heard orgasms are good for healing." She winks before disappearing too.

My men surround me again, and I stare out at The Wastes. "Let's go home."

I help pack up, but I can't ride my bike back, so Jax does it for me. When I tried to swing my leg over, my stomach had me almost screaming, not to mention my shoulder. Dray took one look at me, picked me up, and deposited me in one of the trucks, kissing me hard to distract me from slicing his throat.

So now I'm in the back seat, like some pompous broken ass, being driven back to The Ring. My men ride next to me on their bikes, while Evan is in the seat with me, checking over my stomach, even as I try to push away his faffing hands.

"Stop it," he snaps, pissed. "Your stitches are tearing, you need to be more careful."

"It's fine, I've had worse," I retort as I yank down my shirt.

He sits back with a sigh and stares at me. "Worth, you almost died. You still could if you aren't careful, your body died... Your wound is bad. Really bad. Just for once, do as you're told."

"Not in my vocabulary, Doc, sorry." I wink, sitting back with a wince as my stomach burns with pain, but I ignore it.

The trip doesn't take too long. I spend it looking out of the window, making lists of what I need to do when we get back. They will all be looking to me now, including the other leaders, so I need to have answers and plans. Almost dying isn't an excuse not to have them.

We almost die out here every day. A little sword wound won't stop me.

When we reach The Ring, we pull up to the gate, and the driver looks back at me—he's one of Major's men. "Welcome home, queen." He stops and glances at Doc before looking back to me. "What you did...it was fucking amazing. Don't stop now. I'll follow wherever you lead, we all will."

I nod at him, unsure what to say, and push my door open. I slide out into the blinding heat, stumbling slightly. Gritting my teeth, I force my feet under me and lean casually against the car to gather my strength as my men stop around me and dismount. The looks they give me show they know I'm worse than I'm letting on, but they don't say anything.

Maxen does wrap his arm around me, like he is simply holding me as I pull away from the car, but he takes most of my weight. My feet drag slightly on the sand as I walk. I'm still exhausted and feeling weak, not a feeling I like. Luckily, I shouldn't have any fighting to do today, unless I have to play smack a bitch on some fools.

Some of our people are already here, setting up camp inside the gate. We sent the injured back to be treated yesterday, and those coming in today still need to be looked at, but knowing the Berserkers and Major's men, they won't get checked out unless they are dying or their limbs are falling off.

The gates begin to open for us. We left some guards here in case anyone had any ideas about attacking while we were gone, after all, there are still rogues, scavs, and roadies out there.

When they swing wide, I freeze in horror, scanning the dead and dying. There are so many leaning against enclosures and lying on the ground, some have tops, jackets, and sheets over their faces, their bodies limp. One is covered in a shirt, his bloody, unmoving hand the only part of him I can see.

The injured are wrapped in homemade bandages, and others being treated as water is passed around. I spot men without eyes, and one has half of his face caved in, with blood flowing down it and through the rag he's holding there to try and stop it. Some are missing legs and arms.

The smell of blood, piss, and shit is rife, as is the sweet smell of infection and decay.

Their gazes swing my way, some begging me for help, but I can't do anything. I have nothing to aid them. I feel each stare like a punch in the gut, making it hard to breathe.

So many eyes.

So many expectations.

The odds of a fight never bothered me before because it was just me who risked losing, but looking at these men, faced with the overwhelming loss, is almost crippling.

But then something happens.

A murmur goes through the amassed injured. Some struggle to their knees, their heads starting to bow as I blink in confusion. "What's happening?" I murmur to Maxen, but he doesn't answer.

More and more get to their knees and bow their heads. A big man with half his face bandaged and one of his legs bloody and bent at a wrong angle swears as he tries to get to his knees. He grabs the man tending to him and snarls right in his face. "Help me to my fucking knees, boy! That's our goddamn queen."

I step forward then, releasing Maxen, and fall to my own knees before him, making him freeze. "Don't, stay still, you're injured. Your life means more to me than some gesture."

He shakes his head, and using the man beside him, he drags himself to his knees. "It's not just a gesture, my queen, it is an honour to be on my knees for the woman willing to sacrifice her life to save us all. We kneel for you, for your sacrifice...to let you know we see it. We respect it, and we will follow you always. You gave everything for us, now it is our turn."

I am speechless once again as I stand and turn, looking at everyone bowing to me. The pain must be unimaginable for some, but they still don't move, don't hesitate. One of them bangs his fists on the dirt, and the others copy, the sound loud, like one beating heart.

"Champion, Champion," they chant.

I stand in the middle, astonished, unable to look away from the sight before me. Warriors from all across The Wastes kneel side by side with my moniker on their lips.

It echoes around us, taken up by the arriving warriors. All around me, warriors, hunters, men, and women fall to their knees, calling my name. The first time I came here, I was a slave, no one knew me, I was insignificant...but now.

Now they call for me. Chant for me. Kneel for me.

I wish Major was here to see it, he would be so proud, but in a way, I know he is. He created this place for me, for us, a safe haven. And now it's our home, a place for those lost and damned, a place for people all over The Wastes.

And it is filled with my name.

I soak it up, saturating the part of me that is grieving and angry. I let their honour and belief wash through me until I am full once again.

I reach my hand down to the man closest to me and help him to his feet. "We've lived too long on our knees, brother," I tell the

Berserker. He, in turn, grabs the next man and helps him up, and so on and so forth, until we are all standing.

All free men and women on our feet.

Freedom, it's worth dying for, worth burning the world for.

I didn't give them that, it could only be taken. And they did, so did I.

Eventually, they stop and settle back down, resting again and letting their wounds be treated. My men step up behind me, and Maxen's arm wraps around my waist as we start to walk down the sand-covered track, winding through the empty enclosures and buildings to my rooms.

I make it inside the structure before I falter. My legs crumple under me, and I try to get back up as Dray takes my other side, but I can't, my head lowering in shame. "I can't walk."

Without a word, I am swung up into Dray's arms, and he carries me effortlessly up the stairs to my usual room. Jax opens the door before we get there so Dray can carry me in and lay me down gently on the sofa with a kiss. "Then I will walk for you, soulmate."

But an injured, dying warrior is useless...and left behind. I know my men would never do that, however, so I won't make them watch me die. I will get through this and be stronger than ever.

I have to.

CHAPTER NINE

DEATH'S DOOR

ood and water are delivered to our rooms. I'm too tired to even protest it. I eat some, but I'm starting to feel sick, so I end up sipping water and then crawling into bed.

I hear them fighting about who gets to lie next to me, their bickering making me smile, even as my eyes shut in exhaustion. I feel the bed dip, and then arms and legs wrap around me from either side before it goes quiet and I drift off to sleep, hoping I have no nightmares tonight.

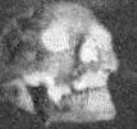

I barely remember sleeping, but when I wake up suddenly, heart racing and body covered in sweat, I know time has passed. Groaning, I slip from Drax's and Jax's arms, stumbling over Maxen's, Thorn's, and Dray's bodies on the floor before rushing to the toilet.

I dry heave and then turn on the sink, cupping my hands under the flow before submerging my face in it. Sighing, I lift my head and meet my eyes in the mirror. They are bloodshot, and there are bags underneath them. My hair's a mess, and my skin is pale and stark. I look like shit.

Feel like it too.

Knowing I won't be going back to sleep with the sick feeling in my stomach, I head out to the balcony to get some fresh air. I perch on the stone railing and look out at The Wastes below.

It's so quiet at night, with only the distant howls of cannibals and ferals drifting on the night air. There is no joyous laughter or fighting tonight. The Ring is dark. Here, I feel Major's ghost so much more than anywhere else, but I also feel at home.

The Berserkers' castle isn't for me. I don't do thrones and torture rooms. Out in The Wastes...I can't lead from there. No, Major was right. This is my home now, my place is here, but I can't look to the past without seeing the ghosts, Vass's and Von's memories flashing in my head. I don't know why I'm remembering my brother now, maybe because it's finally over.

It's strange that I don't really think of my father. I know he's out there, Piper told me, but honestly, I don't miss him. The only father I do miss is six feet under. In fact... Grabbing my sword in clumsy fingers, I silently leave the room, shutting the door gently, and head down the stairs and out the back.

I find the tree and Major's grave beneath it. Wincing as I sit, I stare at the dirt like it will give me answers. Fighting I understand, I am good at, even politics to a degree, but I'm not suited for what is coming now. Maybe if I had more time with him, or if he was here to help me along... I search the dirt where he is buried for answers, but it's just a grave with a body. He isn't here, no, his spirit is everywhere. It's in The Ring where he saved me, in the slave quarters where he healed me, in the pit where he taught me to fight, and in his office where he taught me to read and to love.

I might not have him here physically, but I know his memory is still present. All those lessons and late-night talks stayed with me. He knew I could do this, and Major is—was always right.

"Well, we won," I mutter, not really knowing why I am talking.

The breeze out here is just as hot as usual and blows across my sweat-drenched body, making me frown. I'm used to the heat, so why am I sweating so much?

Ignoring the pull on my stomach, I lean forward and run my hand through the sand there, wishing he could talk back to me. "I guess it's time for politics now, I-I don't know how to do that or get them to listen. I can do the battles, the war... Fuck, I can handle dying, but now they all look to me. They think I have the answers. What if I don't? What if all I have are more questions?"

I let it out here, knowing he can't judge me—all my fears, everything. "I want this to be a better place, the war should mean something... Maybe we could make The Wastes safer. It's not like I'm going out to hunt bounties anytime soon, and I was one of the only ones. Once the dust of the dead settles, they will be back to raping, pillaging, and stealing... I don't want that. But I don't know if I'm strong enough to stop it. How do you change years of lawlessness, oppression, and anger? How do you change the norm, even if that norm is wrong? They are used to getting away with everything, they won't like listening to rules. They think this world is theirs to do as they wish with no consequences. But there has to be consequences, there has to be, Major, otherwise we will just keep killing each other, living one big cycle of death and destruction."

I shake my head, holding my hand up and letting the dirt run through my fingers. "But how do I change the world when I am just one voice?"

I debate it as I watch the granules of sand fall. As more spills from my palm, the pile grows, and when my hand is empty apart from a few granules clinging to my fingers, I almost laugh.

"You get more voices," I murmur, staring at the pile. "Until the world overflows with them, and the only ones who don't speak are the ones who won't ever follow or listen. You turn one speck of sand into a mountain."

This time I do laugh, loudly, but it cuts off into a cough, and I cover my mouth as it hacks through my lungs. Each jerk of my body rips at my stomach, until I fall backwards with a whimper. The agony is too much, I can taste blood on my lips, and when I lift my hand, I spot the crimson on my palm in the moonlight.

That can't be good.

Blinking, I realise time has passed. My hand is on my chest, and I can feel something warm around the wound on my stomach. Lifting my head, I glance down to see the bandage is red...and around it, the skin is too. I hold up my hand, blinking when I get double vision, watching as two hands weave about as I prod the skin. I almost scream when I do, and I fall back with a cry.

Something is really wrong.

My heart is racing, my lungs are tight, my vision is darkening, and my body is on fire. I turn my head to try and find someone, but all I see is my other hand lying in the sand. I watch a huge spider crawl across it. Its spidery legs tickle as its thick, black body stills over my palm, and it turns to me. I observe it helplessly until it finally crawls off my hand and back onto the sand.

Gulping, I force myself to move. My body doesn't want to respond, but with pure fucking grit, I manage to flip over onto my front, biting my tongue at the pain it causes, biting it so hard I taste my own blood.

Great.

Digging my fingers into the sand, I grind my teeth and drag myself across it. Sweat pours down my face, my useless legs heavy and limp behind me. Each drag against the sand sends more pain spiking through me until it blinds me.

Yet still I pull myself, knowing I need to get help. Head down, eyes closed, and teeth clenched, I gouge my fingers in and pull. Dig in and pull. Again, I don't even know which way I am going.

My head starts to get woozy, and I gag when I feel the sand slipping into my wounds. *Come on, Worth, keep fucking going. You did not survive all this shit to die out here like a fucking dog.*

Think of your men.

Of your people.

Of your life still left to live.

Screaming silently, I carry on until I can't move any farther. My body gives out, and I collapse into the sand, unable to see, ears ringing, and blood flowing easily from my wounds, no doubt staining the sand.

I want to cry out for help, but my tongue won't move, and as darkness claims me, I scream for my men in my mind.

Chapter Ten

Bed Bound

I feel the heat first, flowing through me like I have been asleep in the sands for days. My entire body drips with sweat, and my skin burns from it.

Then comes the agony.

Red-hot pokers pierce every inch of my skin, ripping me open, flaying me, cutting me, and I hear Ivar's laugh. Is that where I am? In his torture chamber? It sure as fuck feels like it.

I feel something prodding at my stomach, so I smack it away, at least I think I do. Two seconds later, my arms are pinned down by something heavy, then my legs. I thrash, snarl, and bite, and words spill past my lips, even though I can't open my eyes.

Something sharp stabs into my arm, and then a moment later, coolness flows through me and I slip back into the waiting darkness, this time relaxed and happy. I'm no longer in pain.

When I wake up again, I'm not as hot or in as much pain. I'm lying on something soft, the ceiling mouldy and stained above me. I'm in my room. Turning my head, I spot my guys in the next room talking to Evan, and they all look worried.

I must make a noise, because they quiet and rush in. Jax helps me lift my head while Drax presses a bottle of water to my mouth. "Sip it, babe, tiny sips."

I do as I am told, quenching my thirst, and then they lower me back down, my body still numb. "What happened?" I croak.

Evan huffs and crosses his arms, glaring down at me. "What happened, she asks?" He throws his hands in the air as he leans in. "Did I or did I not tell you to rest?"

"Yeah?" I offer, confused.

His eyes narrow further, his nostrils flaring—oh, he's really pissed. He looks like an adorable little dog when they are angry. "And did you rest?"

I blink and open my mouth, but he beats me to it, pointing his finger at me. "No, you fucking didn't. Instead, I got a rude man waking me up while I was spooning my girl, telling me you almost killed yourself and were now, and I quote, 'sweating like a whore on payday.'"

I snort at that, and he wags his finger. "Not done. So I get up and haul my ass here to find you feverish, bleeding to death, and completely out of it."

I turn my head to Maxen and grin. "What happened? Doc is too busy having a tantrum."

"I am not having a tantrum!" he yells, but we both ignore him. Dray is on the bed next to me, stroking my arm lovingly. He's quiet for a change.

Maxen sighs and crouches beside me, stroking my face. I've scared him, I can tell. "*Mi Alma*, a patrol found you half dead in the sands bleeding a lot. He got you here and raised the alarm... You've got an infection."

"Probably from digging fucking graves or sleeping in dirt!" Evan scoffs before sighing. "It has been brewing for a day or so I would say, but you got the thick of it last night. I don't think it's blood poisoning though, otherwise you would be dead. Luckily, I stole supplies from Paradise, so I managed to knock you out last night and give you some antibiotics to treat it. But you are going to be weak. There is no guarantee these are the right antibiotics for the infection, and without my lab, I can't test you."

I nod, trying to swallow with my dry mouth. I can feel myself getting warmer again, but I don't know if that's just my imagination or not. "So...I could die?"

He lowers his eyes for a moment before meeting mine. "Yes." The room explodes.

All my men shout and gesture at once. Dray has his knife to Evan's throat, who is pale and wheezing but not fighting. Jax stands by my side, but he's quiet, very quiet, and not with us.

"Dray, put him down," I snap and then cough.

That makes them stop, and all of them rush to my side. Jax passes me water, his panic-filled eyes meeting mine. I squeeze his hand when he pulls the bottle away and settle back into the bed. Thorn fluffs my pillows for me until I'm comfortable, his face drawn and lost. Maxen takes my hand and holds it. Drax crawls onto the bed by my feet, watching me worriedly, his hand stroking my leg.

Dray is next to the end again, his weapon sheathed at last. I assure them I'm all right as I watch Evan put himself back together, tossing Dray a glare which luckily my crazy man doesn't see.

When they calm down, I keep my eyes on Evan. "What are my odds?" My voice is calm.

"If you make it through the night, I say we are in the clear." "What can we do?" Dray asks, and the fact that he's ice-cold and composed worries me.

"Ice baths, cold compresses, keep her fever down as much as we can. I will double her antibiotics, which might shut her body down and kill her, but I think it's the only way. You are on bed rest. Eat and drink, even if you don't want to, you will need it. Your body will need it."

"Okay." I sigh.

"Okay?" he repeats. "Just like that, you will do as you're told?"

I snort. "I'm not an idiot, Doc. You know what you're doing, and as much as you might think I do, I don't have a death wish. If this is what it takes, I'll do it."

He smiles at me encouragingly. "You can kick this infection's ass the way you do everything else. Let me draw up those antibiotics. Do you want some pain meds with it?"

I debate it. The pain isn't too bad right now, but it might get worse, then again, I've never wanted to dose with meds to not feel. I would rather feel the pain and know I'm still alive. "No."

He nods like he expected it and leaves me with my men, who are all looking at me. All worried. "All right, stop watching me like I'm already dead, okay? I've had infections before, but this time, we've got a handy doctor," I joke, but it falls flat.

Jax turns my head and stares down at me. "I can't lose you," he whispers, voice cracking.

"You're not going to," I tell him, leaning into him, letting him see the determination in my eyes. "I've been ripped apart, raped, tortured, stabbed, burnt, and worse. They didn't kill me, and this won't either."

He swallows hard, searching my eyes. My poor demon. "Look at me," I snap, and he does. "I'm not going anywhere, I promise you. I'll even do as I am told and stay in bed." I wiggle my eyebrows. "You can join me."

"No hanky-panky!" Evan yells from the other room, making me laugh.

"Hanky-panky? How old is he?" Drax snorts as he reaches over and grabs Jax's arm for a moment. "Come on, brother, you know our girl is tougher than any infection."

"He's right, baby girl, you will be fine. Might teach you to look after yourself more though," Thorn chides and grins at me, flashing pearly whites. His smile softens his face, so I can't really be mad.

"It's simple. She will survive it, or we all die anyway," Dray points out, lounging next to me.

They all share a look, wearing smiles on their lips. "Fuck, you are all insane," I mutter. "Now someone get some cold compresses, I'm sweating like a bitch."

"Sponge bath in bed?" Drax suggests and perks up, tumbling from the bed in his haste. "I'll be right back. Get naked!" He stops at the door and looks back at us worriedly. "Just Tazzy, I don't need to see your cocks."

I laugh, but it cuts off in a pained moan as I breathe through it. Maxen kisses my cheek before bringing his lips to mine, rubbing them against me a hairsbreadth away. His warm breath washes over me. "I'll play nurse for you."

"Yeah? Going to wear an outfit?" I murmur.

He grins, I feel it against my lips. "Anything for you, *Mi Alma*, you know that, and when you're better, I'm going to prove to you just how much I love you."

"I can't wait," I whisper as he leans back and looks at the others, taking charge.

"We take it in turns. One awake at all times, checking on her temperature, making sure she is eating and drinking." He looks to Dray. "Apart from you. I'm betting you're not leaving her side or sleeping."

Dray salutes him. "Correct." He winks at me. "Me and you, soulmate." He seems to debate something before looking up at Evan. "If I cut myself, will I get an infection too so we can go through it together?" Evan blinks, seemingly at a loss for words, so I save him. "Baby?"

Dray looks at me, and I grin. "I love you, but don't, okay? I need you to protect me while I'm out."

His eyes flash as he grips my chin hard, forcing my gaze to his as Evan stabs me with a needle. "I will always protect you, so will your other men... Well, apart from me. Now rest, soulmate, we have some celebrating to do."

I nod and turn back, closing my eyes. I feel them around me. It gives me something to look forward to, getting better and being held and loved by my men. "Celebrate how?" Evan inquires.

I don't bother saving him from this one.

"With my tongue in her pussy and her knives in my chest," Dray answers.

"Hell yes," Jax adds, making me smile. "Or her bouncing on my cock," Drax calls. "Or between us," Thorn remarks.

"All of them." Maxen laughs, and when I peek open an eye, I see Evan blushing furiously.

"Leave the boy alone, the things we do would make him faint in shock," I tease.

"Especially if he saw our foreplay." Dray laughs. "One time, she tried to kill me... I swear I came so hard, I nearly passed out."

"Tried to kill you?" Evan questions.

"Failed, clearly," I deadpan. "I won't next time."

"Save the dirty talk for when you can follow through, wife. If we try to play right now, your men might try to kill me, and wouldn't that be a shame if I had to gut them all?"

Maxen laughs. "You could try. You might be insane and an assassin, but we could kick your crazy ass."

"Keep telling yourself that. I would offer to test it, but I have a feeling my soulmate would kill me if I ruined your pretty boy face."

"Boys," I snap, opening my eyes. "Behave. No maiming, torturing, or killing when I can't join in."

"Party pooper." Drax chuckles as he draws closer. "Now, my queen, where would you like me to cool you down?" he queries, lowering his voice and almost purring. I flip him the bird.

"No dirty talk. You can't get me hot and turned on when I'm dying," I protest.

He pouts. "I can't help that you continually want my dick, princess."

Maxen smacks him on the back of his head. "Stop talking about dicks. We need her to cool down, not warm up." He winks at me. "That can come later."

"You are all pervs," I mutter.

They move around me then as the medicine starts to kick in, and

The Nations

I think the bastard must have given me more than antibiotics, because I'm starting to fall asleep as they place a cold compress on my head.

I narrow my eyes on Evan as I fight closing them, and he grins. "Just had to make sure you did as you were told," he offers.

That rat bastard, I'm going to stab him...when I can move again.

CHAPTER ELEVEN

FEVER PANIC

I slip in and out of consciousness. I can't tell the time or even the day anymore. But I'm hot all the time, sweat covering me and drying across my skin in a disgusting way, yet I can't be bothered to care. One of my men is always there with Dray lying next to me, stroking his knife across his chest and singing to himself. They wet me down with cold water, washing me and placing compresses on my head. They also make me sip water. I try to eat, but I end up throwing it up, and they give up for a while.

But it's still not enough.

I can almost feel the infection spreading, making me sluggish and numb. Numb but hot. So hot. I can barely breathe. It increases every time I rouse, until I am caught between sleep and wakefulness. I have been having hallucinations, because I see Ivar, Major, and Vas, but it feels so real. I toss and turn, and eventually, they have to tie me down, making me cry out.

Dray strokes my cheek and calms me, muttering in my ear the whole time, until I can no longer hear him. My eyes remain locked on the ceiling, my brain stuck between past and present.

I can feel tears streaming down my face and my men wiping

them away, asking what is wrong, but I can't answer, and I slip back into slumber.

When I wake, panic fills me as my dream clings to me. I'm so hot, my head feels like it's about to explode. I hear Evan talking, arguing, and Dray is next to me, speaking to me, but I can't focus on his words.

Too scared. Too panicked.

"Rest? Von never got buried," I scream, thrashing. "He needs to be laid to rest, needs to."

Dray holds me down, getting in my face. "We will put him to rest. Look at me, soulmate, we will, I promise, now stop moving or you will tear your stitches." He looks over his shoulder then as I blink under him. "Doc, she's worse. What the fuck can we do? She's too hot."

I hear Evan mumble, and then Dray swears. "Fuck it. Come on, wife, we need to cool you down."

He scoops me from the bed, causing me to whimper in pain as he strides across the room, kicks open the bathroom door, and starts to run the bath. As he waits, he strips me of my shirt, my pants long since gone, and removes his clothes before climbing in with me. He holds me as the cool water starts to encase my flesh, cooling me instantly.

My eyes close in bliss as I let his strength support me. I hear the others enter the room. They are all worried, but with the cold water lapping over my body, I finally start to drift back to sleep.

"Don't you dare fucking leave me," he snarls in my ear.

"I'm fucking sleeping, you madman," I mutter, making them all chuckle as I groan, my stomach hurting again.

"Take the pain meds, babe, please," Drax whispers, and I crack open my eyes to see him next to me, the cool water stopping the fire in my brain.

"No." I sigh.

Dray laughs as Thorn swears. "Baby girl, it doesn't make you weak. Take the pain meds."

I shake my head and close my eyes. "*Mi Alma*, look at me."

I open my eyes to see Maxen beside me, his eyes pleading and hard. "If not for you, then for us. We've watched you suffer enough. Do you really want to hurt us even more?"

I grind my teeth. "Oh, you manipulative fuck."

He smiles slightly. "Yeah, but is it working?" I groan, and he grabs my hand. "Please, my love, I can't stand this. It doesn't make you weak. It makes you smart enough to know when you need help, and you are smart, Worth, too smart to fucking say no out of pride."

"Please, Angel," Jax whispers, sitting on the side of the bath, stroking my leg. "I like pain as much as the next person, but I can't stand to see you suffer. We both know surrender doesn't mean weakness. I will gladly surrender to you for the rest of my life, but you have to be alive to do so. Take the meds."

"Do it, soulmate, trust in us. No one will touch you or get close while you are out," Dray murmurs.

"Promise?" I ask softly, hating the weakness in my voice. "I will protect you forever, wife, until my last breath." Sighing, I look at Evan. "Do it, Doc."

He mutters, "Thank fuck," and rushes to draw up the dose as I float and cool down.

"You've got this, baby girl. Conquer it like you do everything else."

Their confidence in me helps settle me further, and when Evan comes back and injects me, I think of Jax's words.

Surrender doesn't mean weakness.

It means you're strong enough to know when to bend so you don't break.

I do that now, I bend.

And as the meds kick in and pull me under, I place my trust in those around me for once to be saved, even if the fight is in my body.

I wake a few times during the next couple of days, usually with screams leaving my lips, even though I try to stop them. My body is on fire, as is my mind, and the pain is excruciating. Evan is there to dose me, and they cool my body down with towels, but when it's not enough, I take an ice bath with one of my guys.

They hold me up while I shiver and shake. They sing to me, talk to me. They are always with me, never leaving my side. I'm forced to drink, but I can't eat. Finally, somewhere in the middle of the night, I realise each time I wake the pain is lessening, as is the heat.

The final time I wake up, it's with a gasp, bracing for the pain and warmth, but it doesn't come. I just feel the normal pain from being stabbed, and I'm warm, but not so much that I feel like I am dying.

My men are asleep around me, apart from Drax, who is sitting at my side, his hands holding mine as tears glisten on his cheeks. I spot Evan in the next room snoring softly before turning back to the man beside me. I reach out to brush Drax's tears away. He jumps and smiles as he quickly wipes them away and forces a weak smile on his lips. "Hey, sweet cheeks, don't you look beautiful?"

"Fucking liar," I whisper so I do not wake them. "You okay?"

My funny man has such a sensitive soft side. Underneath all the jokes and charm, he is just as damaged and lost as us. He doesn't often show it, but he does so now, his blue eyes begging me not to leave him like everyone else. His face is pale, and there are bags under his eyes.

"Come here," I murmur, unable to lift my head much.

He shuffles closer, but not close enough. His eyes drop as he tries to hide his fear from me, but fuck that. These are my men, we've been through hell and back, and he doesn't get to shy away to protect me now. I want the raw edge of his fear and anger, I want it all, even if it hurts, because I don't ever want those pretty fucking placating lies.

So, gritting my teeth, I raise my head, even though it almost kills me, and press my forehead to his, running my lips along his reassuringly. "I'm not going anywhere. I'm too fucking strong for that shit, babe. Don't give up believing in me now just because it got hard. Our odds are always life and death."

I feel Jax waking next to me, but he stays still, knowing his brother needs me right now.

"Tazy..." Drax sighs. "I don't know how to live without you. I realised it in The Cities. We spent our lives searching for something, and we found you...and I can't lose you now. I just got you back. I wanted to grow old with you. See you all wrinkly and badass, still riding on your bike and kicking ass. I want to stand by your side as you kill anyone who annoys you, even when we're eighty."

"Eighty, huh?" I deadpan. "I didn't sign up for that long with you fuckers. I'll be crazy by fifty."

I push away my shock at the growing old comment. There was a time I thought I would never see my next year, never mind eighty. But Drax has already thought about it.

"Like you could get rid of us." He snorts and presses closer, his breath blowing over my face as our words are whispered between us on scared, trembling lips. His eyes are filled with hope. Jax squeezes my other hand, offering me strength.

"I don't know, I reckon I could outrun you." I laugh softly.

He grins, his lips catching on mine against it. "We would find you. We would follow Dray, that crazy fucker would catch you."

"True." I snigger. "He would probably chain himself to me."

He chuckles and kisses me softly. "Eighty years would still never be enough with you, Tazanna Worth. You're the love of my life."

"You softie," I tease.

"It was the boobs that made me fall in love, and don't get me started on your ass—"

"That's more like it," I murmur, sighing as I cup his face with shaky, weak hands, annoying myself.

"Sorry if I woke you, sweet cheeks."

"Nah, your brother was feeling me up, it woke me," I grumble, making him smile.

"He is a handsy bastard. You should have seen him when they took us. He laughed right in their faces and declared you would kick their asses for touching what was yours."

"Too fucking right. No one touches you but me, even if it's to kill your annoying asses."

He gasps dramatically. "Is that any way to talk to your husband? And I thought we were the lost boys together! Wait, if we are married... Oh, hell no, if you die, we don't get your crazy killer."

I chuckle, and I hear the others wake up, especially Evan, who yells, "What? Who? What's wrong?" He scrambles off the sofa and falls, and we all watch as he blinks in confusion, waking up.

"We were going on about shaving your head," I murmur as I lie down.

He narrows his eyes on me as he gets to his feet. "Piper would kill you."

"No, she wouldn't. She would barge in all angry, then forget and go off on a tangent, probably about my boobs." I wiggle, trying to get comfortable, and Maxen and Thorn are there, helping me sit up and fluffing my pillows.

Dray is between my legs, and not in a good dirty way. He's just chilling here, like I am a human pillow, with his head over my pussy. Weirdo.

"How are you feeling?" Evan asks, pushing Drax aside and pressing his hand to my head before yanking the sheet down and checking my wound, which looks less angry and red. He leans down and sniffs it.

"Dude, what the hell?" I grumble as he raises his head, his shoulders slumping.

"The infection smell is disappearing." He looks to me then, smiling. "I think you're getting through it."

"What exactly does that mean?" Jax inquires quietly.

"It means she is going to live a long life, annoying and scaring you," Evan rumbles. "Unless she gets her ass stabbed again."

"Only by my cock," Dray murmurs.

Evan blinks, and then it clicks that he said 'ass' and 'stabbed.' His cheeks heat, making us all laugh. "Not an ass man, Doc?"

He rubs his face. "Jesus, I am not discussing that."

"Why? By now you've seen all of me, including my insides." I grin at him as he shakes his head and points at my face.

"No, now sleep, you still need it. I'm going to find my Pip and take a nap. I will see you in the morning." He turns and then looks back. "And I do mean sleep...not the ass—oh, fuck this." He storms out, and we all laugh again.

Thorn hands me some water, which I sip, and Maxen disappears into the other room before coming back with some meat, which he passes to me. "Eat," he demands, so I do, nibbling on it. My stomach feels empty.

"You're cute when you're bossy," I tell him, and he grins, those enticing lips tipping up as I remember his drugging kisses. His eyes narrow though.

"Eat, no dirty thoughts."

I laugh and finish off the meat, watching as he pulls back his hair and deftly ties it in a bun on his head, making his face seem sharper. Jax cuddles against my side, and I lean my head on his. "So, what's been happening while I was out?"

"Nope." Thorn pops my thigh, smacking it lightly. "No work. If you're better tomorrow, you can ask then, but for tonight, you heard Doc, you need to rest."

They all look exhausted. "Only if you do." They start to protest, and I narrow my eyes. "I am not going to die in the next few hours, so sleep before I knock you all out."

"Me first." Dray grins as I wink at him.

"That's the way she treats us after we had to take cold baths all week? I swear my balls shrunk. Hey, sweet cheeks, why don't you check?" Drax says as he stands and starts to pull down his pants.

Thorn laughs and throws a pillow at him. "Put your dick away, bro."

"Sleep, all of you," Maxen orders, crossing his arms over his bare chest as he glares down at us like naughty children. What a man.

"You too, big guy, or else I'm getting my ass up and going to check on everything downstairs."

He huffs but climbs onto the bed, kicking at Thorn to make room. "We need a bigger fucking bed," he grouses.

"That we do. I'm sick of feeling that pipe Thorn keeps in his pocket," Drax comments, and then groans. "It's not a pipe, is it? Dude, not cool, way to show us all up."

Laughing, I snuggle between them all. "I would compare it more to a bat."

They all start laughing as they settle around me, and with the sound of their teasing and their hands on my body, I drift off to sleep, a dreamless, nightmare-less slumber for the first time in ages.

Because of them.

CHAPTER TWELVE

WEAKNESS AND STRENGTH

I wake warm, but not because of the fever, because of the sheer number of hot, sweaty, male bodies pressed against mine. I manage to kick Drax off, who rolls from the bed with a shout and lands on his ass.

The sound wakes everyone, and suddenly, they are all armed, their faces hard, with each one of them holding a weapon. Dray has two fucking knives in his hand as he kneels over me protectively, wearing a snarl on his face. Thorn has a fucking axe and is storming into the other room with Maxen following behind him, holding a sword in two hands. Jax covers me, a knife in his grasp. They are all ready for an attack.

I can't help it, I laugh, and I can't stop when they all turn and peer at me in confusion. Drax drags himself back to the bed and glares at them. "It was me, you idiots. She kicked me off the end." He turns and glares at me. "Mean, babe, real mean."

They all calm down and put away their weapons as I lean back in the bed. "Well, you were annoying me. Now that we are all awake, fill me in on what's happening."

Jax groans and buries his face in the pillow, while Dray settles his head back against my pussy. "Too early, soulmate, go back to sleep."

"I'm awake," I snap, and he looks up at me, wiggling his eyebrows. "Want me to keep you occupied?"

I roll my eyes as Maxen comes over and checks my temperature and stomach. "You can find out what's happened later," he admonishes.

"Fuck, fine. At least help me up, I need to actually bathe this time, I stink."

"You do." Jax grins.

"Bastards," I mutter. "You try almost dying, you wouldn't smell like roses either."

"I'd still fuck you," Drax offers as he climbs back on and cuddles into his brother's back.

I leave them arguing as I sit up on the edge of the bed and, breathing through the pain, get to my feet. I nearly fall, but I keep myself upright, and Maxen is there to catch me just in case, but I ignore his helping hand and shuffle forward. It's slow going, and I feel weak and dizzy, but I make it to the bathroom and collapse on the toilet, panting. "Motherfucker."

Maxen smiles at me encouragingly as he starts to run the bath. "You did really good, *Mi Alma*, considering you were dying about two days ago."

We hear the others coming, and with a wink, he shuts and locks the door in their faces. I pee, uncaring it's in front of him, and slip off my bra after, feeling disgusting as I stand and head to the bath. As I swing my leg over, I groan, wondering if I have the effort to swing the next. Maxen is there, and he helps me without asking, supporting me until I can lie back in the water.

He sits next to me, waiting in case I need help and letting me have a moment of peace. I can hear the others out there, but in here, we are in our own little bubble. "Let it out," he whispers. "They won't hear, and you know I will never tell, *Mi Alma*. Let it all out."

I could lie, saying I don't know what he means, but the look in his eyes tells me not to try. I almost died, and it scared the shit out of me, even though I acted brave for them. I've come close before, but never from an invisible enemy I couldn't stop or kill. It was mental and draining, and yeah, I have a lot of turbulent emotions inside of me.

How does he always know?

I blink and look away before submerging. Once my head is underwater, I scream, just scream, getting it all out. When my lungs are empty, I resurface, coughing and brushing back my hair, but I feel better.

He leans over, swipes more hair away, and cups my wet cheek, his hand nearly covering my entire face as he leans in and kisses me softly, drugging me with his kiss, his scruff rasping along my jaw. "You will always be my champion, bending or breaking."

"How close did I come?" I ask, needing to know.

"*Mi Alma*, I felt your heart stop out in the sand, I felt you slipping away, and there was nothing I could do to stop it. You were just sliding right through my fingers." His voice is rough, hard, and filled with emotions. I watch as he grinds his jaw, trying to hold it together for me.

Climbing from the bath, a bit of my strength returning, I press myself to his front and hold him. He grips my hips, lifts me, and sits me on his lap as he presses his head to my pounding heart. Neither of us care about the water dripping down us.

"I'm sorry," I murmur, and I am. I'm sorry he had to see that. I would hate to watch him almost die without being able to do anything.

"Don't do it again, *Mi Alma*, I couldn't handle it." He shivers, his voice choked, and I feel wetness dripping down my stomach, and it's not from the bath.

We just hold each other as we both work through what happened, and when we feel stronger, he lifts his head. His eyes are red and filled with tears as he presses his lips to my chest right above my heart. I swallow hard, my pussy pulsing as I watch him—such a powerful man weak before me. His heart is in his eyes... No, not in his eyes...

In my hands.

Live or die, they are mine.

"I love you so much. I'm tired of being apart. No more dying," he murmurs, dragging his lips along my chest, making me gasp.

"No more getting kidnapped," I snark back, and he grins against my skin as he trails them across my breasts until I'm aching for him. I knew dying was a possibility, I welcomed it to save my people, but now that I've survived, all I can think of is letting them assure themselves I am still alive.

My men, my husbands. We've been fighting since day one, never having a moment to relax. I want a moment alone with them. I want a million moments until it makes up a lifetime, and it still wouldn't be enough.

I'm weak right now, not mentally but physically, and I can see he's about to protest. But death can come at any moment, I refuse to play it safe when they are before me. I want him, and I will take him. He needs this as much as I do.

I grip his hair, yanking the bun out so it falls around his shoulders as I run my fingers through the tangled silkiness, before dragging my nails along his scalp. He groans, closes his eyes, and leans into me. His hand grips my ass, squeezing now. "*Mi Alma*, you need to rest and heal—"

"Fuck that. I've rested enough. I want you to remind me I'm alive," I order.

His eyes open as I tug on his hair and drag his head back until I can kiss him. I lick at his lips until he opens, and I sweep my tongue in and back out, teasing him. His hands squeeze my ass again as he drags me farther down his lap until I connect with his hardness, making me moan into his mouth.

He rubs me across his hard length as he takes over the kiss, dominating me, making me chase him to keep up as he tangles his tongue with mine. Our teeth clash from the force. My body is his right now, as he controls it effortlessly. My rock, my Maxen.

I writhe against his length as he swallows my moans, his hand stroking up my back until he cups my neck and yanks my head down, changing the angle of our kiss. He pins me against him with one hand, keeping me at his mercy.

I love being in control, but Maxen always makes me weak, always makes me feel like I can trust him to catch me when I'm vulnerable. He's my rock, what I lean on, and right now, I'm doing just that.

He nips at my lips and pulls away, leaving me panting and dazed, my pussy clenching as I remember the way he feels inside me. I wish I could feel it right now. "*Mi Alma*, if I'm going to take you, you're going to be good and take whatever I offer," he murmurs.

I swallow, licking my lips. "Hell yes."

He stands, holding me easily, as he grabs some towels and lays them down on the floor before lowering me down on them gently. Panting, I stare up at him as he slowly strips from his pants and tosses them aside, standing above me naked.

A fucking perfect warrior, his body is covered in scars, and his muscles are everywhere. The V down to his hard cook has me lifting my hips impatiently, his golden chest wide and large. His arms are huge, his thighs thick and covered in hair. I spot his brand, and it only makes me wetter seeing my symbol on him, knowing he is all mine.

He steps on either side of my legs and drops to his knees, eyes on mine as he runs kisses along my thigh and up to my hip before tracing down my other leg. I kick him in the shoulder impatiently, and he catches it, squeezing my ankle as he hooks it over his shoulder and shoves his big shoulders between my thighs.

I can't help the groan that escapes my lips. I came so close to dying, to losing them all. I never thought I would have this again, his hand anchoring me to this world, those dark eyes filled with love as he lowers his head and laves his tongue along my lips.

Teasing me.

His fingers part my pussy as he drags the flat of his tongue up my center before he groans. "Fuck, I will never get tired of your taste, of seeing such a warrior surrender to me, weak for me, screaming for me."

"Don't get cocky," I snap, even as I press my pussy against his mouth. "Less talking, more licking."

He chuckles. "As you command, my queen." "None of that shit," I mutter. "I'm still Worth."

"You are," he promises, punctuating it with a kiss on my clit. "My Worth, our Worth. Tazanna, our love," he murmurs, each utterance marked with a kiss, making me moan.

His finger slips inside me, and I spread my legs, pushing up to meet his tongue and touch. He fucks me softly, adding another finger, stretching me as he focuses on my clit. It's slow and sweet, and when the orgasm rips through me, it almost makes me cry from how unexpected it is. He kisses me through it, and when I sag into the towels, shaking, he kisses up my body to my lips.

I taste myself there as I wrap my legs around his waist. My strength is disappearing, and I want him before I need to rest again. I kick him, and he chuckles against my lips.

Pressing his forehead to mine, his hands controlling my hips, he presses his hard cock to my entrance and drives inside me. I gasp against his mouth, his huge cock causing a twinge of pain, but it soon fades to pleasure, and he waits. Only when I whimper does he start to move with slow, measured thrusts, and at the end of each one, he leans down and kisses me.

"Love you," he murmurs.

I clench around him, the pleasure spiralling back up again, and he increases his pace, pounding into me as I hold on.

I groan, my head tilted back on the tiled floor and eyes closed as he kisses and nips at my neck. My nails scrape down his back, needing to get all my pleasure out and into his skin, to show him how good it feels as he drives into me.

Claiming me all over again.

Proving how much he loves me.

How alive we are.

It's desperate, raw, and filled with our love and fear. Our hands fumble and shake as we stroke and explore each other, his heart hammering, as is mine. Our breathing is ragged, and I see him fighting back his release, so I tighten my legs and lift my head, nipping his lip. He groans and slams inside of me, twisting his hips and hitting that spot that has me moaning as it shoves me over the edge.

He holds me as we come, the pleasure locking us together. When I blink open my eyes, I meet his soft ones as he sucks in deep breaths, his body trembling above me.

"I love you, *Mi Alma.*"

"I love you too," I whisper as we press our foreheads together while we come down together.

CHAPTER THIRTEEN

CONTROL ME

I wash and dress with Maxen's help before I kiss him goodbye. He doesn't try to stop me, and neither do the others. I need some time... I need to gather my thoughts and get back to being me.

Strong.

My body feels weak, and I hate it. It was the one thing I could always count on, the strength hard-won, but now I'm back to square one. Even heading to Major's office has me sweating, and as soon as I get there, I have to sit down.

Sands below, as soon as the wound is healed enough, I need to get back to training and regain my strength. Sitting in his chair, I close my eyes. The room still smells like him, feels like him.

He was there when I was dying. I remember, it was so... Fuck.

Von.

Something I said in the fever haze is sticking with me, and I can't stop thinking about it. "I want to bury my brother," I murmur out loud. We have a few days until the leaders come... Shit, no we don't. We have one.

One day.

Pulling the butterfly necklace out of my shirt, the one I never take off, I run it through my fingers, wishing for his strength and guidance right now. Is what I am planning the right move?

Some will hate it, they will revolt... Others? It will save them, protect them. But am I strong enough to carry it out?

I've never minced my words before, but now I am second-guessing myself. Sighing, I pour a drink and toss it back as I braid my hair quickly to the side. There will be only one way to know.

Try.

I have to try. But first, Von...Vasilisy. Fuck, I want to bury them both. They deserve to be at peace. Even if their bodies aren't here, they deserve to be memorialised and have a place I can go to remember them.

There's a knock at the door, and I sit straighter. "Come in."

Jax pokes his head around the door, and when I smile, he slips inside, shuts it, and leans against it as he stares at me. "You okay, Angel?"

I nod, but he frowns and comes over, falling to his knees before my chair as he keeps his eyes on mine. "Angel...do what you need to do."

I frown, not understanding, and he smiles. "Hurt me, control me."

I jerk back, and he presses closer, turning my chair and forcing himself between my thighs. "You need it, I need it. It's never about pain with us, but control, to give our feelings an outlet. I almost lost you... You almost died. We need to let that out together."

Licking my lips, I debate it, but he's right. Those trusting grey eyes stay locked on me, waiting for whatever I will offer him. He knew I was struggling, too many emotions, too much swirling through me...because he feels the same. My silent demon is unable to let them out any in other way than under my control. He sought me out, and in the quiet of Major's office, I am reminded of just how much I have to live for. But then his eyes flicker down for a moment, hiding away from me, which can't happen.

I might have lost a lot, but I also gained so much...like him. And all my other men.

Reaching down, I grab my knife and press it to his chin, tilting it up until he is staring at me. His lips part on a deep breath, and his pupils blow in hunger. Stroking down his throat to his shirt, I quickly and swiftly slice down. The material falls in tatters to the floor, his wide, built chest on display for me. His heart hammers so loud, I can almost hear it, and his chest is heaving with his breathing now.

"Is this what you want?" I ask darkly as I drop the knife and dig my hands into his hair, yanking his head up higher and further back. He moans, pressing into my hand for more. "For me to control you? To make you beg at my knees?"

"Yes, Angel," he hisses, his throat working. "Whatever you want." "So, if I told you to wait right here while I fucked your brother, you would? If I made you watch as I fucked every single one of my men without touching you, you would, wouldn't you?" He nods, the movement tugging his hair. "And you would love it."

"Angel," he begs, his eyes wild and almost on fire as he watches me.

"When you saw me fall, when you saw me die, what did you feel?" I query, pulling on his hair harder and making him groan.

"I-I hated it," he stutters. "I was so scared I had lost you forever, that I was never going to get to tell you I love you again. To kiss you, hold you, grow old with you... I was fucking terrified, Angel. So scared," he admits, his eyes filling with a sheen of tears.

My silent demon was taught for so long never to speak what he thought without pain following, so I know how big a step this is for him. In my control, he does as I order, even if it's hard for him. That deserves a reward.

Releasing his hair, I stroke down his face before pressing my thumb to his lips. He greedily sucks it in, his eyes on me, before I pull it free and drag it down his chest. "Stand up," I order. He jumps to his feet, and I carry on trailing my thumb down his throat to his chest and over his pecs before twisting his nipple until he groans, his hips bucking in a wild thrust.

Fuck, I love the power I have over this man.

It's heady, and when I'm feeling weak...he makes me feel strong.

He needs this, the pain, the domination, and I need the control and strength of being in charge again.

Dragging my thumb down his abs, I watch them clench, that delicious V making my mouth water. All my men are warriors, fighters, which means they are in insane shape. They have to be to survive. But it doesn't mean I don't love the perks. Running my finger across the low-slung waistband of his jeans, I look up at him to see his head lowered, his eyes locked on me as he waits for my next order.

My other men wouldn't hesitate to grab me and bend me over this desk. Hell, Dray probably would have fucked me already, but Jax waits. For my orders, he would wait forever with me touching and teasing, if that's what I wanted.

His surrender is so sweet.

Dipping my fingers into his pants, I watch him bite his lip in anticipation. "Undo your pants," I instruct as I pull my hand free. He deftly and quickly unfastens them and pulls them down, making me arch my eyebrow. "Did I say pull them down?" He freezes, swallowing as I glare at him.

"No, Angel," he murmurs, knowing I will punish him for it—it's probably why he did it in the first place.

Standing, I clear Major's desk and hop onto it, spreading my legs and ignoring the slight pain in my stomach. "Take my jeans off."

He does it silently, stripping me from the fabric until I'm in my panties. I watch him lick his lips as his eyes zero in on my covered pussy. I make him wait until he's almost shaking from need. "Take them off." He grabs a knife and slices them off quickly. "On your knees," I demand, watching him drop instantly, his hands going to my thighs and digging in as he waits like a starving man.

"Angel, please, fuck," he groans, digging his fingers into my thighs harder as I lean back on my hands and watch him. Seeing his blond head between my thighs makes me moan.

"Please what?" I prompt with a teasing smile.

"Let me taste you, let me feel you alive under my tongue and fingers," he begs, those grey eyes locking on me across my body. "Let me taste your release and know that you are still mine."

Fuck, I almost come from his words alone, from the love on his face, and when he drags his tongue along his lips, I shiver from need, my pussy clamping. "Taste me," I tell him, but my voice is breathless. My stomach twinges from being upright, so I lie down, hating that I can't see him, but when his fingers part my pussy and he takes a long lick, I forget about that and lose myself in him.

"Fuck," I mutter, reaching down and grabbing his hair, pulling on it to get him closer.

Jax circles my clit before lifting his head enough to talk. "Let me look after you, Angel, let me love you."

How can a girl say no to that?

So even though I have queenly shit I should be doing, I lie back and let him eat my pussy. After that, we don't need words, Jax knows exactly how I like it. After all, it was right here at The Ring where I taught him. His tongue dips inside me before flicking my clit, and then he adds his fingers as well. I raise my hips to meet them, desperately rocking into his touch and mouth.

He's right. I feel alive, I feel loved.

All my worries have disappeared with one swipe of his talented tongue. He moans as he licks me, the vibration driving me wild. His quick, thick fingers fuck me as his tongue dips inside me at the same time, before dragging all the way back up to my clit and flicking it. He eats my pussy like he will die without it, as if my pleasure is the air he needs to breathe.

Within minutes, he has me screaming, my hand clenching in his hair as I grind my pussy into his face. He licks me through it, soft gentle strokes, until I push him away with a groan.

He crawls up my body, and I open my eyes to see his lips glistening with my release and his grey eyes alight with happiness. I can't help but lean up and kiss him, tasting myself on his lips. Pulling back, he presses his forehead to mine. "I love you, Angel. Whatever is to come, we do it together, and if you need to whip, cut, burn, or order us behind closed doors to let off that steam, do it. We are yours, however you need us, whenever you need us. I can handle anything... anything but you dying. Promise me, never again," he whispers raggedly, tears in his eyes again. "Promise me you will never leave me again."

I swallow the lump in my throat. When I chose to make that sacrifice, I knew what I was leaving behind, but I thought it was worth it to save my people. I didn't realise how much of an impact it would have on my men. Fear lingers in Jax's eyes. Fear I put there.

Fear that, one day, I will leave. I will die.

I did that, and it breaks my heart. I know my words won't ever be enough, it will take a lifetime of actions and sticking around for him to forgive me, but I'm starting now. "Jax, I'm sorry. I did what I thought was best. If there was any way I could have stayed...I would have. For you and them. No one else could ever make me hesitate like that. I've never feared death, but when I found myself on the cusp of it, I was so scared. Scared of losing you, of leaving you. All I can do is apologise and tell you that I love you." I lean up and kiss him again, but his lips are unmoving.

"Promise me," he demands.

"I can't," I whisper. "If it came down to saving you and dying, I would gladly do it again. This world doesn't guarantee us a tomorrow or a next week, so I can't promise I won't ever die. But I will never leave your side without a fight. Even if I see death coming, I will fight with everything in me, for you, always... Is that enough?"

I hold my breath, searching his eyes, hoping it is. I couldn't bear to lose him, to lose any of them. They are my family, my loves...but what if love isn't enough, with the threat of their hearts breaking one day hanging over them?

I flick my eyes between his grey ones and beg him not to leave. "Please, Jax... Everyone always leaves me. Not you, never you. You knew who I was when you fell in love with me, I can't change that. I'm a fighter, a warrior...a fucking champion. That comes with risks, and life is never certain, but it makes it all that much sweeter. Every stolen moment, every kiss or time we fuck...make love, it makes it that much fucking better, because I know it could be our last." I swallow then as his tears finally fall. "Don't ask me to promise something I can't keep, and I won't ask you to stop trying to save me."

He blinks his eyes shut for a moment before sighing. "I will always try to save you, even when you never want to be saved. You're my love, Angel, you're my fucking everything. The reason I breathe, the reason I fight. You pulled me from my own darkness and made my demons yours. I will never leave you. Not even death could pull us apart," he vows, and I sag at his words. A lone teardrop rolls down my cheek, filled with the fear that I had finally done something to push them away and lose them. He leans down and licks it up before kissing me again. Both of us are telling the other how sorry we are without words.

How much we love the other.

When we break away, we just spend a moment breathing each other in, having a moment of silence before we have to deal with the craziness that is to come over the next few days. "I want to bury my brother and Vass," I tell him.

He nods in understanding. "We can do that, when?"

Another thing I love about these men is that they never try to stop me or question me, they just support me. Always. "Tomorrow, when everyone is here. We start this new North off the right way," I whisper.

"With an amazing leader," he murmurs, leaning down and kissing me. "Not all of them deserve you, it's not going to be easy."

"I know, but easy is boring." I grin, making him laugh.

"You would say that. After all, you married five men."

I groan then. "Don't remind me! I can easily divorce you." I wink as he kisses my chin.

"No, Angel, you can't. Like we would ever let you get away from us."

Chapter Fourteen

A Dream

I find the others waiting for me outside, nosey bastards. When I tell them about the funeral tomorrow, Thorn and Maxen kiss me and rush off to get things sorted so I don't have to. Drax and Dray refuse to leave my side, throwing each other competitive stares. I even catch Drax trying to knife Dray, which makes me spin and glare at them. "Stop it, both of you, or I swear I will tie you up and leave you out here."

"Oh, kinky soulmate, would you at least get me off first?" Dray murmurs, prowling around me before whispering in my ear, "Because we both know I like chains and whips."

Drax grins and winks at me. "As long as you promise to let me watch, sweet cheeks."

"Insane, all of you," I mutter, and storm away.

I hear them laugh as they follow after me. "Yep, and you married us!" Drax calls.

I ignore that and nod at people as we pass, not really sure where I am going, but I want to check on the sick and injured and make sure we have security in place. I stroll through The Ring, and people stop as I pass, and salute and nod in respect, which I return.

When I finally find Nan, it's to see her squaring off with Evan, whose face is red as he throws his hands in the air. We seem to make him do that a lot. Piper is sitting on the shoulders of that new, large man of hers, sipping at what looks like a bottle of rum as she watches the show. Archel is leaning next to her, feeling her up. Beast, as she calls him, is next to her other side, his arms crossed and face locked down in an angry scowl.

"You have been shot, I need to look at it," Evan yells, making me arch an eyebrow as I step to his side.

"You got shot?" I ask Nan, looking her over. I spot some blood on the arm of her cardigan. "Getting slow, old lady."

"I didnyee get fucking shot, it's just a fookin' scratch," she snaps. "Huh, and who shot you?" I query conversationally. He's probably dead, poor man, unless it was foreplay for her, which with Nan, you never know.

"Some drunk idiot." She sniffs. "Thought I was a fucking cannibal, didn't he!"

I try to hold it in, I really do, but the laughter roars from me and right into her face.

She narrows her eyes and squares off with me. "Ya fookin' think that's funny, girlie?"

"It's hilarious." I nod. "He thought you ate humans. I mean, he isn't wrong, you are a maneater." I wink before looking at Doc. "Patch her cranky ass up, will you? If you can find it under all those wrinkles."

"He's not fookin' touchin' me, I'm fine!" she shouts.

I lower my head and narrow my eyes on her. "You will let him patch you up, or I will personally go to your hotel and leave a dead body in every single room."

She freezes then, watching me angrily. "Ya fookin' wouldn't."
"Try me, old lady," I warn.

We have a staring contest before she rips off her cardigan, exposing her bullet wound—which is bleeding, although not too badly—through her bicep. I stare in shock at her arms. They are surprisingly ripped for an old lady, though nothing about her should surprise me anymore. But it's the tattoo on her arm that has me interested. "You were in the army?" I ask.

She looks at the faded ink and smiles. "Aye, when I was a young un, a different world ago."

I blink but look at Evan. "Patch her sour ass up, and then I want a report on the injured." I turn to Piper then, who stops swigging the bottle and grins at me. "I need to speak to you...probably when you're sober."

She nods seriously, trying to feign soberness, even though her eyes are wide and her face is red. "I'm sober, totally sober, one hundred percent sober." She burps and giggles. "Oops."

I hide my smile as I stare at her. "Sleep it off, then come and find me."

"You heard her, Princess, let's get you to bed!" Archel laughs. "Oh, for some horizontal mambo? All aboard the dick train!" she calls, laughing as they pull her away.

That girl. I shake my head at her antics as I look over to see Doc trying to patch up a glaring Nan, poor guy. He has to put up with her, Dray, and me. As soon as he is done, she leaps up and storms over to me, staring me down.

"Come on, I need some advice." I turn, and she huffs but follows after me.

She speeds up and walks by my side as we head back through the building and into the meeting room where I sit, thankful for the respite when my body aches. My men wait outside, giving us peace and quiet. I smile at them lovingly for it, and in their eyes, I see the promise of retribution later. Good, I hope so.

"How ya feeling?" she asks.

"Fine." I smirk. "You?"

"Fookin' brilliant," she mutters and grabs a drink, pouring two and passing me one. "So, what's up, girlie? I thought they would have chained ya down to keep ya resting."

"Nah, that's for later...and it's not to keep me resting." I wink, making her laugh. Turning the glass between my hands, I avoid looking over at the blood staining the carpet. It seems so long ago, but it really wasn't. "Major was right, we need rules. We need leadership."

"Come on, spit it out, lass," Nan encourages, so I lift my head and meet her eyes.

"I want to make a new world, a better one. Under one name, under our leadership. Not a dictatorship...but a—"

"Constitution." She grins. "Very old world."

"I know. Obviously, we would make it workable, but The North is strong. It's clear that if we don't work together, we won't survive. I think we can do that to create a better world. No more Ivars, traders of flesh...just a place to feel safe. For warriors and those who don't fit anywhere else. I'm not saying take away the fighting and bloodshed or the fucking and rough nature, that would be impossible... But ground rules, like Major had here. It worked. What do you think?"

"To cover the whole North?" she questions seriously. I nod, and she sighs, thinking about it. "It would take a strong motherfucker to control all the rough bastards up here." She smiles. "If anyone can, girlie, it's you. I like it."

I grin, taking a drink. "Good, I will present it to the other leaders tomorrow."

"Lass, it will rub some people the wrong way, so make sure it's whatcha wanna fight for. 'Cause ya will have to fight." She winces, and I down my drink.

"I have been fighting my whole life, and I will carry on fighting, this time for everyone's freedom, not just my own."

She laughs then. "Fookin' hell, lass, say shit like that, and you will have them eating out of the palm of your hands."

"Fuck off." I grin. "I guess Major rubbed off on me."

"Too fookin' right he did. It's good, ya finally talking like a leader. Like a fookin' queen. I mean it, girl, if anyone can unite The North once again and forever, it's you. To the Champion." She toasts me with her glass, and I clink mine to hers before she downs it, then burps and wipes her mouth. "Shit, Major did always have the good booze."

"I'm sure you will drink us dry soon enough." I laugh. "I have a plan. We can discuss the exact terms tomorrow, but first thing in the morning, we are having a funeral."

"Oh, fuck, who for now? Wait...are you having a funeral before you kill whoever it is, or killing them at the funeral? I guess that saves time." She cackles before coughing. Grumbling, she grabs the bottle and starts drinking it straight, and when I arch my eyebrow, she grins. "Pain meds for the bullet wound."

"A funeral for Vas and my brother, and anyone else who wishes to bury their dead here. It's time we lay the past to the sands below and start a new future." I grab the bottle and take a swig. "It's time to say goodbye."

"Too fookin' right." She swipes the bottle again and downs it before gasping. "All right, funeral, I'll even wear black and not be drunk."

"How kind," I deadpan, making her narrow her eyes on me. "Disrespectful, you are, kid." She laughs.

"You only just realising that, Deloris?" I laugh.

She leaps to her feet and has a gun pointed at me in a blink. "You tell anyone, and I will kill you, queen or not."

"Sure thing, old lady. Now fuck off, I want to spend some time with my men," I snap with a smirk.

"Aye, I would too if the men I screwed looked like that...all abs and big cocks." She sighs dreamily, and I arch my eyebrow.

"When have you seen their cocks, you perv?"

"Eh, a woman can dream, girlie. Don't take my fantasies away, it's the only thing that gets me through those fat blokes who stick their swords in me." I snort so loud, it hurts and my stomach twinges.

"Fuck, Nan, what an image." She winks and grabs another bottle before ripping open the door. "See ya tomorrow, girlie. Make sure to get a good fucking in, might chill you out!" she calls loudly to make sure my men hear.

Bloody old bitch.

Drax sticks his head around the door and wiggles his eyebrows. "I heard my services for a good fucking were required?"

Thorn pushes him aside and strides in. "Not you. Obviously, she meant me."

Maxen follows, and then suddenly, Dray slips through them all and I hear a grunt. Looking around, I realise he pinned Jax to the hallway outside with knives.

Standing, I stare them all down. "I decide who I fuck, not you..." I grin. "Now, I need a massage. Who wants to do it?"

Five voices all chime in, and I laugh.

I don't fuck them. I do get a hell of a full body massage though. My feet, hands, shoulders, back, and arms are all rubbed, and when it's finished, I am boneless. All of them surround me as we just relax for once, happy in each other's silence. It reminds me of when we first came here, the night I first told them my name. How far we have come since then.

Sands below, I'm even fucking married to them. The cocky bastards were relentless. I wonder if they knew back then this is where we would end up?

Probably not.

"So...sugar tits is queen, right? But there are five of us, and we definitely ain't kings, so are we consorts? Her royal harem?" Drax muses from the floor, my feet resting on his thigh where he cups them lovingly.

"Really?" Jax sighs.

"I'm a king," Dray points out smugly from his position under me, his head resting on my shoulder.

"You're a kinky fuck, but I don't know about king," Thorn mutters from my left, making Maxen laugh on my right.

"He has you there." I snigger, and Dray nips at my neck. "And you love it, soulmate. It has her screaming so loud—"

They all groan and shift. "Stop, we are trying to be good, and now I've got a raging hard-on," Drax grumbles.

"What about that time we had her bent over—" Thorn starts.

Fuck, this is going downhill fast, and I know it will end up with me filled with cocks...which wouldn't be a bad thing, but I'm trying to be good to let my body heal. I do hesitate for a moment, debating it before opening my mouth.

"I'm hungry," I tell them, and they all move so fast, I don't even have time to blink before they are up and ready and pulling me to my feet.

"Why didn't you say so, *Mi Alma?*" Maxen chastises as he pulls me to the door. "Dinner should be cooking in the dining room. Come on, Evan can check you over to make sure everything is okay."

"And clear her for rough kinky sex. I am feeling mighty left out," Dray mutters as he grabs my hand and twines his fingers with me. "Ahhh, but the image of all the blood does keep me going."

"I know," Thorn snaps. "I found him wanking in the bathroom this morning muttering about it. It was creepy."

Sighing, I leave them to compare and talk about dicks, even though we all know I have the biggest metaphorical dick in the room.

When we reach the dining room, everyone hushes and chairs scrape as they stand. I wave them back down, and they eventually sit, and the noise starts back up again. Teasing, laughing, dares, and bets. It's loud, and I smile at the memories this room holds.

Jax slips his hand into my other one, and I wink over at him, knowing he is remembering how he followed me from this exact room before I put him on his knees for the first time. Winding through the tables, Jax pulls me to sit at a big one that's partially empty. When they see me coming, the people sitting there stand and run away, leaving it for us.

Swinging my leg over, I sit down on the bench with Jax next to me. Dray takes the other side, and a few moments later, Maxen, Thorn, and Drax come back with trays of food. They place them down before grabbing some water for the table. I dive in instantly, so fucking hungry. I blame the healing. I devour my food, uncaring what anyone thinks. I might be a queen, but I'm still a Berserker and we are animals.

When I'm done, I sip my water and look around, meeting those prying eyes that are watching us. Even during the end of the world, my relationship is uncommon. People tend to have a lot of partners, but not committed ones. Marriage is also really uncommon, and I am clearly wearing rings.

I don't give a fuck what anyone thinks. These men are mine until the end of time. I found happiness, it just happens to be split between five people. Love is love. As long as everyone is happy, why does it matter how or who it is with?

I give them my dead, cold eyes until they look away, making me smirk. I still fucking got it. When I look back at my men, they are watching me with knowing eyes, and I wink. "Sometimes, you have to remind them who's boss."

Dray leans in. "Remind me anytime, soulmate...with knives, whips, guns...whatever takes your fancy."

Pushing him away with a smirk, I join in on their conversations, loving how easily they all fit together, even Dray, whom I was worried about, but Thorn seems close to him and Maxen is accepting him. Drax teases the shit out of Dray, and Jax just smiles silently.

My back itches, though, from the curious eyes, and old habits die hard. No one would dare attack us here in my own home, but I spent years watching my own back, protecting myself from handsy assholes and people who would kill me in a blink. It makes me hunch over a bit, my hand straying to my knives on my legs. Queen or not, I won't ever be soft.

I've lived a hard life filled with blood and death. I will always be the person who kills first and asks questions later. If you come at me or mine, you are as good as dead.

It doesn't matter if the room is filled with friendlies, Berserkers, or my people, the only time I will ever really relax is behind closed doors with my men, and I have grown to accept that.

Dray feels it, and his hand strokes up my thigh and presses down on my knives there. "They attack you, they have five men to get through first."

"They attack me, and I will kill them, but I'm not growing soft and getting myself killed," I retort. I don't need protecting, never did, just someone to stand with me.

He chuckles in my ear as he leans in and licks the lobe. "But I want to make them bleed for you, to see you watching me as I rip them apart for daring to come at my queen."

Fuck, I shiver from the threat in his voice, from the hard way he holds my leg down. From the raw fucking violence always held just below the skin, like a bomb waiting to explode.

"Are you wet from the thought? I bet you are... When you are healed, I have a plan, soulmate, one I haven't stopped thinking of since I first met you."

"What's that?" I murmur, lifting my eyes to meet Maxen's across from me. His gaze is heating up as he watches me, knowing I'm getting turned on by whatever Dray is saying.

"It's a secret for now, but it will be bloody, and afterwards, I plan on fucking you senseless while we both are covered in it." He nips at my ear, making me gasp quietly, but my men hear it though, and they all stop talking to focus on me. Their eyes darken, their bodies straighten, and they become the predators I know.

And my pleasure is the prey.

I narrow my eyes on them. "Don't," I warn.

"You remember that night outside of here? Where your man was feasting on your pussy, and I was watching and stroking my cock?" Dray murmurs. "I do, I still remember the way you arched into his mouth, the way you screamed for him, the way I came so fucking hard I could barely walk."

Jax leans into my other side, kissing my neck. "I remember. I didn't know what to do. You taught me, showed me exactly how you liked to be licked...tasted, fucked."

Sands below, are they trying to kill me?

I shuffle in my seat, trying to ease the ache forming between my thighs. My pussy pulses as I recall how Jax's tongue felt lapping me and the stark, hungry innocence in his eyes as I made him mine. Claiming him. And when I met Dray's eyes, I had only become wetter. I came hard, knowing he was watching.

Dray's hand traces higher on my thigh, and he yanks my leg open. Jax grabs my other thigh and pulls it towards him as I see the flash of Dray's blade before the flat of it is pressed against my pussy through my jeans, hard. I push myself into it, unable to help myself, even with all these eyes on us. "I dream about it sometimes, the first moment I tasted you. I knew I was yours then and there," Jax murmurs.

My eyes run across Maxen, Thorn, and Drax, who are watching me with a smirk. Their gazes trail down my body possessively, the way someone can when they have seen every inch of you. Tasted you, fucked you.

I should order them to stop, but I don't. They have been on their best behaviour all day, barely touching me beyond massaging and shit, so I'm feeling needy as hell. Flashbacks of the hard way they took me in The Cities fills my head, as do all the ways they fucked me and have yet to fuck me. I'm almost panting now, rocking into the blade.

"If I cut your pants right now and slid my blade and fingers against your pussy, I'm betting you would be wet. You would drip for me even more if I fucked you on my blade, making you bleed and scream at the same time, wouldn't you, soulmate? You love it when I take you to that edge, push you harder than anyone. When I make it so dangerous, we both might die, but wouldn't it be worth it?"

"You need to stop," I say, but my voice is breathless, and we both know I don't mean it. I love it when Dray and I fight, when we fuck like animals and explore just how far we can take pain before it become torture. Some might say that's fucked up, that my past probably messed me up, but I don't care, I love our pleasure.

"Why? You love it, Angel. Can you imagine getting fucked by Dray from behind while you take it out on me... Those nails digging into my chest as you ride me, your blood dripping down our bodies," Jax murmurs.

Dear fucking God.

I almost come from their words alone, and I am amazingly wet right now, and they know it. Fuck, everyone in here probably knows it.

Just then, Evan appears, and he doesn't seem to notice my flustered, wet as hell horny state. "I came to check on your wounds." They all laugh, and I flip them off. "I hate you all," I mutter. Evan looks between us in confusion. "Wait, what did I miss?"

"Oh, just them being jerks." I spin in my seat. "Come on, Doc, leave the assholes to it." Standing, I lead him out and into the closest room, flicking on a light and hopping onto a table as I lift my shirt and lean back.

He steps closer and peels away the bandage, sighing. "Worth... what did I tell you?"

"I have been taking it easy. I haven't killed anybody or had an orgy." I shrug.

"You have ripped a stitch—again," he mutters. "Wait...that's what you call taking it easy?"

"Pretty much." I nod.

"Just when I think you can't get crazier," he mumbles as he drops his bag and sorts the stitch before cleaning and redressing the wound. Once he's done, I drop my shirt and watch as he puts his equipment away.

"How's Piper? She sobered up?" I grin.

His cheeks heat, and I laugh. "She jumped me." He sighs, lifting his head as if in pain. "I couldn't—fuck, I couldn't do it when she was that drunk, so we put her to bed, but she kept stripping to entice us so we, erm..." He scrubs the back of his head. "We had to tie her up."

I manage to keep a straight face for a whole minute before I burst into laughter. "You had to tie up your girlfriend so you couldn't have sex?"

He glares at me. "Yes, okay?"

I howl, I can't help it. I laugh so hard, I'm pretty sure a little bit of pee comes out. When I can finally breathe again, I am hunched over. "Oh God, I needed that today, thank you."

"I'm glad my blue balls cause you pleasure," he mutters.

"They really do." I nod before sobering and glancing at him. "Doc?"

"Yeah?" he questions, frowning at my serious tone.

"I'm burying Vas tomorrow... Will you stand with me? You were his friend, you were one of the last people to be with him." I swallow. "He deserves it, he deserves to be remembered."

He nods solemnly. "He was a great man, he loved you."

"He did, and it got him killed," I mutter before jumping up. "Tomorrow in the morning, once the others arrive."

He stands with his bag in his grip and rests his hand on my shoulder in a friendly way. "He died for what he believed in, Worth, for you. Not because he loved you, though, because he loved you in spite of it."

He turns away and the door opens, and Drax pops his head in with a grin. "Good, you haven't left. So we all want to know if she is cleared enough that we can fuck her?"

I groan and cover my eyes as Drax wiggles his eyebrows. "You know, drop some pipe...give it to her real good?" He opens the door more and thrusts into his waiting hands, humming under his breath.

Doc looks back at me with a pained expression. "Why? Why do I always make friends with the crazy ones?"

"He's serious." I nod, rolling my lips to hide my smile.

With an exasperated sigh, Evan looks back at Drax. "I guess, but easy, no...fuck, I don't know, no rough weird stuff. Who knows what you guys are into."

"Got it, keep the freaky stuff for later." Drax winks before turning to the hallway. "We can fuck her if we do it all soft and sweet like she's a lady," he calls loudly.

Sands below, I'm going to kill them all.

Chapter Fifteen

FINAL GOODBYE

We don't fuck. I bathe with the help of handsy Thorn, and then we all climb into bed, but my mind is caught on tomorrow. They have both been gone a while now, especially Von, but it will be so final tomorrow.

They know, and they shuffle closer, pressing their bodies to mine and offering comfort.

"Tell us about him?" I turn my head to meet Thorn's gaze. "Your brother," he adds, smiling at me as he clasps our hands together. I remember what he told me about his sister and know how it feels, so I open my mouth and start to talk.

"He was so outgoing, always had so many friends and would get annoyed when I tagged along with him. But every night when bad dreams plagued me, he would climb into bed with me and make me laugh until I slept. He was so funny. You would have loved him, Drax. I always wish I got to see him grow up. He would have been an amazing man...but maybe it's for the best. This way, I don't have to see him suffer and die in this world. I can think of him somewhere else all grown up, maybe married with kids..." I trail off, and Maxen kisses my shoulder.

"He sounds incredible, *Mi Alma.*"

"He was," I murmur, my smile widening. "We were really close. I know a lot of people hated their siblings when they were younger, but we didn't. It will be hard tomorrow. He's been gone a long time, but I guess I've always numbed myself and kept moving. Now...now with nothing else to fight for or to stop me from thinking, I'm just—" I sigh, and Jax lifts his head.

"Letting it sink in, Angel, that's what you're doing, processing his death finally."

I nod, tears in my eyes. "But I know wherever they are, whatever comes after this life, he's waiting. With my mum and Vass and Major and Cara." I don't mention the hallucinations I had when I died, it was probably my mind playing tricks on me when I remembered them and heard them.

Right?

The next morning, I am filled with nerves. I slept like shit, tossing and turning all night until I gave up and got up early. Taking extra pride in my appearance, I put on my best black jeans, top, and leather jacket. I braided my hair and left some loose in the warrior's style. I even put on my champion face paint—the red handprint with the dripping black marks. I also place it on my men. They sit before me one after the other, all quiet as I paint them as warriors. When we are done, we head outside together to face the day.

The sun is high and heating up quickly. I'm already sweating as I brief the leaders on what is happening. Today isn't about politics, it's about peace and remembering.

The mood is somber. Last night, the whispers went around about today, so the men are awake and sober, all respectful and quiet. Anyone who isn't is dealt with quickly as I walk through the compound to Major's grave. I would have liked to have buried Vas near his old house, but here with my family is good too.

In procession, we proceed to the burying area with me leading and my men behind me. The leaders are at my side but back one step, showing everyone who is in charge. I keep my head held high and my stride long and controlled, even though my stomach twinges with each step, the stab of pain making me irritable. I don't let it show.

Eyes drop as we pass, and people fall in behind us. I hear whispers that almost make me smile. One from Piper nearly makes me stumble with a chuckle. She calls me a badass. "She looks like a Viking!" she whispers.

Shaking my head, I lead the way around to the tree, swallowing as I stop before it. Major is here, now so will Von and Vass. My family. Priest steps up to the tree to lead the service. He thought it was an honour, but in reality, I didn't know what to say. Men gather at his sides, his angels. The graves are already there looking freshly turned, though there is nothing in them. Two crosses are held in the men's grasps. Crosses I craved words into with my knife this morning.

My words of goodbye from someone who loved them.

Priest steps forward and starts to talk. I try to listen, but my eyes catch on the way the sun shines through the tree here, creating an almost heavenly halo on the ground where they will be forever memorialised. I don't believe in fate or God, but if I did, this would help me feel good about what I am doing. As if it's a sign.

"...gathered to remember those who have fallen, those who were loved by our queen. One a warrior, who selflessly sacrificed his life to ensure her survival, and in turn, provided liberation from the mad king. Another, her brother by blood, slain too soon. Here today, she stands with brothers and family from all across The Wastes—though it may not be by blood, but by loyalty. We stand here today to remember them with her, to carry her pain and grief with us as she carries the burden of their lives." I lift my chin at that, feeling eyes on me, all those eyes. Some watch for weakness, some watch in understanding.

Nearly all in loyalty.

I step forward, away from my men and everyone else, and nod at the warriors holding the crosses. Both step forward with their grave markers and begin the task of placing them into the hardened soil next to Major.

"Though they are gone, we are taught death is not the end. Today, under our redeemer, under the sun who wiped the Earth clean, my angels and I will carry them on to a better life. For warriors and lovers will unite."

Some of the crowd murmurs at that, but honestly, I'm used to Priest's crazy, and for some reason, today it settles me. With my heart heavy, his words of promise that I will see them again someday gives me the grit and determination I need to stand through this.

The smashing of the hammers against the wooden crosses is loud amidst the crowd of gathered warriors. People have come from all four corners of The Wastes for the funeral.

Berserkers.

Seekers.

Worshippers.

Scavs.

Roadies.

Paradise.

Lost...

All in one place, all brought here by one person.

Me.

Not one person talks, their heads bowed in reverence and respect. Arms crossed before them, the warriors chant and sing the songs of goodbye to honour. Their voices fill the air, storming through my blood with each lyric of pain, grief, forgiveness, and remembrance. They sing of death, of meeting again.

Of never walking alone. Even though I stand alone now, it fills me with hope. It fills me with a sense of camaraderie. I might be burying my brother and a man who became like a brother to me, but they will forever be remembered by all of these warriors as their own brothers.

Five men stand apart behind me, their eyes sad and bodies hard.

War wounds cover them, healing but still there. Fresh scars, both emotionally and physically, are evident. I turn back and meet their gazes, the gazes of the men I love. Each and every one of them has their fists over their hearts and their eyes on me, filled with love and sadness for me. We all know this could have so easily been me. I see it in their eyes and the hard lines of their bodies, knowing how fragile and brittle life can be.

For a woman who has taken hundreds, it's only in this moment when I realise just how deeply one death can affect a whole world. How the little whispers and fractures of their life can reach out far and wide on people's hearts. You never know how you can affect someone, or how deeply people love you, so we should hold those we love close and tell them every day, because you never know what is going to happen, and to live with regrets is worse than to not live at all. I whisper it now, my lips moving over the words, and they murmur it back to me.

We love you.

Always.

Smash.

The swing of the hammer comes again as the crosses are forced into the ground, a perfect place to be laid to rest. Here in the sands, under the sun, below the tree carved with markings.

Finally at peace, after all the battles and uncertainty. The end...

A goodbye.

They might be gone, but they will always live on in my heart. And as long as I'm breathing, we will never forget them. I will tell stories of them, and I will spread their love and joy throughout this world, until everyone knows them.

To be remembered and loved is to never die.

"With our hearts joined today, we bid them farewell for now, but not forever. Bow your heads in silence as we remember those we have lost and those who are still with us."

I bow my head and send a prayer up, not sure if anyone will ever hear it, but it feels right. I don't send it to a god or deity, but to my family. To Vass and Von.

I love you, I will never forget you. Until we meet again.

"With the dust of our ashes scattered and the sun lighting the way, our goodbyes are over," Priest concludes and looks to me. "For our queen, for The North, we remember!"

The chant is echoed out among the crowd, and I turn to see the warriors there, screaming their respect and loyalty. I will never be alone, not when I am surrounded by a family of thousands.

I nod and they nod back as my men step closer, surrounding me, offering me their comfort and strength.

As the crowd breaks apart, and the burial song still fills the air as they walk away together, I see him, standing alone to the side with tears in his eyes as he watches me bury my brother.

His son.

He's alone, but I am not. Not ever again.

Chapter Sixteen

QUEEN OF THE WASTES

I turn away as he steps closer. I have nothing left to say to that man who was once my father. He's my past, and I am over him. Instead, I crouch at the edge of the graves, running my finger over the words I carved there. They are rough and raw, not perfect, but for some reason, that seems right.

The sign is easy to read. Hope. That was what his name meant, and burying him means the same. This is our hope. On Vass, I wrote love, because he taught me to love and trust again. He shared his pain and past with me. He may have been a warrior, but he was a lover all the way through. Everyone he touched felt it, felt his true, pure heart. He was a good man. A better friend.

"See you soon. I'll keep count until we meet," I whisper to him with a sad smile. "Got to say, I'm going to win though." I laugh before looking over to Major. "Take care of them, will you? Like you did me. They are my family."

Swallowing back the pain of the finality of my goodbye, I let the sun heat my skin, warming me with a strange sense of rightness. It fills me and all the dark places inside me, and just for a moment, I can breathe easily, no weight, no responsibility. Just a woman soaking in the sun with the crows chirping above us and the slight breeze rustling the leaves on the tree.

It's peaceful. It's home.

I hear him coming up next to me, his steps too loud to be anyone else's. My men walk softer—a warrior's step.

"For so long, all I could do was survive one day to the next. The next second, the next hour, the next week. Always fighting, always on the move, always trying to forget. But never really living." I look up at him then, our past stretched out between us on the ground. His eyes are still glassy with tears, his lips turned down. He looks tanned, probably from living out here. Piper told me he was at The Forgotten with the others. But he's skinnier, and though his arms seem to have more muscle, the result of living above ground is already taking effect. His clothes are old ratty jeans and a tank top, a strange look for him. He's nothing but a stranger, someone I once knew. I've said my peace to him over and over again, so he just needs to accept it and move on the way I did. Sometimes, family are the ones you choose, not the ones you are born with. I've chosen my family, and it doesn't include him.

"I'm ready to start living again." I cut my eyes to my men before looking back to him. "But you're not included in that life. Say your goodbyes to your son, you will always be welcome here, but you aren't welcome in my life or family ever again."

I stand and pass by him. His hand goes out as if to stop me, and I narrow my eyes on him, daring him to try and grab me. Touch me. He drops it with an audible swallow. "I just wanted to pay my respects and to see if you were okay. I heard what happened."

"Why? Why do you care?" I sigh tiredly, sick of this same circle with us. "Never mind, it doesn't matter. I'm tired of wasting my breath on you when you clearly don't listen. Pay your respects." I head over to my men, and their arms wrap around me, solidly, comfortingly.

They knew the cost of today, not just on my heart, but on my soul.

Under the sun-soaked sky, they hold me as I let those final pieces of my past and pain float away on the breeze.

I am reborn.

Queen of The Wastes.

We drink that night. We sit up in what used to be the VIP area for the fights above the empty pit. Around the table are my men and the other leaders, including Piper and her men. I smile as I sit back and look at them all around me. Laughing, joking, and teasing. Telling stories of the war, of previous fights. I wonder if this is how Major felt with me around... Whole?

Looking across the barrier, I nod at those who raise their drinks to me, my eyes catching on my father sitting alone before I drag them away to focus on the pit below. That is where it all started, after all.

That first night, I was fighting for my life, I just never thought it would be this life. If I had, I might have fought harder through all the years to get here faster. To feel so full and loved. Dray leans into me now.

"Remembering the good times?" he murmurs.

Laughing, I look back into those cold eyes, recalling all the times we have shared here, especially when he came down below after the fights... Or the time I came back here, came back home, and he was here waiting like he had been for years, a knowing gleam in his eyes that I would find my way back to The Ring...back to him.

Grabbing a knife, I press it to his junk with a wink, making him chuckle. "Your knives make me hard," he teases, repeating those same words he said to me the night our eyes met across the room.

"I know... Tell me, Seeker King, feel like a fight?" His eyes light up, burning with sudden desire for my blood and body. I know he has been struggling since I almost died, and he's trying to be here for me. But Dray is a brutal feral warrior, and he needs this.

I need this.

To relive that night, but to do it right this time. I tell him as much. "No winnings, no losses. Just us. Fighting...fucking." I press my knife in harder. "The way it should have been that night."

"Soulmate," he murmurs, obviously remembering my injury. But I've fought with worse, and I need this as much as him. Tomorrow, I need to be a queen and make hard decisions. It's going to be a long, hard road to achieve what I have in mind. Tonight, I just want to be Worth, the Champion. His soulmate. His wife.

To feel our bodies pushed to their limits, the crowd roaring for us, cheering and stamping, watching our blood decorating the sands. He won't hold back, I know that, and I love him for it. To win against him, I have to earn it.

I want to earn it. Here and now.

"I challenge you, Dray... Do you accept?"

The table goes quiet, and all eyes are on us now.

"Dayummm, what? I don't know what that means, but it felt right," Piper murmurs, making my lips quirk as I hear Archel lean in to explain. I keep my eyes on those cold ones I love so much.

"Always, Champion. Ready to get your ass kicked?" I smirk as I stand, ridding myself of my swords, leaving me with only the knife I pressed to his junk—Major's knife.

He stands with a chuckle, strips off his cross-chest harness, and hands it to Jax. I suck in a breath as gratitude and happiness fills me. It's a big deal to trust a warrior with your weapons... He's showing he trusts them, considers them friends and family.

I've never loved him so fucking much as I do right now, especially when my silent demon stares down at them in shock and pride. He strips off his sword and hands it to Drax, who clutches it with a wide happy smile, his eyes almost misty. My joker is grateful for his trust.

He hands the whip he carries to Maxen, and lastly, he passes a knife from his leg to Thorn, leaving him with just one knife like me. I look over my men to see them humbled by his trust. Dray trusts hardly no one, he loves even less.

To know he loves this family, that he's accepting our future together...it fills me with determination to make a better future for us. I step back, and he follows, prowling after me, hunting me.

Laughing, I turn and leap over the barrier, landing on my feet, and then I'm moving towards the sand. Heads turn and questions fill the air. I ignore them all as I leap over the stone into the pit and then turn, watching him come. He moves like water, fluid and so powerful. He winds through the tables towards me, his eyes intent on getting his prize.

Me.

When he effortlessly throws himself over the barrier, and in the same stride stabs out with his knife, I laugh. Ducking, I cut along his leg before dancing away. We are usually evenly matched, he has brute strength, but he's also smart and fast.

I'm faster, smart, and agile, but I'm injured. I don't know who will win, either way, he's still my prize. Sometimes, it's not about winning, it's about getting back up to fight another day.

He groans as blood forms on his leg. His trousers have a thin, long hole in them now. He presses his fingers to the wound and then lifts them up to show the blood on his fingertips.

Fuck me.

The crowd goes wild, surging around the arena, shouting encouragements. The king versus the queen. I hear them take bets, I hear my name chanted and called. It's like being back all those years ago when no one knew who I was, when no one rooted for me. But now they do, because they know...

I'm a fucking champion.

"You're getting slow, Seeker," I taunt.

He laughs as he circles me, his knife held inwards, his other hand out and ready. "Oh, really? Maybe I'm just giving you a chance to win, Champion, but if you want fast—" He rushes me then, and there is no more time for talking.

I duck and parry, moving backwards across the sand to avoid his lethal, feral attacks. Even as I do, I feel my panties dampen at the brute strength and force, at the fucking beauty of my husband.

He manages to cut my cheek as I turn my head to avoid losing an eye. Snarling, I duck low and sweep my leg, but he jumps over it and kicks me back to the sand. I tumble backward, rolling over and leaping to my feet to see him coming at me again. Turning, I race to the low wall, and pushing myself to my limit, I sprint up it and flip over him as he ducks low to stab at my legs. I quickly leap onto his back and wrap my arm around his throat and press the knife there. "Yield," I yell.

"Never," he snarls and turns, and rams me back into the wall again and again, until the breath is knocked out of me and I have no choice but to let go. He spins and stands again, but I turn to avoid it and duck under his arm, moving away. Panting, I wipe my cheek and the blood there with a smile at him as I wait for the next attack.

Sweat covers my brow, and my stomach twinges, but I ignore it as the cheers get louder. "Bring it," I taunt.

He leaps at me, pushing off from the sand and flying through the air. I roll to the side as he stomps down at me, again and again, until I can get to my feet. Then we are back in motion, spinning and cutting, each of us trying to get a hit on the other. We fight to the death, every blow meaning to injure and maim.

I block with my arm and hand, cutting it, and he does the same until bloody drops fall steadily to the sand. I hear my men shouting for me, believing in me. Grinning, I feint left and then bring my knee into his cock. He groans but doesn't double over like I thought he would, meaning when I stab, I cut a long line across his chest before dancing back with laughter.

He peers down at it with a small smirk. "Fuck, I forgot how beautifully you fight, soulmate, how fucking hard it gets me when I feel your blade slicing through my skin. When I win, I'm going to fuck you like I should have that night. I'm going to make them hear your screams and know that I'm yours."

Sands below, my pussy clenches at that, imagining the way he is going to fuck me. All sweaty and bloody from our fight, his hands mean...his cock brutal. He will fuck me like we fight, fast and hard, and I can't wait. I ache to end this quickly, even as I hear the chants as they watch their queen and king fight.

He throws the knife to the ground and lifts his fist as he tries to circle me. I pretend to slump on my injured side slightly, and he falls for it, coming for me there. I know it's going to hurt, and it does when he punches it, but it allows me time to tackle him.

He falls to the sand, and I perch on his chest, trying to drive my knife into his shoulder. His eyes gleam with desire as his hand comes up and blocks mine, his strength versus mine, and my hand barely moves downwards now.

I need more force.

Leaning all my weight onto his chest and the blade, I bring my hand down like a hammer as he tries to push the knife away and beat it down. Each slam of my hand against it pushes it closer until it finally sinks into his shoulder. With a groan, his hard cock pressed to me from the pain, he leans forward and headbutts me, sending me sprawling back with my knife left in his shoulder.

Rolling to my feet, I limp for a moment before I shake it out, ignoring the feeling of blood dripping down my stomach, my arms, and my face. He's just as worse for wear, and it makes us both smile widely at each other.

Grabbing the knife, he pulls it from his shoulder and tosses it in the air, catching and retossing it without looking. "Tiring yet, Champion?"

"Never." I wink.

"Good," he snaps, and then he throws the knife. I duck, hearing the whistle of it as it sails over my head and embeds in the wall.

It's on after that. A whirl of fighting bodies and limbs, punches, kicks, and headbutts. He throws me into the wall, and I knock him to the sand. We are both panting yet filled with adrenaline and happiness.

We are evenly matched, but my injury is taking its toll and I'm slowing. He knows it and he knows me, knows that I won't ever give in or stop, and I know he will never let me win. It's one of the reasons I love him.

So instead, he goes to end it now.

Showing me in a burst of energy just what is waiting for me after, he slams me to the ground with one arm and then he's above me, choking me. I struggle and kick, lifting my hips to dislodge him as those icy eyes watch me with desire, even as he drains the life from me.

Eventually, I can't fight anymore, and I stop struggling. To keep fighting...or to tap out? Tapping out means I get him faster, so I do that.

He lets go instantly, leaning down and kissing me before leaping to his feet and helping me to mine. I grin at him as I stride across the sand. I don't care that I lost, I lost to a king. A fucking Seeker, an assassin, and the love of my life. But the crowd eats it up, loving how I fight, even until the end. A queen that knows when to fight another day is a smart one, after all.

He won this round, but we have our whole lives for rematches.

Grabbing my knife, I hold it up to the crowd. They eat it up, and with a laugh, I head underground to where we were that night he found me. I slip into the dim room and wait, knowing he is coming for me.

My heart is slamming, and my pussy pulsing with its own heartbeat as I anticipate our fucking.

I was here years ago when he found me, promising to free me.

It broke my heart all those years again when he never came back for me, but I never have to worry about him not coming for me again. The door flies open, and he's there, filling it, his chest heaving and bloody, his eyes wild, and he finds me in the dimly lit room.

Always finding me.

"Come to collect your prize, Seeker King?" I purr as I rub the blood across my lip like he did all those years ago.

"Yes," he growls, prowling closer. "Then what are you waiting for?"

CHAPTER SEVENTEEN

CHANGING THE PAST

He grabs me and slams me down onto the metal table behind me, the one fighters are sewn back up on. His thumb comes out and runs along my lips, smudging the blood there, before his mouth descends. Our lips meet in a frenzied hurry, our teeth clashing in another fight, but this time, for each other's bodies and pleasure.

He rips my clothes away, and I fumble with his until, with a growl, he steps back and sheds his trousers, then he's naked before me. Gasping, I run my eyes across my assassin. His body is a fucking weapon, all hard edges and muscles, glowing from the sun, and covered in scars and now blood and sweat.

He lets me look for a moment before he is back between my thighs, shoving them open as he drops to his knees between them. Those icy eyes meet mine as he parts my lips to find me wet for him. Hands slick with my blood and sweat, he traces them down me, gathering my wetness before lifting it up to my lips. I suck it clean as he growls, "Taste how sweet you are, how much you are mine."

Reaching down, I grip his head and drag it closer to me. I groan when he flattens his tongue and licks down my pussy before thrusting it inside me, again and again, with sharp, hard thrusts before he stabs my clit with it. He drags me to that edge and throws me over. Our fight was our foreplay.

I scream my release, clamping my thighs around his head as my pussy clenches on nothing. He's on his feet in an instant. His cold, hard face is twisted into a snarl, and his lips are tinted red and glistening with my blood and cum. Using my legs, he drags me closer to the edge of the table, and in one smooth hard move, he slams inside me.

He impales me on his cock, that piercing he got for me dragging along my walls, making me writhe as I cry out. His hands grip my hips so hard before he slides the right one up and through the blood dripping down my side from my injury. "Fuck, I love the way you bleed for me, knowing I'm marking your skin, knowing how hot it makes you."

He slams into me again as I dig my hands into his side to try and hang on, his thrusts are feral and rough, without rhythm. He's in fight mode right now. I can still hear the cheers and stomps from upstairs, our names on their lips, but below them is another battle, this one just for us.

"Fuck me," I demand. "Harder, show me why you won."

He groans and drags me closer, until I'm almost sitting up on his cock, the new angle burying him all the way to the hilt and almost making my eyes cross as pleasure pounds through me. My heart slams in time with his thrusts, and moans leave my lips as I surrender to the pleasure he has to offer.

"Dray, fuck, please!" I almost scream, needing to come again, needing him to fuck me thoroughly so I forget everything for a moment. Everything but him.

My Seeker King.

To tame a creature like this...fuck, the power is heady.

He lifts me with his hands on my ass and drops me back onto the table and into his thrusts. I dig my nails into his shoulders, my head thrown back in ecstasy as he fucks me. He fucks me with wild abandon, no finesse or teasing. This isn't a battle for power, it's a fight to the finish.

I'm so close again already. I can still taste myself on my lips, until he leans in and kisses me, biting my lip. He drags it out between us and releases it with a pop. The hint of pain makes me clamp around him as he roars. Lifting me, he strides over to the closest wall and just slams me into it.

I groan and fight him, so he slams me against it again. My ears ring, my head feels light, and my bruised lip pulses in time with my pussy. Blood and sweat flows between us. His hand lands on the wall next to me, his other holding me up as he pistons in and out of me.

Wrapping my legs tighter around him, I let my head fall back against the wall as I meet his thrusts as much as I can.

The door opens. "Champion, they are—"

"Get the fuck out!" Dray roars, and the door slams. I laugh, which then turns into a moan as he pinches my clit in punishment before sliding his hand down and around his cock as he fucks it into me. "Fuck, fuck. Soulmate, you make me wild. I can't help it, always did, even back then. Every fight, all I could think about was it being me and claiming you as my prize after...or you claiming me and fucking me. Using me."

My breath hitches at that. My breasts smash into his chest, those icy eyes wild and locked on mine. "But now you're mine, mine!" He slams into me and twists, and I come with a scream.

Clamping around him. Milking him.

He roars his own release as it fills me. Both of us pant as he presses his head to mine, and with a gentleness I forgot he was capable of, he kisses me. Our tastes mingle together until we have to break apart to breathe.

"I love you, soulmate. When you are healed, we will fight again. I know you will win, my champion...my queen," he murmurs, making me smile. God, I love this man.

CHAPTER EIGHTEEN

MY ENFORCER

I sleep hard that night. I don't wake up until the next morning, my body sore and aching. Breakfast is brought to me, and I am sipping some water when Evan bustles in. He throws me a glare and gets to his knees, yanking up my shirt to look at my stomach wound. "Oh, I know, I'll ignore the doctor and decide to have some weird ass, kinky fighting foreplay," he mutters angrily as he redresses my wound and checks the stitches. I watch him with an arched eyebrow, as do my men, who are in various stages of undress.

He notices it has gone silent and looks up, blinking. "You okay, Doc?"

"Fine." He huffs, and I grin when he sighs. "Piper said to tell you she is downstairs, and I quote, 'Sorry for being a drunken mess who hit on you.'"

"She didn't hit on me." I laugh.

"I told her that, she then replied that must have happened after you had gone." He sighs and rubs his eyes before sitting back, and I pull down my shirt. "Worth—" He starts. "What do you want her for?"

"Why?" I ask, watching him. His face is closed and tight.

"Because I've been searching for her for so long. I just got her back...I don't want to lose her," he admits without any shame.

"I know, and I don't plan on it, but you have to know Piper won't be happy sitting still. She is co-leading The Forgotten and now a pascha of The Lost... She is never going to sit somewhere safe."

"I know." He sighs. "B-But what do you want?"

I search his eyes for a moment. I know he loves her, but he let his own fears blind him before. "Don't lose her again because you are trying to protect her. I am offering her a position with me. Yes, it will involve danger, but everything here does."

He nods, contemplating my words. "Thank you for being honest." He gets to his feet and washes his hands before coming back and grabbing his bag. "I'll tell her you'll be down in a minute."

He opens the door to reveal Bern. I nod and smile at him as he bursts inside with a wide grin. "Ma queen! You called?" His boisterous face instantly relaxes me.

"I did. Can you make sure the other leaders know we are having a Summit in around an hour, same room as before, and we are not to be disturbed."

"Of course, ma queen!" he exclaims before rushing off to do just that. Maxen comes and sits next to me, and I lean my head against his shoulder as I watch Jax and Drax start to wrestle. They fall to the ground and flip around as each tries to put the other in a headlock.

"You ready for today?" he asks, twining my hand with his and rubbing my fingers soothingly.

"No, but it has to be done, I just hope I can get them to listen." I sigh.

"If anyone can, it's you, *Mi Alma*." Dray thought so, too, when I ran it by him. He's with his people right now. He went to see them after kissing me goodbye this morning. Thorn comes and drops to my other side, sandwiching me between him and Maxen. It's the only time I ever feel small.

Though I could still kick their asses.

"Baby girl, don't question yourself now. The plan will work, and be will be here the whole way to help you," he murmurs, kissing along my neck, which stops Jax and Drax's fight as they both watch me with rapidly darkening eyes.

I point my finger at them and leap to my feet. "No! I have an important meeting to get to. I am a queen," I threaten.

They look at each other with identical expressions of mischief before Drax opens his mouth. "A queen can never be late, everyone else can wait." Then they leap at me.

After kicking their asses and slipping from their roaming hands, I straighten my clothes and head down to talk with Piper. She's waiting downstairs, wearing her goggles on her head. Her brown hair is braided back, and her new mountain man is her seat, which makes me grin. Piper has a way of looking at you so innocently and getting you to do anything because she confuses you that much. I spot Archel not too far away, sitting on the fence and watching her like a stalker.

Her other beast is wandering around, talking with a warrior and trying not to look like he is watching her. Real smooth.

Sitting down next to her, I make her jump, and she clutches her chest. "Fuck! What are you, some kind of silent ass ninja? Though I think ninjas are, by definition, silent, so what are you, some kind of ninja?" she almost screeches.

The mountain man laughs and wraps his arms around her to steady her on his lap as I arch my eyebrow. Her cheeks tint, and she smiles sheepishly. "I mean, good morning, you look good today. Was it the rough fight sex that put the pep in your step—oh God, I didn't say that. I meant your fight was really good last night, not at all weirdly sexual. Fuck, I'll stop talking now."

She mimes zipping her lips shut, and I hear Evan chuckle as he steps past, dropping a kiss on her lips. "That would be the day, Pip. I'm off to help the injured, see you later, be good."

"Everyone always says that to me. When am I not?" she mutters, making her mountain man, Evan, and me laugh as she huffs.

"My pascha, you never behave, it's why we adore you," he murmurs silkily, making her giggle.

"Okay, love birds, break it up, we need to talk," I tell her, and get to my feet. "Walk with me." I stride away, but I look back when I don't hear her. She leaps from mountain man's lap, kisses him, and rushes after me, almost falling in the process.

"Sorry, sorry, okay, I'm here. So I've been thinking. If you're going to ask me to join your little harem, I would be flattered, but I don't like to share my men, so maybe we could do—" I stop and hold up my hand.

"Piper, I can assure you it has nothing to do with you becoming... my bitch." I smirk. "This is about the future of The Wastes and your part in it."

"My part?" she repeats slowly, serious now.

"Your part." I nod. "I trust you, Piper, with my life. I need help to ensure our future is brighter than, well, this." I wave my hand to encompass the injured still outside. "That it never comes down to this again. We have to protect The North, and for that, I have a plan...one I need your help with."

She grins. "Count me in, boss lady. Whatcha need?" "How do you feel about being an enforcer?" I reply.

Her lips part in a wide smile. "Do I get a kickass bike and leather?"

"Sure."

"Hell yes! I'm in! Yo, Clay, go grab some leather! We're about to deal out some ass kicking Mad Max style!"

Shaking my head, I grab her as she tries to rush away. "Wait, let me finish, then you won't be blindsided in the leaders' meeting. This is a really important moment. The soul of our land depends on it."

CHAPTER NINETEEN

FIGHT FOR THE NORTH

Piper and I talk right up until we have to leave for the meeting. She seems excited about my vision, and even gives me some very smart input regarding my plan, tweaking it in a way I hadn't even considered.

She truly will be an amazing leader.

When we arrive at the room for the Summit, the others are there. It seems important to hold it here, as if Major is present and supporting me. It also serves as a reminder of just how easily our North was broken and ripped apart by one man, who could have been stopped if we all worked together sooner.

My eyes catch on the bloodstain, and pain hits me, but it's lessened. The feeling is also filled with warmth and love. Love from his support. I know he would agree with what I am doing here. He would support me all the way, and today, I need to use all of his lessons he taught me.

Dray is waiting on my seat to the left, and I point at Major's chair for Piper. She hesitates when everyone stares but then takes it. Maxen, Thorn, Drax, and Jax are spread out behind my seat as I sit, and the door closes. Bern is standing guard. Nan, Priest, Jon, Piper, and everyone here are ready and wondering what this is about.

"Thank you all for coming. We have some important things to discuss, and I would appreciate you staying silent until I'm done." I run my eyes around them all then. They recognise my serious tone and sit straighter. "The war was a stark reminder of just how far The North has fallen. Never before would The Cities dare come north to take and kill our people. For too long, we have been separated, fighting each other instead of protecting our land and our people."

Sometimes, it's not about being the loudest voice in the room, but the calmest and the quietest, listening and learning.

"I have been a slave. I have been abused, tortured, killed, and tossed away. It will happen to no one else, male or female or child, ever again. No one like Ivar will get through our midst. We are taking a stand against slave traders, rapists, murderers, cannibals, and everyone who is a threat to our new way of life. If you don't like that idea, speak up now. Once this is decided, there is no going back. We show a united front. A new nation...The North Nation. Together."

They frown, wondering where this is going. Dray's hand lands on my thigh under the table, reassuring me. "The treaty we used to bring down Ivar would be extended, and our clans would no longer be competitors, but allies. We would work together to secure our lands."

"Wait a fucking second!" Jon starts.

I narrow my eyes as he leaps to his feet. "Sit the fuck down. Now!" I roar, and he wilts and does as he is told, grinding his jaw. "I wasn't finished. You would have your own lands with borders, you can still punish trespassers and thieves as you see fit. You still rule your people, but we all abide by the same laws. We work together to protect our people instead of hunting and using them like fodder."

"And who would enforce these laws? You?" Priest questions, but he's not being confrontational.

"Yes, and my team of enforcers." I look to Piper then, who sits up taller, her chin tilted back. "A team of dedicated men and women who live and work out there on the road, dealing out justice to those ignoring the new rules."

"And who sets the new rules?" Priest queries, frowning and looking around. "We have existed like this for years."

"Just because it's what you know doesn't make it right. History can be rewritten, and we can do better than those before us. We can start this world on the right path again. We have been given a second chance to do better. This world is a hard enough place without us killing, hunting, and stealing whatever we see. Yes, not everyone will agree, but they will have a choice. We can't let what has happened occur again—massacres, torture, rape. We all nearly died." I look around, taking in their silent, contemplative expressions. Nan is grinning at me. "Our women are raped and killed, our children are taken. We live in constant fear of death. Slavery is rife, as is pillaging and stealing. We live in these clans and communities to band together because it's the only way to survive... Why don't we take back The North and make it one big clan? We would be providing hope for a better future."

I meet each and every eye then. "Aren't you tired of burying your people? Aren't you tired of watching the horrors committed by others with no retribution? I am. I'm tired of the sand running red with innocent blood. It's time for a change, and though that's scary, I think sometimes the fear is what makes it worthwhile. You want to be remembered? To have your legacy live on? Then give them something to remember, to talk about. Be the people who changed The North for the better. Show The Cities just what they were fucking with."

I lick my lips nervously, but I tilt back my head. "We fought a war together and won. United we stand, fractured we fall."

It's quiet for a moment as they all share looks. "About fookin' time!" Nan laughs.

Priest nods for a moment, but seems to be thinking it over.

"And this one?" Priest asks, glancing at Piper. "She is not blessed or destined."

Piper shrinks under his gaze for a moment, her eyes flickering to me. I know it's her concern, that I'm choosing the wrong person to have at my side, but I have faith in her. She should too.

"She's blessed by me. I chose her, and you already said I was chosen, so in turn, that would make her chosen also. She is a warrior, a leader."

"She's a pale face," Jon scoffs.

"Was," I snap. "Now she is more of a warrior than you. She has fought, lived, and almost died for our lands and people. She has experienced its cruelty out there in the dead lands, and still fought for us anyway because she saw the potential. She saw what we could be." I look to Piper then, uncaring about them watching. They need to hear this, but so does she.

"You don't have to prove yourself to me or anyone else, kid. You're a fucking warrior, a hero, a leader, so own it. Without you, we might have lost the war. You put your life on the line for us, never doubt my loyalty to you for that. But you still want adventure, I see it in your eyes. You would never be happy sitting at a desk, leading like that. You want to be out there, and I understand, I was the same. I could use a general, a right-hand woman to help me protect our people, and I'm choosing you. I'm too old to be running around out there in the sands. I've seen it and what the sands have to offer, now all I want is a home. A place to lay my head and rest my feet with my family. It's time I settled down. I'm still a warrior...but now a queen.

"This is your world now. You and the other young ones are our future. I think it was always yours, you were needed here all along. Without you, this wouldn't be possible, and I am forever grateful for our lives becoming entwined." Tears fill her eyes as she watches me, and I reach over and clasp her hand. "A wise man once told me that not every choice you make will be right. It's how you handle the consequences and outcomes that make you a leader. He believed in a sanctuary, in a better world. He believed in us, The North. He told me to never stop fighting, even when it's hard...and you do that. When I look at you, I'm reminded of the way he saw me—a butterfly, scarred, but still able to fly." It seems right to pass this on to her, on to our future. I know Major would have liked that. I can feel him helping me even now in my heart and memories. I hear Nan sniff, but I don't drag my gaze away from Piper until she nods. Then I look back at the others.

"Those men and women didn't just die for me, they died for an idea, a hope for what we could be, and for one blinding moment out there, we all stood as one and we were unstoppable. Let's be that again. Let's create The North Nations, let's create a home. But these are your lands too, and I can't do it without you. You have a choice." I get to my feet. "I will leave for a bit to let you discuss this together, and when I come back, we will vote on the future of our people and The North."

I leave the room without a backwards glance, my men following me. They are always with me, always loving me. I won't say I was lost before I met them or any of the fucking lovey shit. The truth is, they reminded me of who I really was, they brought that girl back, and then every day since, they made me want to be more than just a scared slave running from her past.

They made me want to love. To be fierce and raw.

To be a leader worth following.

They made me want to be a true queen.

Chapter Twenty

Word Is Law

I wait nervously, pacing in front of the building. My men watch me, all but Dray, who is still inside with the other leaders, as is Piper.

"Angel," Jax calls, and it's the fact that it's him that makes me still and turn to face him. "You did everything you could, it's their choice now. This isn't your fight alone, and we will stand by you, no matter what happens. Trust in them, trust in your ability to show people what they already know but are too scared to acknowledge. You are an amazing leader, Angel. Major would be proud." I know how hard it must be for him to speak all that in public, so I step closer and slide into his waiting arms.

How did I ever do this alone? When life gets hard, you need someone at your side with encouraging words or to even hold your hand. Doing it alone is harder. I did it for many years, and I am tired of that, so I lean into them now.

This queen doesn't need a king, she needs the five men behind her who will have her back when it gets hard. I never wanted to need someone. To me, that felt like a weakness. I wanted to stand on my own two feet and never be overshadowed by a man again, but now I'm realising that made me very lonely.

Not every man wants to overshadow you, and needing someone can be a good thing. To everyone else, I'm Worth, the Champion, the Berserker Queen, but to them, I'm just theirs. And they are mine. I never have to prove myself or be on guard, I can just be me, and for a woman whose life was a constant battle, that peace is worth all the pain I had to suffer to get here.

I let them comfort and assure me. Their love fills me as I wait for the decision regarding the souls of our people. If they say no, I won't stop fighting to leave a safer world behind than the one I was raised in, so a young girl can be free and happy, so no other women or men have to go through what I did.

So they won't carry the scars I do.

I've earned every scar and brand on my body, and I refuse to be ashamed of them. They are marks of survival, of my strength. My journey to the throne and to this moment, it was hard, and at times, I didn't think I would make it out alive. But now I'm here, and I have a duty to make the world a better, safer place. I have a duty to that little girl stolen from her father, forced to watch her brother die. Whose innocence was stolen, whose body was made not her own, who never got to love.

Or laugh.

Or be free.

I owe it to every single person still to come, and I will not fail them the way so many failed me.

I will never stop fighting, no matter how many times I am knocked back down. No matter how much it hurts.

To live is to feel, and that includes pain...but also love. Happiness and hope...and hope is a powerful thing.

"It's time," Drax murmurs. I pull away and, steeling myself, head back with them behind me. When I open the door, the room is as quiet as a tomb. I sit and look out at them.

My heart races, my palms are sweaty, and a fear unlike any other fills me. Fear they will be too scared to take a chance. Fear can be a powerful emotion, it can bring even the strongest to their knees. I'm just hoping that today they overcome that, and we can become something better than we are.

"Are we ready to vote?" I inquire. There is a slight tremor in my voice, but not enough for them to notice, only me and my men.

They nod, and I begin with Dray, meeting those icy eyes as he smiles. "Don't even ask, the answer is yes. My people and I will follow you anywhere and support your new vision, soulmate."

I offer him a smile and move to Nan. "Nan, how do you vote?" "I say let's give the new North a fookin' chance!" she exclaims.

"Priest, how do you vote?" I ask nervously, knowing he could go either way.

"I—" He looks around before tilting his head back. "I will follow our great Lord's word. You were chosen, we follow you. To a new North."

"Jon," I prompt, and he frowns, looking at the table. He controls nearly all the scavs and roadies now, almost every stretch of land between here and The Rim, so we need him on our side. "Jon," I repeat. "I need your vote."

"I want to vote the way Reeves would. He trusted you, followed you. I say...if you think it's possible, let's do it."

"Piper?" I question with a smile, a feeling of victory flowing through me, but I have to ensure it's what they all want.

"Fuck yeah! Shit, I mean yes." She winces, making everyone laugh, including Priest.

"Then it's done. We are starting fresh," I murmur, shocked. "So, where do we begin?" Priest asks.

Where do we begin? What would Major do?

"First, we need to agree on rules and punishments, then we will announce it and see how much opposition we face," I suggest, and look around. "Rules and laws... I have a few I was considering."

"Well, let's fookin' hear them, lass," Nan snaps.

"Some are obvious." I smirk. "No eating people." A murmur of consent goes up at that. No one likes people eaters. "No raping. You can still keep what you kill, but no slavery. We kill if we have to, not for fun." I look around at them.

"They obey the rules set forth and those of your leader, anyone who breaks them answers to me, my general, and her road team." I wink at Piper. "My hunters. Anyone who has a problem with it tonight can raise their concerns...and go through me."

"Through you?" Dray queries, and I grin at him.

"If they can win or kill me, the rules won't last, but we all know that won't happen. However, this isn't a dictatorship, so we will put it together, and anyone who doesn't want to be a part of that and doesn't want to kill me for it can head south."

"Welp, that should be fun." Piper laughs.

"Any others, you think?" I ask, wanting their input.

"I would ask that we are still allowed to make our own rules for our clan and dispense justice accordingly. My angels need punishment as reminders," Priest proposes.

"Of course, as long as it does not break the slavery or raping laws," I point out.

They are ones I won't budge on.

"Torture," Piper offers. "No being should be tortured unless sanctioned by a leader or the queen."

"That's a good one." I nod. "Any others?"

"I think ya got some good base laws, girlie. You can add as we grow and change. Ya will realise what needs to be said then."

Nan is right. "Good, any other questions?" "When does this commence?"

"Tonight." I grin. "No time like the present. You will all be needed there as a show of support to assure your people you are on board with this. We are all in agreement, correct? The North is to be one nation, governed by us."

"The North Nations. I like it," Jon remarks.

"No," Nan interjects, "not The North Nations... The Nations!"

"Yes! The Nations. That is perfect," Priest agrees. "Too fucking right." Dray grins.

"Then it is done. We will announce it tonight," I declare, and they all stand, knowing the meeting is over.

Everyone leaves, apart from Nan, and she stares at me, her shoulders bare of her cardigan, showing off her new scar.

"I'm sorry Reeves isn't here to see this," I tell her.

She nods. "I'm sorry too, but it happens, girlie. Least he died for something, and in a world full of senseless death, that means everything. Don't sully it, death comes for everyone eventually."

"Even you?" I snort.

She laughs hard. "Girlie, please, death is scared of me."

"Too fucking right." I toast her and wink at the scar. "It's badass."

"Ain't it? All the boys will love it." She turns serious as she stands.

"I hope ya prepared for the fight ya have on your hands, girlie," Nan offers.

"I'm always ready for a fight. I'm the fucking Champion, after all."

Chapter Twenty-One

The Nations

The meeting went very well, and now we have a plan and a new home. The North, The Nations, together as one. I know not everyone will agree, mainly the dicks who want to rape, torture, and kill, but we need the rules and punishments for those who think any other life is not as important as their own.

They still have free speech and choice, and can do whatever they want, but we have to be able to protect our people. I will fight and die for this, for the right to protect all those children still to come.

Children like Vass would have had. That Ethan would have had.

That Piper might have.

It's going to be chaotic tonight, but I thrive on that. There's a knowing in the air as I head back to get ready after finalising the arrangements for this evening. They know something is coming, but they don't know what.

I just hope those who choose to leave or break the rules run and run fast, because until the day we die, we will stop them. We will kill those willing to harm others. I'm not perfect, I have blood on my hands, but I know how precious life is, even if I have taken a lot of them.

I've killed mad kings and controlling governments, and now I'm ready to show what I have learned from that. We need leadership, control, and yes, even some people to answer to.

I am already psyching myself up for tonight, for the fight that is to come. Like when I used to be in The Ring, I cannot afford any weaknesses or distractions. They will be out for blood, and they will notice any hint of vulnerability. If I show weakness, I die. Tonight, I have to be the Champion, the woman who became queen. I have to be strong, sure, and confident in what I say.

And I have hope they will listen.

I dress not just like a queen, but like a Berserker. My men help me. They paint my face and dress me in leather pants and a crop top, showing off my brands and scars, and yes, my new wound I got from saving The North.

Piper paints my chest in her pascha colours. She is also dressed as a queen tonight, with her face painted, her hair wild, and her crossbow on.

Dray helps me strap into my two swords, and I add knives as if I am going to battle, which I guess I am. Someone will challenge me, I know that, and I will win.

I have to.

Time to remind them why I'm the Champion, why I'm queen. When they are done, I look every inch the warrior Berserker Queen. My hair is braided in a style Piper calls Viking bitch. My face is hard and set, my weapons visible. And to it all, I add a crown.

I don't know where Thorn got it from, I don't even ask. He just stands before me with it in his hands. "It's time you looked like the queen you are, baby girl." He places it on my head securely. It's black, inlaid with roses and skulls. It's beautiful and perfect for a Berserker Queen, and when I look in the mirror, I finally see the woman they all see.

A queen.

One worth fighting for. One worth loving.

I won't be able to fight in it, but it will have the impact I want, showing them why I am making rules, why I am changing the way we live—because I can, because I fought for us and these lands again and again.

One more fight.

One last time.

"Let's go, they are waiting," I murmur, and as a group, we leave the building. The announcement is being held in The Ring. I couldn't think of a better place to fight for our future. Piper and her men are with us, and Dray is at my side with the other leaders, who are already here and waiting.

Tonight's the night everything changes, I can feel it in the air. A purpose, a knowledge that this world will never be the same again, no matter the outcome.

We reach The Ring's entrance, where I can hear them talking as they wait, the conversations nervous as they await our arrival. Tilting my head back, I watch the outside, readying myself for what is to come.

I am surrounded by my family, those who love and support me, and it offers me the strength I need to face this new challenge.

Piper is standing at my side, ready to face the wolves at our door together. My general. She suddenly gasps and reaches up, straightening my crown. "It was tipping." She grins. "You've got this, you fucking badass bitch. Show them who's boss."

They all go in before me, and I hear the urgent whispers, the confusion. So lifting my chin higher, I step inside. I look at everyone and no one as I stride through their masses. They part for me. Most pay their respects as I pass, and I keep note of those who don't. When I reach the front, I step up onto a raised table to see everyone and so they can also see me.

The other leaders are gathered to my left, my men to my right. This is going to be harsh, bloody, and will undoubtedly end in death, but it needs to be done. I run my eyes across the gathered warriors.

They are dirty and bruised, and scarred from the war we just won, but now we are fighting a very different one for the heart and soul of our North.

"I asked for this meeting for a reason. I hate long speeches and beating around the bush, so I will be blunt. I ask you to wait until the end to respond or react." When no one offers a protest, I begin.

"The way to the throne has been paved by blood and sacrifice, and I will never forget those who brought me here. Who has loved, and where possible, given hope for a better world. One that started with a slave girl." I run my eyes over the crowd harshly as I raise my voice. "But this is so much bigger than you or me, this is about more than individuals. This is about The North, about our future, and what kind of legacy and world we want to leave behind for our children...and their children!" I almost scream before quieting. "We survived by becoming what we needed to be—brutal warriors and survivors—but now we need to adapt again, because this world needs thinkers, inventors, artists, and lovers. It's our job to bring them back and protect them. To create something we are proud of...a new world, a new North—The Nations."

There are murmurs, but my leaders step forward in support. I meet their eyes again. "I know what you are thinking, change is scary, but to stay the same is madness. We almost lost our lands! But together, we defeated the threat, and now we need to work together for the best interest of our people. It's time The North was reborn." I swallow nervously, but the support of my men allows for me to carry on under all these eyes and expectations.

"Starting here, with us. One world ended, and in its place, madness took hold, but no longer. Together, we can make this place safe for everyone. That's why starting now, The North will be known as The Nations. What that means is all clans will be joined in unity under my leadership." I hear some cheers and some roars of anger, but I narrow my eyes. "Quiet!" I scream, and to my surprise, they do.

"Slavery and the hunting of humans is over, and I have a team of enforcers ready to follow out the wishes of myself and each leader here. This isn't a dictatorship. I will lead, but bend to the will of my people. Each clan will still follow the laws set forth by each leader and will be approved of by the council here today. We have voted, this is what we think is best for The North. One North, together at last, governed by those who were selected and fought for their place, following the laws of our people."

"Who sets the laws?" one screams.

"What laws?" another roars.

I let them get it out, but they start to get riled up, so I grab my sword and point it at them, and they quiet once again. "We do! We have voted on them. They are as follows. No eating people. No raping. You keep what you kill. No torture. No slavery."

With each law spoken, I sense the tension rising. We are about to explode. To try and tame a group of warriors will lead to nothing but blood. I have to be willing to die for what I believe in. And I am. I let them see that now.

"Listen to me! I am done bending the knee. I am done quieting my voice. I came from this very fucking place, I spilled my blood on this very soil. When I was just a slave, a man here...he saw something I did not—a woman willing to fight and die for what she believes in, a woman willing to fight for those who can't. His death will not be in vain, nor will any of those we have lost along the way. There has been too much death!" Some nod, others cheer.

"Our new future is built on their bones and sacrifice, and I refuse to let it be for nothing." I swallow and raise my chin with a smirk, a come at me gesture of a fighter. "So those who don't or won't follow the laws of our new lands set forth today...I suggest you run. Run fast, run to the fucking south and never come back!" I scream as I swing my sword in a warning arc. "Because I will find you, and I will kill you if you ruin our new future. This is our world now! And together, we will start again! For the dead! For The Nations!" I scream.

In unison, like they practiced it, my men and every leader steps forward and slams their feet and hands into their chests. "Long live the Berserker Queen! Long live The Nations!"

It's quiet for a moment before the crowd erupts. They fight, they scream, and they roar. I see the bloodshed happening already. Factions are dividing, and clans are turning on each other like I knew they would. "Quiet!" I shout, but this time, it doesn't work.

Dray jumps onto the table next to me. "Fucking quiet, or I will kill you all!" he bellows, the demand so loud, it reverberates around and everyone stills, the threat very real. "Every Seeker who disobeys will die, so listen to my fucking queen or feel the cold steel of my blades!"

"Does anybody have a problem with that?" I yell. Some people step forward, and I smirk before leaping down from the table. "Because they can go through me." One steps back instantly. Others stay, making me grin as I ready for the fight. "Those who wish to leave The Nations, do it now. Those who want to stay, who want to kill me and take back their way of life now, you will die at my blade."

I see their hesitation as they debate whether or not they want to fight and die for the ability to do whatever they want. But one of them gets brave and steps forward, and all other warriors step back, creating a circle for us to fight in.

"This should be good." Dray laughs, and I hear my men taking bets on how I will kill him. It makes my smirk widen into a smile.

Other warriors, warriors I fought side by side with, chant their support for me. The man is big, and his dirty blond hair is bushy and tied back. His face is almost square, with thin lips and big eyes. His nose is crooked, and a scar cuts across his sweaty cheek. He's muscular, his chest bare, and his legs are encased in jeans. He already has an axe in his thick, meaty hands as he prowls around opposite me.

They should know better by now. They may look like the ultimate warriors, they might be used to being the best, the strongest, and the fastest...until me. I will always win, because I am fighting for love, for the future, whereas they are only fighting for hate.

I will win. His blood will coat this floor and mark a new future.

"You will not change us! We are warriors. We fought your fucking war, we died, and now you want to take away our choices? Fuck you and fuck your crown!" he yells, and some echo his statement. I focus only on him, knowing the others will be carefully watching those who joined in. He will be a warning to those who still wish to trade in flesh and kill and rape.

"You spit on the sacrifice our people made. You are only fighting for yourself," I snap, keeping my feet spread and my weight on my toes, my hands loose as I hold my sword and wait. He's cocky, and it will be his downfall. He will die with my sword in his belly and my name on his lips.

"Enough talking, false queen. Before this is through, you will be on your knees with my cock in your mouth as I show them what you are really good for." He laughs, but no others laugh, even the ones who supported him before.

The bloodthirsty warriors watching know what will happen. Their bodies itch with the need to fight. I feel my men's anger at his words, but also their unwavering confidence in me and my ability to win. Swinging my sword, I wave my other hand at him, gesturing him towards me. His eyes narrow, his nostrils flare, and with a loud cry, he rushes me. He swings his axe in a strong downward stroke, hoping to end this quickly despite his words.

I duck the swing easily and stab upwards into his arm before pulling my sword free and twisting away. He screams, his arm dropping uselessly to his side as he turns. I smirk as blood drips down his arm. He switches his axe to his other hand and comes after me like a man possessed, swinging and screaming. I duck and weave each blow, dancing around him effortlessly with my speed.

He's slow, lumbering.

Laughing, I tap his back with my sword, and when he turns to swing, I duck before slipping up through his guard and slicing his face, then I move away again. Circling him as he pants and bleeds, I let everyone hear my taunts.

"You are slow, pathetic. All the years of pillaging and bloodshed haven't made you a warrior. You are nothing. A fucking useless parasite draining the life of The North. And you know what? You will die at the end of a woman's blade. I bet that really angers you."

He roars again and rushes me, almost stumbling from the blood loss and exhaustion, but I'm not tired. I am used to fighting when my body is screaming at me. I am used to surviving no matter what. When others fall and give in, I keep going. I am a warrior. I am the fucking Champion.

I am a queen!

As he swings the axe above his head, I smirk and drop to the sand and slide towards him. With my own warrior cry, I slice through his legs. He falls to his knees with a roar, his axe falling uselessly to the ground with an audible clank. Jumping to my feet, my heart pounding as adrenaline pumps through me, I step behind him. I rip his head back with my hand, and I press the sharp edge of my sword to his throat as I lean in, making sure my words are audible to those gathered.

"I always follow through on a promise. Your blood will cover my blade. I will kill for our Nations. I will kill those who stand in our way. Mark my words here today, no one will stop what is to come! To The Nations!" I scream as I slice his throat.

I hold him there as his blood spurts onto the sand, as he chokes on it and fights in my grip. I keep my eyes on the crowd, making them watch as his life drains away into the ground below, and only when he stops moving, do I drop him like the trash he is. I step over his prone body and place my sword in front of me. "Who's next?"

Two more men step forward, and the crowd roars with anger, spitting at them. "Traitors! Long live the Berserker Queen!"

I let my head fall back with a yell as I join in. "Long live The Nations!"

When I lift my head again, the chant echoing through the space, I grin at the two men. "Are you ready to die today? I sure am."

Some might call me crazy, some might think what I'm fighting for isn't worth it, but I can't settle down and start a future while our world lingers in the ashes. It's time to break free from that darkness and move into the brilliance of the sun that fills our world.

It's time we became who we were always meant to be.

"Two men stand before me, two men amongst something much bigger. But never think you are worthless or small. Without you..." I look around them, meeting my warriors' eyes. "Without you, each and every one of you...this world wouldn't be what it is. Today I kill, today I face death for every man and woman gathered here. For the children we have lost, for the women who have died, for the men who have grieved and hardened. I fight for us."

They chant my name, and they call for the men's deaths. They know now, they understand what we are fighting for and just how willing I am to protect and die for them. Lifting my bloodied sword, I point it at the men. "Begin."

They are smarter than the first man, they are slimmer too. Both are tall, although one is slightly smaller, with a bald head and vicious eyes and a snarl tugging at his lips. The other is a ginger with long, unkempt hair. Both are dressed in more than rags, showing their station and are working together as a team. No doubt for years. I'm betting they are flesh traders from their obvious anger and intelligence. One of many who work across The Wastes...well, who used to work across The Wastes. Not anymore.

They circle around me, trying to split my attention. It doesn't work. I look forward with a calm expression and wait. I listen to each small movement they make, their breathing, and everything fades but the bloodlust pumping through me. I hear a small scrape as one pushes off from the sand, and suddenly, everything is in motion. I turn and stab into his gut as he charges before spinning and pulling my sword free. I disembowel him and then engage his friend, who yells in anger.

He's smarter, faster, a true opponent. He meets my sword and pushes me back, slicing my cheek in the process. Grinning, I reach up and smear the blood across my face, looking as it covers my fingers. "That's the only hit you will ever get, boy." Then I show them just how much I had been holding back. I show them why I always win.

Why they never will.

I throw everything at him, chasing him across the sand like a true Berserker. Wild, untamed, bloodthirsty, and unstoppable.

He stumbles back under my onslaught, barely managing to block each wild swing, until suddenly, he can't. He spins with the force of it, and when I dance around him, I see half of his face ripped open as he screams raggedly. I end it quickly, impaling him on my sword, my arm around his back as I hold up his weight. "Today, you concluded your final flesh sale—yours," I murmur in his ear before stepping back and kicking. The force sends him backwards, pulling him from my blood-soaked sword.

He falls to the ground with a loud thump as I pant, my sword held at my side. "Now, does anyone else have a problem with The Nations—" I don't get to finish.

The sound of the gun firing is loud, and I turn too slowly.

CHAPTER TWENTY-TWO

NO MORE DEATH

I don't close my eyes, wanting to see my death coming. I do flinch, however, waiting for the agony of the bullet ripping through my chest and ending my life. It's a coward's kill—they took a shot when I wasn't looking.

It makes me angry. This is how I will die? By a coward's bullet? But the pain never comes.

I blink, and he's there, his body blocking mine and taking the bullet meant for me. I hear his grunt as it hits home, and then he falls to the ground next to me from the force of his jump and the bullet. I stare, open-mouthed and shocked, as The Ring erupts in chaos. The traitor is detained, my men rush to my side to check me over, and just a step behind me is the man who took the bullet meant for me.

My father.

His face is pale, his mouth is opening and closing, and his eyes are dull with shock as he lies on the ground. My sword falls from my hand, forgotten on the sand as I drop to my knees next to him, my eyes catching on the hole torn through his chest. It's raw and bleeding, like crushed meat. His chest is ruined.

He's dying.

His hand reaches for me, bloodstained and shaking. I take it automatically, cold and numb. I have made my peace with him, and I do not really hate him anymore, but that doesn't mean I want him dead. Because right now, I'm staring into the paling face of a man who helped raise me until the world went to shit. Who kissed my scrapes, who brushed my hair at night and read me stories of kings and queens. I'm looking down at not just a stranger, a man who gave up on me and made many mistakes, but the man who once loved and protected me.

He smiles slightly, his lips trembling and red with his blood. "It's okay," he croaks before coughs rack his body. I don't know what to say, and he tenses for a moment, but he carries on, and I forget everything but him. "At least I was here this time."

"Da—" I start, but he grips my hand harder.

"No, I'm not asking for your forgiveness. I'm just so fucking happy I got to save you for once, and that I finally made up for my mistakes. You are an amazing woman." He coughs again, and I look up helplessly for assistance, but his voice drags my gaze back. "Your mother would be so proud of you, of the person you have become." His back bows as he screams, and I scream with him.

"Help me!" I yell, even though I know it's pointless.

"No, baby, it's time. I'm just glad I got to save you this time, that I wasn't too late or too scared. I'm paying my penance. I should have died that day. Instead, I got to watch you grow into this amazing woman, the woman who will change the world. Never stop fighting for that, never let the fear blind you like it did me. I love you forever and a day, my girl," he promises weakly. His eyes become glassy as Evan drops next to him and starts working on his chest, but when he sits back with a shake of his head, I know.

He's going to die.

He swallows hard, and I blink away some tears, my own emotions mixed. "Show-show them what it means to be a true queen," he rasps, blood dripping from his lips. "Love-love you," he slurs as his eyes start to turn cold.

"No!" I scream. "Look at me!" I demand as his hand goes slack in mine, but I grip it harder and lean down. "Please, fuck, don't do this!" I yell. "I lost one father, I can't lose another!" I beg and look up wildly. "Help me!"

But no one does as I stare down at my father. A man I once loved, then hated, then said goodbye to. But this goodbye is permanent, it's forever. I can feel him slipping away in my arms. His eyes locked onto mine, scared but accepting. His blood pumps into my hands and onto the ground.

I lean down and sing. I sing the song Vass sung to me. I let my broken, grief filled voice carry around the arena, and it is taken up by everyone here until the thunder of it is roaring. Our pain one. My dad smiles at me. "For once, I know what it feels like to be truly loved. Thank you," he whispers.

It's not fast. I grip him to me, keeping his head close as I rock and sing like a mother would her child. When it's done, and I know he's gone, I set him down gently and close his eyes, pressing his hands to his chest to cover the horrendous wound. Leaning down, I kiss his sweaty, cooling head. "I forgive you," I murmur. Sitting back, I meet the eyes of my men. They are broken, they are angry, and they are worried. Not for me.

For him.

For the man who just killed my father.

I'm numb and too tired to care. I stand and look at the man in question who's being held. He looks scared but determined, his head tilted back, and when I step closer, he spits at my feet. "He died like a fucking animal, the stink of his shit still lingers, and you will die the same way, you fucking slave bitch."

It's fast. I grab my knife and watch in cold fascination as it slices through his neck. His eyes widen, his mouth opening and closing as his blood squirts all over me—into my eyes, my mouth, and dripping down my body. I simply blink, watching as he falls, and those holding him let go with disgusted sneers. Crouching, I press my knife to his chin and meet his eyes. "You are the one dying like an animal now, traitor."

I watch him until he's dead, then I stand. Blood-soaked, exhausted...and broken once again. Because with him gone, with my father dead, I realise no matter what, I still loved him. But everyone is looking at me now, expecting me to break.

I can't. I won't.

"Does anyone else have a fucking problem?" I almost scream, no doubt wild and crazed looking. I want to fight, I want to cause pain. I want screams and death, anything to make me forget, to get this...this fucking pain out of me.

I feel my men step up behind me and reach for me, but I shake off their hands. "Do you?" I roar.

All the warriors gathered drop to their knees. I see the respect in some of their eyes and fear in others, and that is what stops me. One man's mistakes shouldn't cost them all their lives. I stumble back in fear at myself, at what I have become. At what I might have done. I feel arms again, and as they wrap around me and lift me from the ground, I let them.

"Come with me, soulmate," Dray murmurs into my ear.

I close my eyes for a moment, shivering in his grasp. My men and the other leaders, including Piper, close in front of me, protecting me, shielding me from view.

"We will now answer any questions," Priest announces.

"But first, someone rip that fucking bastard to shreds and feed him to the ferals!" Piper yells.

I am pulled away before I hear anymore. Time seems to pass in a blink, and when I realise where we are, I start to struggle. We are below in the slave quarters. The door shuts with a resounding bang, and my men stand in front of it, stone-faced.

I bite at Dray's arms so he tosses me away. I land on my feet and turn with a snarl as he smirks. "Come on, queen, show me what you've got," he taunts.

I fly at him, my crown dropping from my head and skittering

forgotten across the floor. I scream and slash with my knife, which is still covered in blood. Dray laughs and bobs and weaves out of the way easily, spinning and spanking me as he goes. It only enrages me further until I'm seeing red.

All I can think about is spilling his blood, of replacing the feel of my father's on me. He teases me, taunts me. "Come on, soulmate, you can do better than that."

I spin, chest heaving. My other men stare at me, blocking the door, keeping me here until I can think clearly. With a yell, I turn back to Dray. I feint kicking him, and he goes to block my leg, but I smash my fist into his nose. The crunch of the bone is loud, but instead of screaming or howling, he laughs as his eyes water and blood flows, but he doesn't care.

"Good, more," he urges, but the sight of his blood freezes me in place. I don't want to hurt him. I don't. It's not his fault, he doesn't deserve my rage, but he's the only one who's here and he's willing to take it. He sees the hesitation in my eyes and narrows his own. "Don't get weak on me now, soulmate. Fucking bring it. Unless you're scared? Too slow? Too injured? Maybe not fit to be the Champion anymore?"

He carries on, circling me as I clench my fists. "Stop, I don't want to hurt you," I mutter.

"No? Weak, that's fucking weakness," he spits, and his taunting hits home, even as I try to ignore it. I know he's lying, saying whatever he can to get a rise out of me, and trying to get these emotions out, because we both know if I keep them in, they will rot.

Maxen stays leaning against the door, but the others step forward. Drax and Jax move in opposite directions around me as Thorn stands in front of me. "Do it. Hit us, kick us, fight us. Get it all out, baby girl. No one can hear or see you. Scream, fight, cry, we don't care, but don't fucking shut us out."

I swallow, tears blurring my vision, and Jax attacks. I automatically duck, and then I have no time for thinking. They all come at me in a flurry, one after the other, until I can only defend myself, exhausting myself with no time to think on what happened or my roiling emotions.

I focus on the movement of my body, the feelings of my sweat dripping and my heart hammering, and before I know it, I'm not just defending, I'm attacking. I kick and punch, sweep my leg out, and fling myself around them. It doesn't matter that there are four of them, it doesn't matter if I'm outmatched, I don't give up.

I keep fighting because that's what you have to do. You get knocked down, you get back up. You break, you put yourself back together, and you never, never fucking stop. Because if you do, you might as well be dead. To be in pain, to feel is to be human, I know that. I've had my fair share of trauma and pain, but also love and laughter and even now, at my lowest, when I don't think I can do it anymore, I surprise myself.

I can lie down and give up, or I can keep going, just doing the next thing and living in the moment. Not an hour from now, or a day or a year. My current breath slowly turns into the next and the next, and before I know it, those breaths will get easier, I just know it.

Because to be strong isn't about just your body, but your state of mind, and fighting the demons inside your head is the biggest battle you can ever face. Every single person who wins, whether it be just that day, just that one stand, they are all fucking winners.

All champions, every single one of them. I am too.

They blend into one, and I don't even know who I'm fighting anymore. It is a whirlwind. My body starts to flag, but I push harder, feeling my stomach start to bleed again. Good, I should be bleeding, but when hands cup my cheeks and lips seal to mine, I freeze, and all that ice melts into desire. I taste him, take his breath like I can't live without it. He's my lifeline in the dark haze, and he pulls me back to life. Hands touch me, stroke me, and comfort me, and it's too much.

The softness overwhelms me.

I break the kiss, ripping my mouth away, and scream. He catches me as I sag and holds me in his hands as we fall to the stone floor. "No more," I whisper. "No more." I feel the others draw closer, and their arms join Dray's. They kiss and hold me, offering their comfort, but I am still cold.

"I want no more fucking funerals!" I shout. "No more of those I love or care for dying. I can't take it! Their blood fills my hands, their cries fill my nightmares... I'm so fucking tired of grieving. So tired of burying people... Please...please promise me, no more funerals."

Maxen steps away from the door after watching to make sure no one got hurt. He stops before me and cups my chin, making me meet his eyes. His own are hard and filled with such determination and love, it stops my cries.

"*Mi Alma*, breathe, no more funerals. I promise, no more, breathe for me. Let us hold you, we will put you back together again. Just breathe for us. No one will ever hurt you again, ever. Do you hear me? We will kill them all if we have to. No more tears, beautiful, they wreck me. That's it, breathe, feel us, we are here, we will never leave you. Not ever, it's us for life, *Mi Alma*. Breathe."

So I do.

HELP ME FORGET

I'm lying in bed with my men, and I don't want to get up. If I do, I have to face reality, so for a bit, I'll lose myself in them. I will let them take me away, comfort me, and make me happy before I have to become Worth the queen again. I don't remember how we got back here, but we did without seeing anyone. The moon is high in the sky, shining through the balcony, but I know soon it will be sunrise again, and I will have to bury my father. I will have to pretend I am not in pain, I will have to be the queen they need and are expecting, but here...

Right now, I'm just *Mi Alma*. Baby girl. Angel. Baby. Soulmate.

I turn into their reaching hands. Maxen's chest is there, always behind me, always my rock. He's the closest one, so I smash my lips to his. He groans, his hands going to my ass and gripping me, dragging me across his chest until I am straddling him. He knows I'm using him, I can feel it, but he's willing to do whatever I want as long as I am okay.

"Help me forget," I plead against his lips, not for the first time. He inhales, his hands clutching more tightly before he rumbles,

"You heard her, Jax, on your back," he demands. He lifts me up and places me on Jax, who lies down next to him. I drop my hands to his chest as I peer down into those hungry grey eyes. His hands go to my hips as he waits for me to dominate him. But this isn't about my strength, this is about my weakness, and when I feel Maxen behind me, I sigh in relief at not having to make a decision. At not having to be in charge for once.

He wraps his hand into my hair, making a fist and yanking my head back. "You will do exactly what I say, won't you?" he murmurs.

"Yes," I hiss, rubbing myself against him, relenting to his control, surrendering to my husbands. I give them control over me, losing myself in the pleasure they promise.

"Good girl. Are you nice and wet for us?" he asks and reaches down, dipping his fingers inside me and grunting. "Not good enough. Drax, get over here and make our girl wet."

Drax laughs and slips in next to me, uncaring about his brother being there. "Hell yes, now that I can do." He grins up at me and then spins upside down and presses his mouth to my pussy, licking and sucking automatically. Fast and hard, no teasing strokes. I groan and rock against his mouth, whimpering when his fingers spear into me, knowing just how I like it. Within a moment, I am nearly coming, and they must know.

"Stop," Maxen barks.

Drax groans but pulls away, sitting up with wide, lust-filled eyes. His lips are parted and glistening with my cream, his chest heaving. "Fuck, I forgot how good she tastes."

Maxen slides his fingers back across me again. "That's better. Now, *Mi Alma*, you are going to ride Jax's cock, aren't you? He's going to put his hands up so the only thing touching you is his cock. You are going to ride him so good, make him wild and come, and then Drax will fuck you." He licks along my neck as I moan. "And then Thorn and me together...and then if you can still walk, the crazy bastard can have you."

Jax lifts his hands and presses them to the wall, his abs clenching as Maxen helps me hover over his dick. At Maxen's urging, I drop down. impaling myself. I cry out at the intrusion, the slight edge of pain making it feel all the better. I start to rock automatically, and Maxen goes back to kissing my neck and whispering dirty things in my ear.

I can feel all the others staring, watching, so I tilt back my head and lose myself. Letting myself just feel, I use him and ride his cock, chasing my orgasm, which is building again.

"That's it, ride him. Fuck, you should see how beautiful you look right now. Everyone else gets to see you, but only we get to see you like this, and I love it. I love how I can hear your heart hammering." He licks along my neck. "How I can taste your need. I can't wait to be inside you, to feel that tight pussy wrapped around my cock as two of your husbands fuck you."

I flicker open my eyes to see Jax's teeth gnashed together, his eyes narrowed and bones grinding, abs tight, his hands shaking against the wall to undoubtedly stop himself from touching me. It's torture, a form of domination, and he loves it.

"Look what you do to him. You make us all weak. One touch, and we are gone. One look, and we are yours, always. Our bodies are for you to use, our hearts are yours to protect, and our weapons yours to wield."

His cock is so thick and it curves upwards, so it drags along my inner walls, hitting that spot over and over. The feeling of him inside me, Maxen's words, and the others' eyes have me screaming my release as I rock my hips. Jax roars, and I feel his cock jerk inside me as he fills me.

When the trembling stops, I open my eyes, panting, but I have no time to recover. Maxen lifts me free and holds me to his chest as Jax rolls from the bed and Drax takes his spot.

I crawl up his thighs and lick his cock along the way, making him groan. "Get your fine ass up here, baby girl. I want your pussy, not your mouth." He drags me up and drops me onto his cock, his brother's cum slicking the way, but a few thrusts in as I bounce on his cock, he stills and smirks. "Remember in that room when I almost died?

We were in this exact same position... Shall I show you what I really wanted to do with you then?"

My mouth goes dry, but I nod. He holds me tighter and flips us over so he is above me, the new angle making me moan. I wrap my legs tighter as his hand presses to the bed next to me. He slams into me, harder with each thrust. "I wanted this, you beneath me, wanted to watch all that worry and heartache melt away to lust. To see you come and writhe, to feel your nails in my back, to fuck the woman everyone wants or hates."

"Drax," I beg, kicking his ass. He's already building me back up with each twist of his hips, and when he leans down and closes his lips around my nipple, I forget thinking and even breathing.

I ache to come, but something is stopping me, holding me back. My body vibrates with desire, and lust pounds through me. I'm at the edge, but just as I am about to fall over...the pain comes back.

The screams. The blood.

I close my eyes and shake, thrashing my head as I try to get it out. But then Maxen is there, and he grips my chin. "Eyes open," he snarls meanly, as Drax's thrusts speed up, punishing me for forgetting where I was, for trying to remember.

My eyes flicker open and meet Maxen's, and he presses his cock to my mouth. "Can't stop thinking? Fine, you'll think about my cock in your mouth and Drax's in your pussy. In fact... Thorn," he barks.

Maxen leans over and whispers something to Drax, who grins down at me before pulling free of my pussy. I whimper and reach for him. They can't stop, because then I will remember.

He moves, and I spot Dray watching from a chair, sharpening a knife. Those cold eyes are locked on me, heating—he knows what's coming. They will have me...and then he gets whatever is left.

He will push me over the edge of madness, our bloodlust mixing with desire, until we explode in a force that might kill us all.

One look, and I shiver from it, because I know tonight, he is over being nice, over being gentle—well, gentle for Dray. Tonight, I get the Seeker King. The assassin.

But not before my other husbands. I am lifted, so I close my eyes, trusting them as I am placed back down onto a chest, and then there is a cock at my pussy. Bigger.

Thorn.

He rubs it along my wet center, bumping my clit and making me cry out. In one smooth, harsh thrust, he slams into me. The size of his cock stretches me, and I groan in pain.

But that pain, just for a moment, eclipses the other pain in my heart. Then he starts to move, and the pain fades to pleasure as I slump.

Drax, I realise now, is pressed against my ass and, working with Thorn, he lifts me so he can press his cock to my other hole and pull me down onto it.

More pain comes.

I beg for more, reaching out wordlessly. It deserves to hurt, I need it to hurt.

My head is yanked to the side, and I open my mouth, my gaze clashing with Maxen's. Thorn starts to move, pulling out as Drax slams in, stretching me to the border of pain and pleasure. Their cocks fill me until I can barely breathe.

And then Maxen pushes into my mouth, right down to the back of my throat and pulls out in a slow, measured thrust. Those eyes anchor me, forcing me to feel the pleasure starting to crawl back through my body.

My hands grip the sheets, twisting them as each cock, each push and pull, sends me higher. Hands rove across my body, pinching, twisting, flicking, and sliding. Each one pushes me higher and higher. Maxen's thrusts speed up until my mind blanks. My body is the only thing feeling now, and all those sensations explode through me until I can't move.

Can't think.

Can't breathe.

And then I scream my release.

I think I black out a little. I hear Thorn's grunt, followed by

Drax's sigh in my ear, as they fill me with their release, and then something is splashing on my chest.

I force my heavy eyes open to see Maxen stumbling back.

Then I am empty again as they pull from me, and as soon as they do, the pain and thoughts return, making me shake in fear.

"Dray, you are up. Make it hurt, make her body scream louder than her mind," Maxen orders.

In one sentence, he described exactly what I needed before I even understood—pain, the fight, to forget.

I am lifted and placed gently on the bed. I feel well used. My body is sore, but not sore enough, and when I climb to my knees, I feel their cum drip from me like a mark, which makes me shiver in pleasure.

Dray stands as the others leave the room and go next door, giving us privacy. They aren't stopping us tonight, aren't holding back. Those cold eyes meet mine as he prowls towards me. Turning my head, I keep him in my view. He's a wild animal and could pounce at any time.

I shiver under his dangerous gaze. He doesn't even need the knife in his hand. He is the weapon, and right now, I'm the prey. From one breath to the next, he is on me.

I fall back to the bed, his lips wrapping around my shoulder as his teeth dig in. He yanks open my thighs before he slams his fingers inside me, making me yell and jerk. I lift my hips to try and dislodge him. He snarls, digging his teeth in deeper, and then I am flipped.

He pushes my face into the bed and wraps his hand in my hair, holding me there as I feel his cock pressing against my pussy. He's ready to fuck me right here.

I thought I wanted to be dominated, controlled, but that's not who I am. Not with Dray. He's mine to tame, to fight and to fuck, and he will bow down to me before I let his cock inside me.

I twist, ripping out some of my hair, but the flare of pain only spurs me on as I throw myself at him.

We fall from the bed, fighting each other, our hands and feet clashing. I land a punch, and his head whips to the side before it jerks back around with a snarl. His legs lock around me and twist us, but I roll us again and we slam into the wall. Grabbing his head, I smash it into it again and again as he yells. His cock jerks beneath me, rubbing against my dripping pussy in his desire.

He pulls free from my grasp, and I see the blood forming along his temple, and then I am thrown. I land on my ass across the room and roll to my feet, crouching as I watch him get to his feet.

Nothing of Dray is left. This is a mad animal, and it sends a bolt of desire straight to my heart.

I can never hurt him, never kill him. I never have to hold back, and that is addictive.

"I was just going to fuck you," he snarls, stroking his hard cock, his piercing glistening in the dark. "Now I think I want your blood too."

"You'll have to pry it from me," I taunt.

He flashes the knife again, and as I watch, he drags it along his lip before his tongue darts out and licks along the blade. "It can be arranged, soulmate."

One second, we are talking, and then, we are fighting. Not teasing, not play fighting...actually fighting.

He slashes out with the knife, and I duck and weave around it, bringing my knee up to smash it into his junk, but he grabs my knee and twists me, throwing me into the bed. I slam into it hard, jarring my jaw, and then the blade is at my throat as he drops to his knees behind me, pressing his cock to my ass as he leans in. "I could slice your throat right now and fuck your body as you die, soulmate."

"You wouldn't dare, you like the pain I give you too much," I pant, rubbing back against the blade and his cock.

"That's true, I prefer you alive. To taunt, to tease." He drags the knife down my throat, drawing blood. "To pleasure."

Reaching back, I wrap my hand around the sharp edge of the blade and yank it free, cutting my hand in the process. The sudden pain has me gasping, even as my pussy clenches.

He groans at the sight, my bloodied hand wrapped around the blade, and he grinds his cock into my ass. "Fuck, wife, that's so hot. Cut me, mix our blood together as we fuck."

Our fighting so easily turns to sex, always has with him.

I turn and meet those icy eyes that burn only for me. I slice out quickly with the knife as I turn, cutting his cheek. I watch the blood well and start to drip down his cheek. His chest heaves, and his cock stands at attention, making me clench my thighs together.

He picks me up and throws me again. I bounce, my legs hanging off the bed, and suddenly, he is between them, making me laugh. He yanks them up and presses the balls of my feet to his shoulders as he lines up at my entrance and slams inside.

We both groan as he thrusts in deep, that piercing dragging along my walls, his hands gripping my hips so cruelly. I slice again, down his chest, and he grunts as his cock jerks inside me. Eyes wild, he starts to rut into me like an animal, harder and faster, pushing me up the bed from the force. My already sore pussy aches, and that edge of pain has me crying out as I lift my hips to meet each desperate thrust.

He growls, the sound vibrating through me. Eyes on him, I run the blade down my chest, over my belly, and press the flat edge to my clit, just pressing the cool metal there as he slams into me. The tip is probably inches away from his dick, but it only spurs him on.

Those cold eyes flick from me down to the display, driving him wild.

This man can kill thousands and lead warriors so fearsome, people cry at the sight. Yet one look at me, and he's lost. Tapping my clit with the knife, I groan before dragging the wet metal back up and around my nipples.

Grunting, he leans down and stretches my legs as he follows the path with his tongue, but then he suddenly pulls free, and a moment later, he is back. He drags me up, sits on the bed, and drops me back down on his cock, making us both gasp. I place my hands on his chest, confused until he produces a thin, needle-looking knife.

He hands it over. "Pierce my tongue, I want to feel it against your nipples and clit."

Shaking, I take the knife, wanting to feel that myself. He sticks out his tongue, trusting me. Freezing on his thick cock, I find the center of the tip and, with a sharp strike, sink it through his tongue. He groans, thrusting up into me, and I quickly yank out the needle before I rip his tongue. A moment later, his hands come up, messing with his tongue, and when he pulls back to show me, I see the matching bar through it.

"On your back, let me lick you," he demands.

I roll free, and he's between my thighs in an instant, dragging his tongue along it. When his piercing hits my clit, I almost scream. Laughing, he sucks it into his mouth, the cool edge of the hard metal pressing against it, making my hips jerk as I tumble over the edge of another orgasm.

Two seconds later, his cock is back in me and ramming into me harder than before.

I'm still riding the high, so I barely come down before I am thrown back into it, and he follows this time, his cock filling me as he comes. We are locked together, panting and bloody. He kisses me, his tongue tangling with mine, and I groan at the sensation of the bar. I taste the blood and smokiness which is all Dray.

And not once did I think about my dad.

Chapter Twenty-Four

The Ring

"Dray," I start as he sharpens his sword while the others are eating breakfast. He just got back from checking his new piercing with Doc on my request. Evan apparently sighed, but said it was fine after cleaning it. "I need your help."

We got up early this morning before the sun even rose and buried my father. My heart still twinges in pain at seeing him lying there next to Von, but it doesn't hurt as much as it did with Major, which causes guilt to fill me, so I plan on staying busy to forget.

I fucked all my pain away last night, I can't let it come back.

His head jerks up instantly. "With orgasms or murder? I'm down for both, soulmate."

I can't help but smile. "Neither at the moment, crazy, just a normal favour. No murdering, torturing, or maiming... You might be able to swing some threats to get it done though."

"You got it, wife. What do you need?"

"A present for Piper." I grin and outline everything that needs to be done. When I've finished, he hops up, kisses me soundly, and rushes off to do as I asked. I turn to the others but frown when I spot them whispering to each other. They smile when they catch me staring.

"Do you need us today, baby girl?" Thorn asks. "Why?" I hedge.

They share a look. "We have something to sort out, we will find you later, *Mi Alma*. Try to take it easy," Maxen offers as he stands and kisses my forehead. "Thorn, stay with her. I don't want anyone getting any ideas about trying to attack her when she's alone. Yes, you can take care of yourself, but I would still feel better if he was here," Maxen says straightaway, no doubt sensing my rising defensiveness.

Drax and Jax kiss me and rush after Maxen. "Stay with my wife? All day? Just us two? Not a problem." Thorn grins, flashing me a deep, dirty smile which has me groaning and shifting in my seat.

"We have work to do," I huff.

"Sure we do. My work is to get into those pants and make you scream my name again." I can't help but laugh as he wiggles his eyebrows at me.

After eating and getting dressed while only being felt up twice by Thorn, I manage to get out of the door without him, as he said, getting into my pants, though it wasn't easy. I want to climb that man like a tree all the time, but I have things to do. The leaders will need to leave soon and get back to their own clans. I need to check on the injured and make sure our people have no concerns or worries.

To keep busy...to forget.

I start with the injured. Thorn walks behind me like a bodyguard as we head through The Ring. Some offer me contemplative looks, but no one attacks me. They might not like some of the new rules now, but they aren't stupid enough to fight me for it. I do get some pitying looks as well, no doubt waiting for me to explode in grief.

But strangely, I am okay. Maybe it's because I said goodbye to my father a long time ago, and this just feels very final. Maybe the pain will hit me again when I'll least expect it, but for now, while I can function, I will.

When we reach the wounded, I find Evan there treating a Berserker warrior. He has blood on his face, and he's shirtless, and his tattoos are on display, which is strange for Evan. Maybe he is finally settling into the world above the bunker.

"Wait, where did the hot nurse go?" I hear as I turn the corner. "That's my girlfriend, you Neanderthal idiot!" Evan growls as he wraps the man's leg.

"You calling me dumb?" the warrior roars, almost throwing Evan backwards, but I cross my arms as I stop behind him.

"This man is my friend. You will treat him with the same respect you show me," I demand as the man withers under my glare, and then I turn to Evan. "And you, she's your girl, make it known. Otherwise, these men will just see her as something to win, though I'm betting Piper might kick their asses for it."

He grins. "That she would." He nods, and I follow after him as we circle the injured. He checks in on as many as he can.

"Can you give me an update?" I ask, noticing there are less wounded today. I pray that's not because they have died.

"Three died overnight, not much I could do. I did an amputation this morning." He looks down at his chest. "Hence the lack of clothes. Blood gets everywhere when you don't have a proper surgical unit." He sighs. "But other than that, they are steady. They are recovering, but it will take time. Some are idiots and refuse treatment, thinking they have had worse before," he mutters.

"Warriors." I grin. "We are tough fuckers."

"Yeah? Nothing tough about a blood infection that you won't let me treat," he snaps, rubbing his head. "Honestly, they will need checking on, but there isn't too much I can do now. When were you going to send Piper on the road?"

"A few days, if that works for you? She can do supply runs until then for more medical supplies."

He nods, his eyes distant. "That might work. There's an old, abandoned research facility under a hospital somewhere to the east. We could do with more antibiotics and equipment. I'd also like to set up a proper medical facility here. I've found a suitable room."

"Do it. I'll speak to Piper and tell her what you need her to get." I smile at him. "You're doing amazing, Doc, just be firm with them. They respect the truth and threats, not much else."

He nods, and someone shouts his name, so he rushes off to help them. I linger and speak to the warriors here for an hour or two before heading out to find Piper. We follow the shouts, finding her sparring with Jago in the pit. Archel is watching before he jumps in, both of them double teaming her, but she holds her own. I watch with a grin. She's a good fighter, really good, and every time I see her, she gets better.

Her mountain man is observing from the side with the other Lost, his mask in place. The crowd cheers, and I jerk my eyes back to see her knock Archel on his ass before Jago takes her down. I whoop and cheer as they get to their feet, panting and sweaty.

She shields her eyes from the sun and runs them around the viewers before they land on me. "Hey, Worth! Come kick my ass!"

I shake my head, but the crowd hears her and starts cheering for it. She jogs over, grinning up at me. "Come on, Champion, everyone loves a bit of girl on girl." She winks, making me laugh. "Teach me your greatness, I am your padawan."

"I don't even know what that means. If I fight you, Piper, you won't walk for a week," I tease.

"Oh, big words... Prove it," she retorts as she steps back with a wide grin.

"Kick her ass, baby girl." Thorn laughs.

"Worth, Worth, Worth!" the others chant, so, with a sigh, I throw myself over the ledge and land on the sand and walk towards her.

"First blood, no weapons, no holding back," I inform her, as I throw my swords and knives to the side. "We fight dirty here, Pip," I tease. "Don't think I'll go easy on you 'cause I like you. I'm the Champion. I was born from blood and flames, so when I fight, I always do it to win." I grin as I circle her. "Hear them screaming my name? Because they know even if you knock me down, I will get back up. I never give up." I lean in. "And neither do you, my friend. One day, they will scream for you. I might be the Champion, but you? You're a damned fucking fighter through and through."

She smiles, even as her eyes flicker nervously.

"Don't worry, I won't kill you." I laugh as I step back, my hands at my sides. "First shot is free," I offer.

She hesitates but swallows and rushes me. She's good, fast, and smart. She feints high but goes low, but years of fighting to survive, of watching my opponents like a hawk, have me spinning out of the way. I kick her ass lightly as I laugh.

"Good, really good, but you shifted your eyes to where you were going to hit. It's a clear signal, keep them on mine," I instruct, pointing at my own. "Never indicate where you are going to go. Surprise them, keep them on their toes. You're small and fast, but they will always be bigger, so wear them down. Use their size against them, make them use their energy, and when they are exhausted, end it."

"Teaching me your tricks, hot stuff?" She laughs, pushing back her hair and leaning down slightly.

"Don't tell anyone," I tease, and then I'm done talking.

I don't go as fast as I normally would. I'm not fighting to the death here. We trade blows, dancing across the sand. She is only a fraction behind me, and what she lacks in finesse, she makes up for in attitude. She never stops, even when I hit her side and kick her legs from under her. She just flips back to her feet. When I almost knock her out, she gets her ass back up.

I respect that.

She reminds me of, well...me when I was younger.

I step back as she wipes her mouth and the blood there, but I don't call time, wanting them all to see why I picked her. This isn't about me winning and showing off, this is about making the gathered warriors understand why I picked her to be my right-hand woman over everyone else. She has something they never will—heart.

She has the soul of a champion.

She spits her blood to the side, panting slightly, and she has sweat on her brow, but she still smiles. "That all you got?" She laughs. "I was expecting more."

"Oh, girl, you're going to regret that." I laugh, and then I stop holding back. She can handle it, she can handle me.

She doesn't even get time to swear as I throw myself at her. I wrap my legs around her neck and throw us backwards, flipping us. I roll to my feet as she groans. She gets to her feet, but slower than before. She punches out and hits my tit, making me narrow my eyes as she freezes.

"Oops, honest mistake, didn't mean to hit your boob, shit, fuck!" she cries out as I headbutt her. She stumbles back, and I sweep my leg, but she jumps it, eyes narrowed.

There are no more words, which is surprising from her. She manages to land a few punches, one solid one to my injured shoulder, which makes me grunt, but good for her. She spotted my weakness and wasn't afraid to use it. I kick her stomach and bring my knee up to her face, but I lessen the blow so it doesn't break her nose.

She falls forward, so I grab her shoulders, spin her, and wrap my arm around her neck and throw us down, encircling her waist with my legs. I hold her as she bucks and fights, until eventually, she taps out. I roll away and get to my feet, looking down at her.

She lies there panting and groaning. I lower my hand to her, and she stares at it. "Fuck, you're good. Is it weird I'm wet from that?"

I laugh as she claps my hand, and I pull her to her feet and step back. "You're good, Piper. Keep practicing, and one day, you'll even be able to hand me my ass."

She perks up at that. "You think?"

"I know it," I reply, and look at her men. "Go enjoy your loser's prize. Meet me later before the evening meal, I have things to talk about."

I turn away and run to the wall, throwing myself up it. Thorn reaches down and hauls me over the edge, keeping me in his arms when I get up there. "Fucking hell, just when I think I can't love you more…" His eyes are soft as he brushes my hair from my face. "Baby girl, you're a goddamn miracle."

"I don't know what you mean," I murmur, leaning into him.

"You did that to show everyone not to come after her. You almost let her win, and you did it for her to give her more confidence. Baby girl, you are a queen through and through, and I'm so lucky to be at your side, getting to watch you lead and save our world."

He drops to his knees before me, grabbing my hand and placing a kiss on it as those smouldering eyes roll up to meet mine.

"If I could, I would ask you to marry me all over again, but instead, I'll ask this. Tazanna Worth, will you stay married to me forever? Even when I'm dumb, and even when I make you angry, will you stay? Will you be my queen?"

That motherfucker. I fight back my tears as I stare down at him. "Always," I murmur.

I hear others whoop as he jumps to his feet and lifts me, swinging me in a circle. I laugh as our lips meet hungrily, and he groans, squeezing my ass as he rips his mouth away.

"I need you, right now," I tell him.

"Yes, my queen, your needs are my orders." He grins and turns away and rushes to the closest building.

I hear the whistles and comments of those gathered, but I don't give a fuck. Thorn storms through the corridor of the main building and steps into the closest room. He kicks open the door as I kiss his neck and slams it behind us, pressing me against it. I grunt at the sudden impact, but he swallows the sound, his lips crashing to mine.

This isn't my sweet lover, this is Thorn, the man who fucked me like an animal after not seeing me in The Cities. This is my husband, my warrior. I dig my nails into his shoulders, kicking his ass to get him going.

He grunts into my mouth before yanking down my shirt and bra. His fingers find my nipple and flick, twist, and tease until I'm gasping into his mouth. I bite at his lip. "More," I demand.

He pulls away from the door and stumbles across the carpeted floor. It's dim in here, since the window is covered in cardboard, but the holes let fragments of light through, enough to see by as he throws me onto the closest table. It creaks but holds, and he sweeps everything from the top. It all falls to the floor with a loud crash, but we are too busy seeking each other out again.

His lips are on mine as his hand dives into my trousers and panties, finding my wetness there. I gasp as he slips two fingers inside me, his thick digits making me lift my hips to fuck myself on them as he swallows all my needy sounds.

"Baby girl." He flicks my clit with his thumb before he pulls it free. I pant, watching as he steps back, rips off his shirt, and unfastens his jeans, freeing his hard cock. He's a masterpiece, all hard muscle under his glistening onyx skin. Those hungry eyes remain locked on me as I pull off my own shirt and toss it away. My bra soon follows, and he grabs my boots and throws them over his shoulder before stripping me of my jeans and panties, leaving me bare before him.

His tongue runs along his lips as he looks over my body. "Every time I think you can't be as beautiful as I remember, you're better. You drive me crazy."

Grabbing one of my legs, he presses my foot to his chest where I can feel the pounding of his heart as he kisses along my thigh and across my pussy. Soft, featherlight kisses. Thorn is the biggest of all my men, so he can't just slam into me as much as we both want him to.

His tongue darts out and licks along my pussy. I drag my foot up and hang it over his shoulder, then grip his hair and drag him closer as he chuckles. His fingers dive back into my pussy as he licks and sucks me. I grab my breasts, rolling and twisting my nipples as I fuck myself onto his face.

I can't help but cry out as I come, grinding against his tongue and fingers. He kisses and licks me through it then lifts his head, those dark eyes almost feral. His fingers grip my thighs as we watch each other, caught in a trap together. The world outside fades away.

"I bet you're still too tight for my cock, aren't you, baby girl?" He grins. "I guess I could help with that... Tell me, have you ever fucked a sword?

I blink, unsure what he means as he grabs one of my swords, the one without the skull on the top, and presses it to my pussy, making me groan. "It's smaller than me," he murmurs almost casually, "but should stretch your tight little pussy nicely, and if you're good, I'll even let you come on it before I fuck you."

"Fucking hell," I groan, dropping back to the table. I can't help but just breathe as he slowly pushes the handle of the sword inside me. It has slightly raised bumps that have me moaning as they drag along my walls. At first, he slowly pulls it out before pushing it back in, twisting as he goes, but when I lift my legs onto the table and raise my hips to fuck it more, he groans and speeds up.

Fuck, fuck, fuck, this is so wrong, but it feels so amazing. The handle hits that spot inside me, and when his mouth comes down on my breasts, attacking them ferociously, his teeth and tongue wrapping around them, twisting and flicking, I feel myself almost coming again. "Thorn," I whimper. "Fuck, I'm s-so close," I pant, my eyes squeezed closed.

He grips my chin. "Eyes open. I want to look into them while you come, and when you are coming down, I'm going to slam my cock inside you. I'm going to fuck you so roughly, they will think I am murdering you in here with the noises you will be making."

Fuck. Me.

His filthy words send me over the edge. I come around the sword with a scream, and he pins me down as I do. I try to keep my eyes on his as, with an almost mean smile, he yanks the sword free of my pulsing pussy. Then he's there, ripping open my thighs and pressing his cock to my entrance, and between one blink of my eyes and the next, he slams inside me.

The edge of pain has me arching away from the wood with a snarl and ripping my nails down his chest. He groans and starts to move, fucking me hard and fast like he promised. I wrap my legs around him as I sit up, the new angle making him hit even deeper inside me. His hands go to my hips and pull me to the edge of the table before he growls and turns, slamming me into the nearest wall.

I use him as leverage to ride him, meeting his thrusts. Our eyes are locked together, our breaths mingling. The rough loud slap of our bodies, our moans and groans, do sound like we are fighting. He slams me into the wall with a grunt, dropping me onto his cock harder and faster, both of us fighting our release. Our bodies come together like two lost puzzle pieces.

I hear laughter as people walk past, but I don't care. They could walk in and I wouldn't even make him stop, that's how lost in him I am. Only my men make me like this, make me forget everything but them. Make me drop my guard until I'm just a woman fucking the man she loves.

Our foreheads press together, our lips touching as his hips stutter. He fights to keep the same rhythm, but when I purposely squeeze his cock, he roars and just fucks me relentlessly with hard, quick thrusts. His huge cock borders on the edge of pain, but that makes it all the better, and with one more twist of his hips, I come with a scream.

My eyes close. He yells his own release and stills as I feel him fill me. His head is pressed to my shoulder as we both shudder and rest against the wall. I wrap my arms around him and hang on as our hearts race in sync, our bodies sweaty and satisfied.

"I love you," I pant.

"I love you too, baby girl," he whispers, kissing my shoulder. "Now and forever. Let's get you dressed and fed before you go kick some more ass."

"Too fucking right. You know the way to a girl's heart." I laugh.

"Only yours, Taz, only ever yours," he vows.

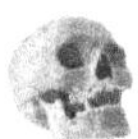

I eat, but I don't see the others. It makes me wonder what they are up to. I'll torture it out of them later, but for now, Thorn is right. I have queenly duties to take care of. There will be concerns on what this means for the future, and I have to listen to disputes and settle them as well as reassure those who are worried.

We do it in the pit. I sit on a table and pretty much hold court. Priest comes, as does Nan, though after the first ten people, she gets bored and wanders off to 'get drunk and laid.' Jon is there, but he is mostly watching and taking notes. He's nervous and unsure of his opinion, but that will change over time. Priest is surprisingly helpful, and with his angels around the space, I have no worries about being attacked.

"Next!" I call. A Seeker troops in, and I frown. Usually, they would go to Dray, but he simply nods at me and presses something into my hands.

"I was told to say this," he mutters and sighs. "Soulmate, I miss you and your body already. I haven't killed anyone yet, I will save that for us to do together later." He blushes, and I grin.

"Thanks."

He rushes away like the hounds of hell are on his heels, and I open the wrapped package and laugh. It's a patch for a leather jacket, hastily made, that says, 'Worth's bitch.' I'm not sure who it's for, but imagining one of my guys wearing it makes me laugh harder. It's just what I needed right now.

Thorn leans next to me, offering his voice when I need his opinion, and he has a very good mind for strategy. I always knew he was smart, but he is able to look at the concerns from all angles and come up with a solution that suits us all in such a way that it doesn't feel like a compromise.

Another man comes in, a scav. His chest is bare and filled with scars, his face is flat, and his nose is almost cut off. One side of his hair is missing. He looks wild, and when he speaks, he has a loud booming voice that matches his massive frame. The more he talks, though, the more I realise how much of a teddy bear he is, and I relax.

"Ma queen," he begins. "I'm Lochlan. I was part of a bandit crew. I was drafted to help win the war against that Cities scum, and I would like ta stay, if you will have me? I appreciate a good leader, and that you are. Strong enough to hold the crown, with good morals, unlike that mad king scum." He spits on the ground then, making me smirk.

"You think you can follow a woman?" I inquire, knowing some men can't. It's better to know now.

"Women, man, both? I don't fucking care. No offense, but a leader is a leader. I don't care what is between ya legs so long as I believe in what ya preaching, and, queen, I do. You got good ideas. I'm tired of killing, I want to start a life. I want to have a home here, and I know a lot feel the same. If ima kill, I want to kill to secure that." He pulls his axe out. "Ma blade is yours, queen, if you will have me."

I look him over as he waits. "Of course, everyone is welcome here."

He drops to his knees, his head bowed. "For The Nations, for the Berserker Queen."

"Those bandits...you know where they are? Are they still killing people?" I ask.

He looks up. "Aye, they were when I left. I joined them because I couldn't find anyone else and it was hard living alone, never liked the way they did shit though. They steal and kill, working out of an old plant to the north. It's surrounded by the fuckers, they have firebombs and warriors."

I smirk. I could send Piper, but she isn't ready to do that kind of thing. "Anything else?"

"They kill anyone who passes. They don't care who they are. I don't like that, they need to be stopped. I wish I was strong enough to do it alone," he answers with self-disgust.

"Never be sorry for wanting a helping hand, and everything is not black or white. It isn't good or bad. You've done bad things, right? We all have, but you can choose to be better, and you are. I will take care of them. If you would like to come with me, that would be a big help, since you know the layout."

He grins and jumps to his feet. "Would love to. Just let me know when!"

"Good, get some food and rest." He nods and leaves.

"Worth—" Thorn starts.

"I know, but Piper would be killed. How can I speak of change when I know of people killing my people just outside The Ring? No, we go, and we kill them all. Our last mission. I will plan it in a few days, and we will go at night, kill them, and be back before light."

"Good plan." Priest nods. "I will send some angels with you."

"Thank you," I tell him. I raise my voice. "Next!"

And so it goes. I listen to them all and help when I can, and they leave feeling better. I'm beginning to think this might actually work, but hours later, I am tired, my head is killing me, and I am hungry, so I call it a day and bid Priest goodbye to go in search of food.

We head to the cafeteria, grab a table, and eat, but it's quiet without my other men. Thorn keeps me laughing and distracted, which means he's in on whatever they are up to. I've just finished eating when Piper turns up at my table.

"So you wanted to see me?" Piper asks as she sits opposite me. Her cheeks are flushed, and I smirk, knowing exactly what she has been doing.

"I need you and your men to do a medical run for Evan. He will tell you what he needs, and he knows of a facility. Consider it your first job as my enforcer, if you accept."

She almost squeals as she leaps up. "Yo, mountain man! Grab your explosives! We are going on an adventure!" she screams across the room. Jago sighs as he sits down next to her and Archel laughs.

She sits between them, almost bouncing, but Jago puts his hand on her head to force her to stay seated. "Brawler, let her finish."

"Right, sorry, go ahead, just excited, sorry, keep going," Piper blurts, looking at me with a crazy smile. No wonder she has so many men, she needs them to keep up with her.

"Like I said, get the supplies and get back. Evan and I have a deal. He can go with you on enforcement and track runs once the injured are sorted. This will be your base, of course, but you'll be on your own out there, Piper. So load up with weapons and never be too care- ful." I narrow my eyes. "I mean it, I want you back in one piece, understood?"

"Yes, sir—I mean ma'am, I mean queen. Fuck," she mutters. "When do we leave?"

"End of the week. Evan is compiling a list, so until then, I suggest you check on your bikes and get them up to scratch and prepare. I'm not sure how far east it is, but you are bound to encounter ferals and cannibals."

She rubs her hands together. "Yes, sounds fun. Team Piper for the win!"

We all blink at her as Evan comes and sits down. "I thought we agreed we were still searching for a name?"

She rolls her eyes and looks at me. "It's a work in progress. Okay, so end of the week."

"Yep, get your other people back home. We will discuss trade routes tomorrow and make sure we all stay in communication as much as we can across The Wastes," I inform her as I sip my water and then stand. "Get ready for the ride of your life, girl." I wink and walk away, with Thorn holding my hand.

Time to find my men and see what they have been up to.

Chapter Twenty-Five

At The Gate

They are in the room when I get back, and they are all quiet as I walk in. I prop my hands on my hips. They all smile at me innocently, but I'm not buying it. "Okay, cut the shit. What have you been up to?"

Just then, the door opens and Dray strolls in. "Soulmate, I have what you requested," he announces dramatically, placing the jacket on the sofa for me to inspect.

I grin as I look it over. It's perfect, and I hope Piper will love it. I carefully fold it and place it on the table to give it to her before she leaves on that run. It's a good luck gift, and also to welcome her as my right-hand woman.

"I still want to know what you fuckers have been up to." I narrow my eyes on them and swing from them to Dray. "Are you in on this?"

He just winks, that bastard.

"It's nothing bad, baby cakes," Drax offers sweetly. I turn my glare on him, but he just grins wider.

"*Mi Alma*, it's not. I promise," Maxen soothes.

"Then tell me," I demand, crossing my arms.

"No, it's a surprise. You are going to have to trust us," he retorts, the fucking asshole. Because now if I ask, I look like I don't.

"I do trust you...I'm just curious," I hedge.

"Nope, it's a surprise, Angel. You will just have to be patient," Jax states finally.

"Fuck, I hate being patient." I groan. "Fine, you owe me." "I think we can come to a deal," he growls hungrily.

All eyes swing my way, and Thorn laughs. They watch me with lust as Maxen gets to his feet. I point my finger at them. "No, you are being secretive, you don't get my pussy."

"Really?" Drax asks, stepping closer and licking his lips. "I bet I could convince you with my tongue inside you."

Oh, that's not fair. Dray joins in, circling me. So what is a girl to do when faced with five, horny men? She grabs her sword. I press it under Dray's chin and tilt his head back. "Tell me and I'll fuck you."

"Soulmate, cut me and I'll fuck you," he promises.

"I only have one vagina, put your cocks away," I order.

"But you have a mouth, an ass, and two hands," Drax reasons, circling me. His warm breath blows across my ear as his hand strokes down my side. "Plus, Thorn has had you today. I've missed you, baby, missed that pretty little mouth around my cock and watching my brothers take that pussy of yours. Watching you give yourself to us."

My panties are wet and my pussy is pulsing, even as I fight it. I don't even know why, other than I feel like I'm turning into a sex crazed woman. One look, and I'm theirs.

Jax's eyes are dark as he drops to his knees before me and rolls them up submissively. "Make it hurt, Angel. Ride me, use me, do whatever the hell you want to me... I might even let it slip what the surprise is," he teases, knowing he already has me hooked.

Maxen is standing there watching it all with a smirk on his lips as he pulls down his hair while I watch. He knows I love it around his shoulders, love fisting it as he fucks me.

"I'm supposed to be resting," I protest, but it's weak, even to my own ears. I tilt my head to give Drax better access as I still hold Dray with the sword, but now he's rubbing himself over his jeans as a bubble of blood forms at the tip of the blade, where he is pushing against it.

I hesitate, unsure what to do, when I decide fuck it, and just go with it. I drop the sword, and they are on me in a second. Hands and lips trace across my body, so many I can't tell who is who. There's a pinch of pain as my shirt is ripped away, and then lips wrap around both nipples. My jeans and boots are stripped off. All the while, I stare at Maxen, whose eyes remain locked on mine as I pant and shake, my body overloaded with all of my husbands' attentions at once.

Maxen stares, watching me, protecting me like always so I can be weak. Someone's fingers drag along my pussy, and another set of hands push my thighs wider as a mouth suckles my clit. More hands drag down my back. I close my eyes and give myself over to it, focusing on the pleasure from their hands and mouths. There's a sharp bite of teeth on my shoulder, which makes me groan and jerk, pressing my pussy harder against whoever is touching me.

Hands slide around me from behind, cupping my other breast and squeezing hard, and a cock presses to my ass and I whimper, unsure where to hold onto. I open my eyes and glance down. Drax is paying attention to my breast, Jax is on his knees still, his lips around my clit and eyes locked on me. Thorn's fingers are inside me, which means Dray is behind me.

"Is she ready for me?" Maxen calls.

"She's wet as hell, aren't you, baby girl? I think she likes all of us worshipping her," Thorn comments.

There's a knock at the door, and I ignore it, reaching down and cupping Drax's head, but it comes again, more insistent. With a growl, I rip away, grab my sword, and open the door. I glare at the man on the other side. I must look crazy, naked, and wild with a bloodied sword. His eyes widen before he slams them shut.

"My queen—I'm—fuck, I'm sorry!" he rushes out. "I wouldn't have disturbed you if it wasn't important."

"What is it? And talk fast," I demand.

"There is... There are people at the gate. I can't even explain, you have to come and see."

I slam the door in his face. Fuming, I slip into my clothes. Great, now I'm going to have blue balls. "Later, *Mi Alma*. For now, you have duties," Maxen soothes, obviously reading my face.

I rip open the door again and storm past the man, my men in tow. When I get downstairs and out in the open, men are rushing to the gate. Even at the late hour, most are awake and security is on patrol. I shouldn't be mad...but fucking hell, that was going to be amazing.

It doesn't take me long to wind through The Ring. When I reach the gate, I freeze. On the other side are women. Lots of women, some tough looking, some younger, some children. I step through the gate as one moves forward. She has a cut down her face, the scar jagged through her lip and eyebrow. She is beautiful in a terrifying way. Her body is all muscle, and she has a gun at her hip, her body encased in dark clothing.

"Worth?" she asks in a deep voice.

I nod, looking at them. "That's me. Can I ask why you are at my gate in the middle of the night?"

She smiles slightly, and I don't know which is scarier. "I am Mother and these are my people. We have lived on the move across The Wastes for years...but rumours have been getting louder and louder about a slave queen, one freeing The North of its tyranny, and then we heard the announcement. She has made it a nation with no slavery or killing or raping. We took a vote, we had to see if it was true. Is it?" she demands.

"It is. I killed those who opposed it. No one will ever be hunted in The Wastes again...unless they themselves have committed a crime." I raise my chin. A murmur goes up through the amassed women. It's hard to tell in the dark, but it looks like there is around thirty of them.

"Good, we want to join you. We have been searching for a home for so long, somewhere safe to raise our children. Our men died or were bastards. We stayed alive by sheer will and hiding. We are tired of that, and we want a permanent place. We want safety for our children, can you guarantee that?"

I step forward. "I vow it on my blade, if you wish to come in, to stay, you are welcome. No one will touch you, or I will rip them apart myself." I look at the men gathered behind me, all hardened warriors, scary. "Isn't that right, men?"

"Too fucking right!" one person shouts.

Others join in, and I look back at the woman, Mother. "So, Mother?" I ask with a smile. "Do you want a drink?"

"I would love one, Worth." She steps forward, holding out her hand. I shake it with a grin.

"Call me Taz," I offer, and it feels right on my tongue. "Then call me Clarissa."

I look to the women behind her, most scared as the children hide between their legs, and peace settles within me. I made the right choice. There are already changes occurring. Women are coming forward to create a life and a community, because they now feel safe under my new laws.

The North is changing, the world is rebuilding.

Chapter Twenty-Six

MOTHER

I lead the women inside. I inform the guards to get Bern and Piper, who rush over a few moments later. "Clarissa, these are my generals. They will assist your people in getting settled if you wish to accompany me."

She nods and turns to her people. "We have to have faith. Go with them." She looks at me. "We aren't giving up our weapons, you can understand."

"Of course, I wouldn't expect you to. But if they attack any of my people without just cause, there will be consequences," I inform her.

"Understood."

I leave her to talk to her people. They glance at me every so often before, as a group, they move towards us. Piper and Bern lead them away. I spot Bern glancing back at Clarissa with a wondrous look before he rounds the corner. Poor man looks like he's seen heaven. I can't blame him, she is a woman to be reckoned with, that I can already tell. When she turns back to me, I nod my head, and we walk to the cafeteria where my men clear out as we sit.

She takes the seat opposite me as Dray brings us both a drink and leans in to kiss me before walking away. Clarissa watches the action with a strange intensity. "I almost didn't believe it, a woman leading all these men? A woman killing the mad king?"

"Women are the stronger sex." I shrug, and she laughs.

"Hell yes we are." Her grin fades. "How did you do it? You can understand my hesitation, my people have followed me for years, they expect me to protect them."

"Then let's get to know each other. I think you will find we have both suffered enough for a million lifetimes." Her eyes twitch at that, telling me I am right. Her aversion to men, the cut, the gun... I'm betting she was a slave like me. "If you feel safe enough after, you can stay. You are welcome to leave at any time. All of the clans work together now, so you can stay here, or we can help you get set up somewhere else."

She nods, narrowing her eyes as she holds the drink. I sip mine to show her it's not poisoned, and her lips quirk at that as she takes a drink. "I was a slave to the mad king, stolen as a child. I was tortured every day for years before they threw me here to fight as a punishment. It was meant to be a death sentence, but I was good, and I only got better. I won my freedom." I look around. "This has become a place for breaking chains, if you can understand that. There was a man here, he helped me."

"What happened to him?" she asks kindly.

"He died, he's buried out back," I reply with a grimace. "I spent years as a bounty hunter until my men came north, and the rest, as they say, is history. We fell in love, but Ivar found me. I killed him, but not without losing greatly. I thought I was finally safe until The Cities came north. You heard of the war, I assume?"

She jerks her head in acknowledgement, so I carry on. "We won and took The North for ourselves. The other leaders trust me, they fight alongside me, and those who don't wish to can leave."

"Isn't that one of those leaders? The great Seeker King?" she spits, and I narrow my eyes.

"Watch your tone. I'm friendly, but insult my husband, and I won't be so kind," I snap.

She laughs at that. "I like you," she admits. "I guess it's my turn then. I was young when I married. We were together for years. He was older and had to move away for work...to the north, just a few months before the world went to shit. We escaped the old cities down south, farther south than what even exists anymore, and came north. I tried to find him for years with no success, and then I was sleeping one day with some other travellers when we were attacked." She sucks in a breath and takes a drink before carrying on.

"The men with us were slaughtered, our possessions were stolen, and the women were taken as slaves. Through the years, I was sold a few times, and the last time, I managed to escape. I took the others with me. Ever since then, we travelled across The Wastes, trying to survive and outrun those who would hurt us. We found more like us and saved those we could..."

I pour her another drink, and she nods in thanks and downs it. "We lost some, of course. It wasn't easy. We were always

searching for a place to stop, to settle down, but we never found one. Over the years, women have had children, either from rape or their choice, and the more we have, the worse I feel. They need stability, they need safety, if we were to lose one of them—" She closes her eyes and shudders.

"Like I lost mine," she grits out brokenly, and I reach over and grab her hand. One tear drips from her eye before she chases it away and looks at me with glassy eyes. "I never wanted a child. I hated that it was growing within me, but when he came out...he was the love of my life. And they took him and killed him." She swallows hard, and I understand her pain. I let her know I see it. "I can't let that happen to them, so I'm here, begging for your help. I will do whatever it takes. We have seeds, and one of the older women is a botanist who is sure she knows how to grow them in the soil. I-I will give my body if that's what you want—"

I squeeze her hand and harden my eyes. "Clarissa, look at me and listen. Thank you for sharing your story. I am sorry that happened to you. I can't change that, but I can change your future. You are safe here. Your body is your own, as is your freedom. I want neither, I want your happiness. I want to see this world flourish instead of sinking into bloodshed. Your people look to you, my people look to me. That weight...it can be crushing. I know it, but if you let me, I swear I will shoulder that burden with you. Here" —I look around— "I found my home." I look to my men and smile. "I found my happiness" —I look back at her— "and my purpose, and if you give it half a chance, you might find the same." I stand then, because I can't make this decision for her.

"This is your choice, that I swear. You can leave now or tomorrow or the day after that, but I think you are right. I think you need a home, and this home here needs a heart. It needs children and laughter, it needs a reason to fight. Together, we can make that happen. Think that over, eat, sleep, and shower, whatever you need. We have a very good doctor also. Talk to my people and yours. I will find you in the morning if you are still here." I turn away. I will not force her decision, even if my heart hurts for what she went through.

She is older than me, has to be over thirty, but for some reason, I feel the years between us are nothing. Our pain is the same, our past is similar. Women out there all have stories like us, and if this can be their mecca, their hope, then I will die happy.

"Thank you, Taz, for listening, for understanding, and for offering me hope when I had none," she calls.

I look over my shoulder and smile as softly as I am able. "Seeing a child again? You brought us all hope, Clarissa, and those women out there trust you, never doubt who you are."

I leave with my men then, and I have a skip in my step. This is the beginning, I can feel it. I hope they choose to stay. As I wander through The Ring, I hear a child's laughter, and it makes me smile wider. I never wanted children, and I never will, but they are our future and all my warriors know it. I see the longing and protectiveness wash over those who are gathered here.

Shades of grey, the world is filled with them, but sometimes, a rainbow shines through and lights up that monotone in its brilliance.

I slept only a few hours. I spent the rest of my time trying to ensure the women's safety and housing in case they chose to stay, not to mention food and water supplies, so when I finally head out, I am wide awake and have been for hours. I find some of the women eating outside. They are cautious still, but seem more relaxed since we haven't pounced on them. I even find Nan sitting with Clarissa. They are laughing, and as I approach, they both grin at me.

"Girlie, there you are. I see you be adopting some stray warriors," she teases. She jerks her head at Clarissa. "This one's good, she handles my shit too."

"Fucking hell, that's a compliment, you old bitch."

Nan huffs and looks at Clarissa. "No respect, these young ones, I tell thee." She stands and points her finger at me. "I can still shoot ya, I don't give a fook about a crown. Now, I have adopted all these women and little children, they are staying," she declares and wanders away. I watch in shock as two kids grab her hands and walk with her. I wonder if they would if they knew what she was capable of.

I have to say, the most shocking thing about all of this is the fact that Nan has a maternal instinct. Who bloody knew? I sit next to Clarissa in the shade of the building, our shoulders brushing as we watch the others. "Are they all okay?"

"They will be. A lot have suffered, they are relearning how to live. I think we all are," she murmurs and then looks at me. "I've been thinking about what you said all night... We took a vote. We want to stay, for now, if you are still happy to have us."

I smile wider. "Of course, you can leave anytime. I spent the night drawing up plans for some extensions for lodging and increasing our food and water supply to accommodate everyone. Piper is also going on a run soon, so if you need anything, you need let her know, especially for the children."

"We have a pregnant lady, but we also have a midwife, and she will need more supplies," Clarissa says as if to herself.

"Sounds good," I respond.

It goes quiet then, and I let the sun heat me.

"Do you want to meet them? They all want to meet you...the Champion." She laughs, making me groan. "One of your men, Bern I think, was telling us stories of you."

"That bastard, I'll kill him," I mutter.

"I don't know, he seemed nice," she offers. Ooohhhhh.

Sands below, at least someone will be getting laid, because I still have blue balls after last night.

Chapter Twenty-Seven

Battle Time

I spent the afternoon meeting Clarissa's women. They seemed hesitant at first, like I was some savage beast, but when they got to know me, they welcomed me. They offered suggestions, showed me their seeds and their children, and I left them near nightfall with a smile on my face, but as I walk away, it fades to a determined snarl.

Tonight, we attack the plant to the north. I have been sending messages out all day and getting my men ready. We must attack and be back before Piper leaves. I know they have a surprise for me, but it can wait until tomorrow. Tonight, I'm just a warrior, a warrior who will stop those bastards to the north.

Lochlan, the name of the warrior who gave me the information, is coming as well. As are Priest's angels, Seekers, my men, and Jon and his scavs. We are taking thirty people in total—not too many to draw too much attention, so we can still sneak into their plant before they know it, but not too little that we are struggling to win.

Excitement courses through me as I go to get ready, the adrenaline pumping through my veins. I have missed the thrill of the hunt, and I know this will be my last one. It's a sad day, but I am ready to move on to my future... That doesn't mean I won't enjoy tonight, however, and the blood spilled in the sands. It's what I am good at, after all—protecting people and killing.

And they will die tonight at the ends of my blades.

Most women have one last hurrah before marriage, at least that is what Piper said, and this sort of feels like that. One last adventure before I settle down into queen life.

My men are waiting when I reach the room, their faces stark and hungry...for battle. Stern, tall, and fucking dangerous, they have my panties wet in a second, and I remember how we left off last night. I wish I could finish it now, but the bloodlust will have to do. They help me dress in my leathers to help me blend in, and then they start strapping on weapons. My whip is coiled at my side, and both swords are sheathed on my back. Blades are attached to nearly every inch of my body. My hair is plaited and made into a crown on my head by Thorn. Once dressed, I grab the paint and quickly place it on my face before turning to my men. We are sneaking through the dark to massacre men, we are warriors, champions, and we wear our paint with pride.

They all stand still as I cover their faces in black and red streaks and symbols before stepping back and looking them over. I have to bite my lip on a groan. They look incredible, good enough to eat, and like the true fucking warriors they are. Their bodies are hard, muscular, and on display, their weapons ready to kill, and their eyes are dark with excitement. And they are all fucking mine.

Sands below, I'm a lucky bitch.

"Are you ready, soulmate?" Dray asks, his leather pants so tight, I can see each indent of his muscles. His chest, sides, arms, and back are strapped to the teeth with weapons, and his crazy smile is in place as those blue eyes flare with excitement. For blood, for death, and what will come after...

"Always." I smirk, my eyes flickering to my silent demon, Jax, next to him. His blond hair has been slicked back and stained so he blends in better with the dark. His grey eyes watch me, as always. His body is covered from head to toe in black clothing and weapons. His brother, Drax, is next to him. His chest is bare and painted like our faces, and he wears his crossbow on his back and blades at his sides. He smirks at me as I look him over.

"Want me to bend over, babe, so you can check out my ass too?" he teases.

Rolling my eyes, I look to Thorn next. He has an axe at his hip and a sword on his back. His huge muscles are on display, and his onyx skin is gleaming in the light. His face is calm and collected, his normal smile on his lips as he watches me. He might be the most serene and soft, but when it comes to fighting, he's a fucking Berserker. The memory of watching him has my legs clenching together, and he winks at me as if he knows my thoughts.

Maxen clears his throat, drawing my eyes. "Are you ready, *Mi Alma?*" he queries, but I forget his words as I stare at him. His bottom half is encased in trousers similar to what he wore when I first met him. This time they are black, tied at his thick waist, and they balloon out to his feet from there. His chest is bare and streaked with paint, his huge arms and chest calling to me. His hair is tied back similarly to mine, accentuating high cheekbones and full lips. He only has a few knives and a sword—he is the weapon, after all.

He chuckles and steps forward, tipping my chin up with a finger before kissing me solidly. "Soon, *Mi Alma*, but first, let's go destroy those bastards...then later," he promises.

"Yup, later we destroy you," Drax calls. I peer around Maxen to see him fake thrusting into his hands and spanking the air, making me grin, even as I roll my eyes.

"Ready," I tell Maxen, and lean up and kiss his lips. "But later, you're all mine."

"Promise?" he murmurs.

Chuckling, I pull away, zip up my jacket, and head to the door, looking back at them as I wink. "Come on then, husbands, let's go kill some scum."

"Fuck, that's hot, soulmate. Tell me how you are going to kill them, in detail—"

Laughing, I lead them outside, ready to go into battle.

The men are waiting at the gates, already on their bikes. I nod at Jon and say goodbye to Priest and Nan, leaving them in charge while I go. Piper is there too, pouting because I won't let her come and 'kick some ass.'

"You've got years to kick ass. Tonight, I'm trusting you," I tell her, "to protect those women and my people, and if anything is to happen to us, to lead my people."

She straightens then, her face hardening, serious for once. "I won't let you down," she vows.

Grinning, I lean in and press my head to hers in a warrior's good-bye. "I know you won't," I murmur, before striding to my bike, swinging my leg over it, and revving the engine. We will use lights until we get close, and then we will cut them and go on foot, surrounding them before sneaking in. Lochlan informed me of some high windows we could scale, which Jon will, and a back door which they don't guard, since ferals sometimes wander through the parking structure that leads to it—that's my entrance. Priest's angels will distract them at the front door.

It's a good plan, and I am ready to leave when Clarissa suddenly appears at the gate. Her expression is hard and determined as she stops next to my bike. "Be careful. I would hate for you to die when we just found you," she offers. I nod, and she inclines her head before turning and hesitating.

With a muttered curse, she heads over to Bern who is near me, grabs his head, jerks it down, and kisses him. All the warriors whistle and catcall, and I smirk, watching as she pulls away, spins on her heel, and storms off. He gapes after her, his mouth open and eyes wide in shock.

Laughing, I lean into my bike and grin at him. "Stop drooling, lover boy, it's not a good look."

"Ma queen..." He groans before shaking his head and looking at me. "Women are confusing."

"That we are," I agree. "That we are."

Circling my fingers in the air, I spin my bike around and ride next to him, smacking his chest. "But that means she likes you. Keep on doing whatever you are doing, and maybe you won't get a knife to the gut." I wink before gunning it, leaving him to mutter behind me.

We head out into The Wastes. The sand blows back into my face, so I quickly cover it with my bandana and gun it harder. We don't have a lot of time to kill, but I want this done by sunrise. As the world stretches on in front of me, the moonlight lights our way. My bike rumbles between my thighs and I relax. I no longer feel pressure or worries about ruling. Right now, it's just me, my bike, and the battle to come.

I will miss this. Maybe I will have to get out and do this every so often. It's strange how it relaxes me. The sand will always be my home. I spent years hunting and wandering through them, and I guess that's hard to shake. The lights of The Ring soon fade, plunging us into darkness. The purr of the bikes behind me makes me grin, our lights barely penetrating the dark sand surrounding us.

Somewhere in the distance, I hear the ferals screaming and roaring, then I hear gunfire and grin wider. Fuck, I love The Wastes. Even with the new laws to protect people, this place is still wild and untameable. I can't imagine a world before this now, before the sun and the sand and the desolation.

This is all we have, and we have to love it and do better than we have done before. The world is a living, breathing thing, and it must be respected.

Lochlan circles my men to ride at my side and help direct me with hand signals since he's unable to be heard over the roar of our engines. The closer we get, the quicker my heart beats. My grin grows, and my body prepares for the battle to come. I don't know what to expect inside the plant, as he calls it, but I sure as shit know what will happen.

We will win.

The miles are eaten quickly until, in the distance, lights pierce the dark.

Huge lights—the plant.

Chapter Twenty-Eight
Battle Time

Leaning against my bike, I use the sniper rifle to check out the plant. It's all like Lochlan described. The lights tower into the sky, wrapped around the giant, circular, ancient creation. The building in front of it is made of brick with high, tall windows, and railings and walkways surround it.

At the front, lots of men are either patrolling the chain link fence or sleeping on overturned cars and ripped out busses. String lights illuminate their base, with two big double doors behind them. There is a fire roaring, which is easy to spot from here. They aren't worried about giving their position away, which makes me respect their numbers more. They are unafraid of an attack, even asking for it.

Cocky bastards, it will be their downfall.

But the farther around the plant, the darker it gets, with a nearly pitch-black, sunken in underground parking garage behind it. Only a fence stands in our way between that and the entrance. That's where we go in. Putting the sniper rifle down, I look back at my men.

"You know what to do. Get into position, no one breaches until I do. You know the signal." I pass the sniper back over and look at

Lochlan. "You are with me. You know the layout better than anyone, so you can point out sentries and access points."

He nods, and I turn back to the plant rising from the sands like a beacon. It's time we clean up The Wastes, starting with these bastards. When everyone is ready to go, we move silently. No one is talking now, we all know what to do. We stay low, moving quickly over the sand as we circle around the plant out of view of the lights.

I hear some growls and chattering yips of ferals, and make sure to stay on high alert. Lochlan said they come through here sometimes, they might even be in the dark garage. They liked to hide there and pounce on their prey. They would also be drawn to the noise and lights of the plant, but we have to get through them to get into the plant. Easy enough, right?

When the rolling sand hills turn into a flat section of old, broken concrete leading to the fence surrounding the garage, I still and hold up my hand, watching and waiting just to make sure. When I spot nothing or no one, I rush across, covering the distance easily. Thorn deftly rips back a hole in the fence, and we slip through.

The concrete turns more solid under our feet, still cracked with holes in places, as it tilts down into the dark garage. Crouching at the top of the entrance, I cock my head and let out a low whistle, trying to attract anything that lingers down there. After all, it's easier to kill them up here with the light and room to fight.

When nothing emerges, I sigh and grab one of my swords anyway. Something is waiting down there in the dark. I can feel it. The tension, the eyes watching me, anticipating. "You stay quiet," I murmur to everyone behind me. "Even if you are being eaten, no screams. It will draw more and alert those inside the plant, and then we will be surrounded and outnumbered. Understood?" I snap.

When everyone murmurs their assent, I stand and crack my neck from side to side, swinging my sword. "Then here we go. Eyes on every corner, lights on, we are in for a fight down there. If it's ferals, move away, their bite means death, so stay out of their reach and kill them from a distance if you can."

I hear weapons being pulled and readied, and when it goes silent again, I start down the ramp. Torches flicker on behind me, shining into the dark, and lighting my way only just. It barely touches the walls that rise on either side of us, and when we reach the bottom of the ramp, it doesn't reach half of the parking garage.

Licking my lips and keeping my breathing even, I step into the garage. I kick a rock and it rolls into the dark, interrupting the silence. When nothing jumps out, I look around, following the lights circling our location, illuminating the wrecked and abandoned cars and the graffiti on the floor and ground. The skeletal remains and burn marks. There are even old skeletons hanging from the ceiling in warning.

Lovely, their interior decor is quite inspired. I love a good skull decoration.

We wander farther into the garage. Lochlan stays by my side, steering us towards the door he knows is back here. Until, suddenly, we hear a crash. I look over to see a scav falling over what looks like an old barrel. The sound reverberates, filling the air as it rolls to a stop and smashes into a car. I wince, tightening my hand on my sword as growls echo around us.

We put our backs together, staring into the dark as the sound of growls and the snapping of jaws gets louder. "Get ready!" I hiss. There is no point in staying too quiet, they know we are here.

A light catches on a blur of a creature dashing around cars, and I widen my stance, ready to go. Another light catches on it, and Drax fires. The yelp is loud as he hits his target. He aims and fires again, taking out as many as he can before they get to us.

"Keep firing!" I order, even as one of them leaps at me from the dark—mouth open wide, fangs ready to snap and injure, drool and saliva dripping from his mauled lips. Those dark, soulless eyes meet mine. I swing out effortlessly, slicing through its throat. It falls to my feet, and blood runs across my boots as I hear the others fighting their own ferals. Grunts and gasps are the only noises that fill the air around us. We are staying quiet, even now, as we fight for our lives.

I hear a pained groan and know someone has been injured, but they don't protest or scream, and we keep the ferals back, slicing and hacking. Our circle moves apart slightly as we face them, creating more room to manoeuvre. I lose track of them as they fly at me from the dark, some leaping, some skidding, and some prowling. I hack, slice, and cut. Blood runs down my sword and hands, and across my boots and legs. I refuse to think, I simply let my body take over.

One manages to slice its fangs across my arm, and I hiss. It enrages me, and I spin and slice faster until no more come from the dark. Standing there panting, sword held at the ready, I keep my eyes on the shadows.

Someone comes to my side, looking at my arm, but I don't look away. "I'm fine," I tell them. "Let's keep moving. Any dead?"

"Nope, but one of the bastards bit off my fingers," someone hisses.

"Bandage it and stop whining," I snap. "Lochlan, lead the way. Dray, up front."

I stay at the back as we move across the garage, my eyes on the shadows. I keep my sword ready to protect us in case they attack again. I spot at least one standing on a roof of a car, its head lowered and mouth open in a snarl as it watches us, but it doesn't attack, probably realising we will kill it.

Others surround it, probably the alpha of the pack. I keep my eyes on it as I walk backwards, trusting my people to get us out of here. "Door," someone murmurs.

"Anything behind it?" I ask.

"No, it leads into an entrance and a staircase, shouldn't be anyone there," Lochlan replies.

"Then get fucking moving. They aren't attacking right now, but I have a feeling that's going to change."

I hear the creak of a door, and cool air blows in behind me as we start backing into the entrance. The alpha leaps from the roof and prowls towards me, his pack following. Fuck.

"Quicker," I hiss.

I'm just moving through the door when they leap. Maxen yanks me through all the way as Thorn slams the door shut, pressing his shoulder against it as we hear them hit the metal with a howl. "Well, fuck," I mutter, looking back at them. "Wasn't that fun?"

It's bright in here, and I have to let my eyes adjust. The power must be on, since the strip lights shine above us. The space is small, a simple rectangle leading to stairs going up with more lights above. Written on the wall in dripping red is 'Gates to Hell' with an arrow pointing up.

"That's blood, isn't it?" Drax sighs. "Why do they always use blood? That's so creepy."

I wink over at him as I start up the stairs. "Pussy." "I'll give you pussy, sweet cheeks," he mutters.

The stairs creak under our weight, but they don't collapse, which is good, considering how long they have been here and what they have probably withstood. At the top of the stairs is a barricade—wood pieces held together with giant spikes pointing down. It's probably to stop the ferals. I don't spot a gap in it, so I step back, run at it, leap over, and land on the other side with a thump. I look back with a grin. "This way."

"If I could, I would marry her again," I hear Dray mutter. "Get in line," Thorn jokes.

Lochlan sidles up to my side as I head down the only corridor to the left. There is more writing and warnings on the wall, as well as arrow and bullet holes. The hallway starts to fill with doors, all made of wood. Some are missing, and some are half broken or wedged shut, but we have to check those that can open just in case someone is inside. We can't have them coming up behind us. I take the first one, kicking it open and rushing in, but it looks like an old storeroom. It's filled with overturned metal filing cupboards, and old ruined papers are spilled everywhere.

The next one is a cleaning cupboard with a half nudie pic on the wall. Drax whistles at it, making me smack him. The next three are wedged shut. Maxen takes the first, and I watch him clear it, but he comes out stern-faced. "Anything?"

"A body, female, tied to the wall... Looks like she was eaten by fucking ferals," he snarls.

I grind my teeth and look at Lochlan, who pales. "I swear they didn't do that fucking shit—fuck, maybe they did."

I clap his shoulder. "You can make up for it now. Let's kill the fuckers who did that to someone."

He nods, his eyes lost and angry. The hall ends in another door, and I look to him as he blinks, obviously thinking back on everything he saw here and wondering if he could have done anything about it. Grabbing his head, I hold it tight as I glare at him. "I need you here. You want to make up for it? Then fucking help me. What's behind this door?" I snap.

He licks his lips and clears his throat. "You're fucking right, sorry. It's more stairs, it leads up to reception. From here on, they will be crawling everywhere. They have no set routine. Apart from two men stationed in reception, the rest sleep, fuck, eat, and patrol wherever the fuck they want apart from Inferno, who will be in the boiler room at the very back."

"Right, so we go in quiet. Low. Dray, you're with me. We sneak up and slit their throats, no fucking noise." I look at him as I speak.

He grabs a small knife, and I do the same as he grins at me, his hand snaking down to my ass as he comes to my side. "I love assassinating people with you, soulmate," he murmurs dreamily.

"Killing first," I remind him.

He puts his hand on the door and winks back at me. "I was thinking at the same time, but fine, soulmate."

Grinning, I nod at him, my knife ready. He opens the door slowly and we creep through, staying low as we slide up the stairs, crouching there and looking into the room to find them. It's a dump. There are two holey, dirty sofas in the corner with a table and a lamp. The floor is covered in blood, dirt, sand, and rubbish. There are more wooden barriers on a door farther into the plant, but I spot a corridor to the right. To the left are toilets, the door is open, and I hear someone peeing from here. Another guy is leaning on an overturned counter in the corner eating.

The whole room is dark apart from the random torches, leaving plenty of shadows, which is good for us. There are holes in the wall that give us glimpses into the rest of the plant, and we need to be careful to avoid them.

I look to Dray and nod at the toilet, telling him I'll take that one. He grins, and we split up, moving quickly. I make sure to avoid the light so as not to cast shadows as I slip across the wall to the left and to the toilet door, ducking my head around.

Luckily, it's dark in here too, with only one torch shining up into the ceiling. The man has his back to me, his legs parted and cock out as he pisses opposite me. His back is to me, and his weapon is on the sink at least two meters away. Idiot.

There are two stalls to the side, one without a side, the other without a door, so I can clearly see they are empty. Smirking at how easy this is, I rush across the floor. He must feel me at the last second, because he turns, but I catch him before he spins fully around. My arm locks around his head, and I slice my knife across his throat. I quickly cover his mouth as he kicks and jerks, the warm blood spraying everywhere, including the wall.

His ragged breathing as he dies is loud, but not loud enough to draw attention. When he finally stops moving, I lower him to the ground and turn. Dray is already at the door with blood splashed across his face and his knife dripping blood in his grasp.

"Good?" I ask quietly.

"Easy. Too fucking easy," he murmurs before striding across the room, sliding his knife away as he goes.

His hands tunnel into my hair, yanking my head back as his lips smash against mine. Groaning, I tangle my tongue with his, kissing him back desperately before we break apart. We are both panting, and there is undoubtedly blood smeared across my face now too, which only makes him grin.

"Let's get the others before I bend you over and fuck you," he growls.

Smirking, I follow him back out front, watching the corridor as he opens the door and beckons the others upstairs.

They look around as I head to the corner and glance around it. There is a man at the end, sitting in a fold away chair, with his head lowered to his chest as he snores. His shaved head catches the light of the two barrel fires near him. Ducking back, I put my finger to my lips, and everyone falls in behind me. How the fuck do we do this? I look to Dray, and he peeks around the corner for a moment before moving back to my side. He pins me to the wall, his lips going to my ear. I didn't mean *that* quiet, but I can't really complain. If anyone will know how, it's the assassin.

"I can slip halfway down, then monkey crawl across the ceiling using the exposed bars, drop down behind him, and snap his neck."

I shiver at his words, and his tongue darts out and licks my ear.

Focus, Worth. "Do it if you think you can." "If I do, do I get a reward?"

"Yeah, I'll use my whip on you later," I tease.

He moves away so quickly I almost fall. I watch him go with a smile and a shake of my head. Peeking around the corner, I watch his progress, unsure if he can pull this off. He's good, but it's an open corridor, so all it would take is the man looking up.

I watch open-mouthed as Dray jumps up, catching the bars in the exposed ceiling, and then lifts his legs and starts crawling along them like some kind of ninja. When he reaches the end, he throws his legs over the bars and then releases his hands, dangling upside down behind the man. With a wink at me, he fists the man's head and snaps his neck quickly. He sits the body back down, then flies off the bars and dusts off his hands.

"Easy," he calls.

We follow him down the corridor and past the dead body to the left. It opens up into a metal tunnel, which ends abruptly at the large main room. Standing there out of sight, I look around and whistle.

Fuck. I see what Lochlan meant. It's huge, with three layers of rail- ings and walkways, two in the air and one on the floor. But these crazy bastards have built ladders and wooden planks between them, so it's basically one giant maze system. I spy men sleeping and wandering around everywhere.

"Okay, where first?" I mutter to Lochlan.

"You need to hit at once, or they will gang up and regroup. Find cover though, they will firebomb you," he suggests.

Turning back, I look over my men. "Okay, ten each level. Maxen, you're with the first ten with Thorn, Jax, and Drax second. Dray, you're with me and Lochlan. Split yourselves up. I am going low, we are going to get Inferno."

"We'll take the top," Drax offers, and Jax nods. "We can pick some off from up there too." He winks, and I grin.

"Middle then. Be careful, *Mi Alma*," Maxen murmurs.

I nod and look them over. "You don't fucking die, you hear me?" I demand.

My men all grin, and I turn before I hesitate and stride down the metal stairs to the right, the men walking behind me. I duck behind a huge pipe at the bottom and watch my other men split up, climbing and finding cover before we are seen.

A shout goes up, and I see Drax duck a firebomb that explodes behind him. He gets to his knees and fires. It causes chaos, and everyone starts shouting. They fire and more bombs explode. Fuck this. I push from behind the pipe with my men and start firing on those down here.

They turn in confusion. Their weapons are pointed up, which is why I manage to take down two and my men another three before we have to throw ourselves behind crates. Fire explodes over the top and front, and I grunt. "I fucking hate firebombs," I mutter.

Lochlan pulls out two, and with a crazy grin, he lights them and tosses them. Two seconds later, we hear them explode and screams follow. Laughing, I grab one and throw it. "Okay, so maybe they aren't so bad," I tease. Looking around the crate, I spot a man coming towards us with a sword. I wait, crouched at the edge, and when he gets ready to strike, I dive out and disembowel him.

Grabbing the bottle at his hip, I light it and toss it to the others and rush to the next pipe. We do this time and time again, slowly making our way across the room. We have to duck behind cover when they fire from above, but Drax is making quick work of them, thank God.

I spot Maxen and Thorn handling them as well, so keeping my head down, I trust my men to get the job done. My focus is on getting to Inferno and killing him, they can handle the clean-up.

When we duck behind an old forklift, Lochlan moves to my side. "There," he murmurs, pointing at a steel door towards the back. It has a ramp leading down to it, and a warning label on the front saying 'Forge,' where they have drawn a skull over it.

Adorable.

Ducking as more flames burst before us, I roll my eyes. "I am over these fuckers fighting like pussies."

"What are you going to do?" he asks with a frown.

"Show them how Berserkers fight." I grin and look at the man next to him. "Draw their fire, I just need to get close enough so they can't light them."

He nods and leans around the barrel. I stand and turn to see the six men hiding behind a makeshift fort of sandbags, throwing fire-bombs like pussies. Withdrawing my other sword, I swing them in my hands as I storm swiftly across the distance. They are so focused on the others, they don't see me until it's too late.

Jumping over the sandbags, I grin at them. "Heads-up, fuckers," I call, as I slice my sword across one of their throats, and as his throat slits and he falls back, I spin to the others. They fumble for their weapons at their hips, relying so heavily on the firebombs, they are unprepared for hand-to-hand.

One drops his machete on the floor, and I trap it under my boot and tap his chin with my sword. When he jerks back, I turn and slice, opening up his chest. He screams, and the other four converge on me.

Laughing, I spin and slash. I block with both swords as one brings down a hammer, trapping it between my blades before I headbutt him. I knock him back, and his hammer falls to the floor, so I leap into the air and kick him backwards, spotting the spikes behind him from another forklift. I kick again, and he stumbles back, impaling himself on the spikes. He screams and gapes down at them as I duck an oncoming assault.

I manage to disembowel one, and then the two others circle me. Holding my swords ready, I grin at them. "Not so strong without the fire, are you, pussies?" I spit.

"Fucking slut!" one of them hollers as he pants, holding a butcher knife in his meaty grasp.

"Original. I wonder if your boss knows you are getting your ass kicked by a girl." I flutter my lashes and then rush them as they try to think of a comeback. I stab both swords out, and they are standing so close together, the blades spear through both chests. I kick out the legs of the one on the left. He falls to the floor and slides off my blade, coughing and sputtering as he dies. I turn to the other, yank my sword out, and kick him over.

Looking around, I grin wider before a groan sounds, then I glance up and spot the man impaled on the forklift. He's sweating, grunting, and screaming, but also slowly pulling himself off the spikes. What a determined bastard, you have to give it to him. I watch in curiosity, wondering if he will actually manage it.

The others join me, and we all stare. "Knife says he doesn't make it," Lochlan bets.

"You're on," I mutter. "He's a determined little fucker, isn't he?"
"Sure is. I bet that hurts like a bitch." He laughs.

So, in the middle of a raid, we stand there watching this man slowly struggling to pull himself off the machine. He gets so close to the edge and then starts to sob. "Ah, dude, what are you doing? I bet on you, and now you're going to sit and cry? Pathetic," I snap as I stride over. Grabbing a fistful of his greasy hair, I yank it back and slice his throat open. His blood sprays across me as I hand the knife to Lochlan. "Yours. What a disappointment. I see why you left."

Just as I am turning to head to the door, I hear a yell. "Heads-up!" Jax calls, and I step back just as a body hits the cement in front of me and splatters.

Looking up, I throw him a thumbs-up and step over the man with a laugh before heading down the ramp, the others following after me. When we reach the old rusted steel door, I look to Lochlan, who grabs the handle. I'm always first through the door. It's my responsibility. "Anything I should know?"

"He has a flamethrower," he tells me.

I blink and look at the door again. "Fucking great."

Sucking in a breath, I nod at him, and he yanks open the door. I have a split second to take in the scene before I throw myself forward, rolling across the floor to hide behind a wire fence as Inferno takes aim and, with a roar, fires.

He was waiting for us. Standing in front of a melting forge, which is still burning, six men wait with him. He has his flamethrower in hand, and his bald head is glistening with sweat from the heat in the room. His body is huge and scarred, and one of his legs is bent weird, probably broken before. He is a big fucker, and as the flames flow past me in a stream, I know this isn't going to be easy. He's got reach, so all it would take is for him to aim true, and it would be barbecued Worth.

The ramp leads down to the forge where he is, and to the right and left where I stand are wire fences surrounding what looks like inclines leading up to stairs. I crane my neck to see they go up to the platform above the forge. Great. So no real hiding spaces.

The others are trapped at the door. I narrow my eyes on them as they try to get in the room, warning them to stay back. Surely he will run out of fuel soon? But he's walking now, and the flames increase as he draws closer. The heat makes me slide farther to the side. His men laugh and shout encouragements, and he's shouting too, but over the roar of the flames, I can't hear much.

Any minute, he will turn the corner and I will be crispy. Looking to the ramp on the left, I growl, knowing I have no choice. I rush up it, keeping low, and stop at the top of the stairs, which is right over where he is searching for me.

I have an idea, a terrible idea, but as the others spot me and start to take aim, I know I have no choice. Sheathing my swords, I climb up on the railing.

Really, this is a shitty idea.

Sands below, don't let me become dinner.

Leaping from the railing, I land on him. He stumbles and drops the flamethrower, falling near the forge. The others rush in and start to handle the other men, and I trust them to take care of it as I face Inferno.

He turns with a yell, his eyes wild and narrowed, his mouth open to show his toothless orifice. Lovely. His muscles bulge, glistening from the fire behind us. Sweat pours from me, it's hotter in here than out in The Wastes. "Traitor!" he roars when he spots Lochlan behind me. I step in his way and draw his gaze.

"Eyes on me, you big bastard." I grab my sword and wait. He lumbers towards me, all swinging fists and slow movements. Without his little flame toy, he is no match for me. Smirking, I punch before slipping under his arm and gliding behind him, tapping him on his back.

He whirls with a yell, swinging wildly, and I duck before stepping away and bending backwards to avoid another meaty fist, but I don't see the one coming from the right. He might be slow, but he's got a lot of power, and it sends me flying towards the forge. I roll over the floor and almost right into the fire until I grab the edge, singeing my fingers to stop my momentum. With a hiss, I yank my fingers back, ignoring the ache in my jaw from his punch. I can feel blood where he has cut my cheek as well, but I leap to my feet to meet him as he stomps my way.

I manage to circle him until his back is to the forge, that is how cocky he is. I hear the others fighting, but I focus fully on the bastard in front of me. No one makes me bleed but Dray. This fucker is going down.

"You punch like a little bitch," I taunt, spitting blood on the floor. "Now I know why you have such a big flamethrower, it's to compensate." I look down at his cock to make sure he understands. After all, he doesn't seem like the sharpest tool in the shed.

"You'll die like all those other cunts!"

"Yeah, that won't happen, but thanks for trying. Say hello to all the others who have." I grin as I take a running start as another crazy idea forms in my head. I can't get hit again, he's too strong, so the element of surprise is my only option, as is my speed.

With a spin, I leap and roundhouse kick him, pushing him back. I do it again and again, landing kick after kick until, on the fifth kick, he falls. He tries to grab my foot, but I fall backward to avoid it as he falls into the forge. He roars as he tumbles into the flames. Standing, I head over and wince as I watch his body become encased in the blaze, melting him as he is slowly devoured by the flames until I can't see him anymore.

"Guess you lived up to your name." I laugh as I turn to see the others watching me with a grin. "What? Too cheesy?"

Lochlan chuckles just as my men come through the door. They look around with raised eyebrows. "Late to the party, as always." I wink. "Don't worry, I cleaned up, now let's check the whole building. I don't want any of these insects left alive."

I look to Lochlan then. "What about any women?"

He shakes his head. "I wouldn't say so, but honestly, I don't know."

"Then we check." I nod and grab my sword. "Let's go."

The main room is a bloodbath. There are bodies everywhere. Some of my men go high to double-check everything, while I head through another door at the back which leads to an office. There are two overturned desks with old papers everywhere, a broken mug, and even a fucking globe. There is a white board with a bloody handprint on it and the wall has scorch marks. In the corner of the room is a bed on the floor.

"Inferno slept there," Lochlan explains. "Nice digs," I scoff.

There is a door at the back with two chains crisscrossing it that catches my eye. "What's that?" I ask, jerking my head in that direction.

"I don't know, I was never allowed in here," Lochlan replies.

Heading over, I tug on the chains, but they are locked. I look around for a key, but I don't see one, so I grab the axe at Lochlan's hip, heft it up, and bring it down on the chain. It jangles but doesn't break, so I do it again and again until it snaps with a resounding clatter and falls to the floor. Turning, I grin at him as I pass the axe back. "Well, it's open now." Yanking the door open, the first thing that hits me is the smell. I turn away and cover my mouth. I've smelled some shit as a slave, but holy fuck. I almost gag before grabbing my bandana and covering my

mouth. The others cover themselves as well as I peer into the dark.

It's pitch-black and seems to lead down, but I have no way of knowing. "Get me a light," I demand as a bad feeling starts to build in my stomach.

The more the trapped odour escapes and fades into something manageable, I know what I am smelling.

Rot. Decay. Death.

Something is lit behind me, and I close my eyes as it's tossed inside the pit, illuminating exactly what I was dreading seeing. I hear the swears behind me, and even some whispered prayers as we stand and stare.

The room is pretty big, probably an old storage room, if the shelves pushed against the back are anything to go by. That's the only furniture though—no light, no bed, no blanket. Just four solid cement walls and the floor. Dark and cold.

And filled with blood-covered, naked corpses. Some even have missing limbs.

One closest to the door is turned my way, and her face is completely smashed in. It's so bad, I spot her brain escaping. Flies buzz, and my stomach rolls as I run my eyes over them all.

There has to be over a hundred, and when I spot the two small children at the back, tears fill my eyes.

"Fuck, fuck, fuck." Lochlan dry heaves. "I swear, I never knew," he cries. "I didn't know, I swear I didn't know!" He stumbles back as I look at him. "I worked outside on protection. They didn't let me—" He shakes his head as he falls to the floor and grabs his head, muttering to himself.

"Get him outta here," I bark, my voice rough with anger and grief, and then I look back into the room. I hear the others leading him out as I step into the space. I have to check if any of them are alive, even as much as I don't want to go in there. I would never forgive myself for not making sure.

I have to close my eyes when they clash with that of a girl no older than ten or eleven. Her face is bloodied so badly, all I can see are her piercing blue eyes, open and empty. Her little body is broken. I have seen so much violence and death in my life, so much senseless pain and torture.

And this is why I'm fighting now, this is the fucking reason why I'm making a new North. So tragedies like this never happen. So that girls can be safe. So that people like Clarissa never end up dumped and forgotten in a pit of death.

It only hammers home how important this change is.

Crouching down, I press my fingers to a neck, and when all I feel is ice-cold skin, I move on. I make sure to check as many as I can, trying not to think too much about the limbs I have to move to get to them. By the time I've reached the other end of the room, I feel filthy, like I will never be clean again.

Standing in the mass of bodies, my heart aches for the senseless loss. I've killed a lot in my life, mainly to survive, and other times it was a job, but it was always a necessity. I didn't hate it. In fact, I liked it. I'm good at it. But I never killed for fun, for the pleasure of death.

The fact that these poor women and kids had to die at a sick man's will, their hearts broken, their hope gone...to think they thought no one cared, it pisses me off.

I've been there, and that lack of hope is what kills you faster than a blade. Right now, staring around, I have all the motivation I need to see The Nations through. I will kill every single flesh trader myself if I have to.

No more fucking senseless death.

No woman will ever be hopeless. They will know I will always come for them, always protect them, always avenge them.

"Baby girl?" Thorn calls, and I look up to see him and Jax at the door. I take one look at him and have to turn away.

But then they are there, both of them. Their arms wrap around me, offering me their strength. "I couldn't save them," I whisper.

"I know—"

"I couldn't fucking save them!" I yell, smashing my fists into his chest before pressing my head there.

"Baby girl, you can't save everyone, but you sure as shit are trying. Stop being so hard on yourself. Think of all the lives you have saved here today by stopping them. Think of all the lives you will save in the future," he whispers, as Jax kisses my shoulder and holds me.

"Maxen, Drax, and Dray are making the others pay. Want to see? Might make you feel better," Jax murmurs. "Others?" I echo.

"They found more men holed up in the basement. They went there when the shooting started and set up traps. We lost a man, but we got them," he informs me.

Sucking in a deep breath, I step from between them and slick back my hair. "Yeah, let's go," I state, trying to stay calm when my heart is filled with such hate.

Thorn leans in and kisses my forehead. "There's our fucking queen. Head up, baby girl. Just a little longer, and when we are back and you are in our arms, you can break."

I let them lead me from the room with the intent to come back later and sort the bodies. For now, I want to see what my other men are up to, and hopefully, it involves blood and pain. With the way I am feeling right now...I need both.

I find them in the main area of the plant. There are five men on their knees, with my men in front of them. Dray is circling them, running his knife along their faces. Drax is perched on a crate, aiming at them with a teasing grin. Maxen is standing before them like an avenging god with his arms crossed as he stares them down.

Lochlan is muttering as he paces back and forth. I keep my eye on him as I step up next to Maxen and look the men over. They are all glaring, all pissed as hell, yet I see some fear in their eyes. They know what we are capable of, and they know they are next.

"Who knew about the bodies in the back room?" I ask.

No one answers, so I turn, and with a wink at Drax, I grab his crossbow and take aim.

"Who knew?" I repeat through my teeth.

Their eyes dart to the man on the left, and without a word, I fire. The bolt embeds in his eye as he falls backwards. The others yell and try to get up, but my men stop them as I turn and hand the crossbow back to Drax, who licks his lips. "That was so fucking hot, babe."

"You knew too?" Lochlan yells, and I look back to see him pressing his blade to one of the man's faces

I should stop him, but I don't.

"Everyone fucking knew. If you are pretending you didn't, traitor, then you're an idiot." The man laughs, spitting in his face.

We all step back, knowing what is coming from the tension in his shoulders.

Lochlan whirls and smashes his fist into the man's face. I watch with an evil smile as he screams and does it again and again. When he's done, there is nothing left of the man, just bloody pulp as Lochlan stands there panting. His fists are covered in blood, and there are tears in his eyes. I know guilt, I see it in him now, but only time will help him heal.

He storms away, and I look to the last two men. "Did any of you touch those women?"

Their lips clamp shut, so I wander over and crouch before them. "If you don't answer, I am going to start cutting and won't stop until your skin is covering the floor like a rug... Now, did you touch those women?"

The one on the right narrows his eyes. "No."

"Liar." I grab my blade and slice down his arm, cutting deep until the skin flaps open and hangs as he yells. Grabbing his throat, I squeeze and stop his scream. "Now tell me the truth, or your penis is next."

He gulps against my hand as I let go. "Yes," he hisses in pain. "We both touched them, we all did."

Nodding, I hold the knife to his neck and look into his eyes. "Remember them as you die, as you choke on your own blood, and piss and shit your pants when you're terrified, and we all watch you die. Remember them," I snarl, before slitting his throat.

It sprays across my face as I punish him. I knock him back to the floor to choke and die a painful death. I look at the other man then. "Did you know their names?"

He swallows, and that is answer enough. With a snarl, I slice his throat and leave him to die as I turn and look at Lochlan. His face is drawn in guilt and anger, but there is nothing I can say that will reassure him, so I step closer and clasp his shoulder.

Just then, Jon runs into the room, face panicked. "Get out, get out now!" he screams. "The forge is exploding!"

Fuck.

I turn and start to run, and everyone follows as we sprint through the machines and to the front door. As we race down the corridor, our boots and panicked breathing is loud. I almost slip in some blood, but Maxen yanks me up and throws me forward. We don't bother going through the back entrance. Dray throws himself into the front door, opening it. We all burst out into the open and have to duck behind the stone wall encasing it as those left outside take fire.

The first explosion comes from behind us, and I turn to look at the building. We are trapped and need to move now, or we are all dead.

"Fuck, we left the women! We can't leave them!" Lochlan yells and stands. I try to yank him back down, but he turns towards the building. He isn't going to—fuck, he is. I throw myself on top of him, tackling him to the ground as fire whooshes over my head. Just then, we hear the growls and yips of ferals, and I whip my head around to see those from below the plant attacking the men firing at us.

One is assaulted near us, standing on an abandoned bus. His screams fill the air, as do the growls of the three ferals attacking him as they shake him from side to side. Lochlan uses my distraction to drag himself from under me. I reach for his ankle, but I'm too late. He rushes into the building, right into the flames of the imminent explosion. Getting to my knees, I stare after him with an open mouth, debating going in after him and dragging him out, but the earth rolls beneath us as the explosions begin from the gasses caught in the plant.

Dray throws me over his shoulder and starts to run, our people following us as we wind between ferals and assailants, killing any that get too close. When we are behind the fence, he throws us behind a sand dune, and I turn with a glare.

"What the fuck—"

"You were going to go in after him and get yourself killed, soulmate," he snaps.

"I was—" Just then, a giant explosion bursts from the building. Lifting my head, I watch the mushroom cloud billow into the sky before it suddenly falls, and all the debris and air fly towards us. I bury my face in Dray's chest, and he buries his in my shoulder. The earth rolls and shakes. We can feel the flames from here, and rubble and dust cover us as we huddle behind the dune.

When it's over, the world is quiet.

I lift my head hesitantly and look around. One of our men has a pipe shard through his chest. Blood runs from his mouth and his eyes are empty—dead. But all the others seem okay, apart from a few cuts and bruises, covered in sand and dirt.

Swallowing, I get to my knees and look over the dune to the plant. Or where the plant once was. All that is left is a towering inferno. I spot ferals and half burnt bodies littering the scorched ground before it. Everyone is dead, the women inside burned... Lochlan.

I spot a body not too far away, probably thrown from the blast, so ignoring my men, I stumble to my feet, slip down the sand, and land next to him, turning him onto his back. I wince at what I find. His face is half burnt away and melting, the skin on his chest too, and one of his arms is missing. His mouth is locked open in a scream, his teeth visible, his other eye gone and melting down his blackened face. Half of his body is basically a skeleton. I can see the bones underneath the melting skin. Turning my head away, I try to control my gag.

He's dead.

A hand lands on my shoulder, comforting me, and I lean into it. I look up at Thorn as he peers down at me with a sad expression. "You couldn't save him, baby girl. You tried, but that man needed to face his demons, and in the end, he chose to give up his life to try and offer peace to those women."

Standing, I lean into his side as I stare down at Lochlan. The man wasn't a saint. He made mistakes—fuck, we all have—but he didn't deserve to die like this. It was his choice though. And in the end, he chose to die with his guilt rather than live with it.

The fire is still burning, but we have nothing to put it out with. There is nothing for it to spread to, though, so soon enough, it will die down. "Let's go home," I mutter. Turning, I spot my people spread out behind me.

They are covered in blood and wounds but victorious. We came here and completed our mission. We stopped a slave trader threatening our North, our Nations. We lost lives, and as I feel the blood drying and flaking from my body, I remember why I wanted a home.

A forever.

I'm still the Champion, but I'm also a queen, and tonight has shown me there will always be enemies, but it's not just my job to stop them anymore. My soul has enough scars and darkness, it might be time to let someone else bear the weight.

As the sun starts to rise, the brilliant rays shining across the sand, I know this is my last adventure out here. My next one involves The Ring and my men, nothing more.

It's time to hang up my swords and become the queen they need. To rule The Wastes for as long as I live.

Thorn's hand twines with mine as we watch the fire burn. Even when it goes out, the fire to make this land better, to protect people, will continue in my soul. That fire will never extinguish, even when we are gone.

Our dreams and the difference we make will live on.

Chapter Twenty-Nine

MARRY US

I'm exhausted and covered in blood, so I don't even think twice about my men's choice not to join me in the shower. We got back just after sunrise, so the heat is slowly increasing as I strip off and get into the shower. Leaning into the wall, I let it wash me clean, and when I step out, I dress with a frown... Why didn't they join me?

They take every opportunity to feel me up. Fuck, are they up to something bad?

Probably, they promised me something was happening. Ripping open the door, I narrow my eyes as I hunt for them, but they aren't in the room. Storming into the bedroom, I freeze at the material on the bed, along with a note.

I pick it up, and my mouth drops open.

Mia Alma, soulmate, angel, baby girl, sweet cheeks,

We are yours and you are ours, but we want everyone to know. You never had a family or a traditional life growing up, and we want to give you that. We want to

show everyone just how much we love you and plan to spend the rest of our lives together.
So, will you marry us...again?
If yes, wear the outfit and meet us by the tree for our wedding ceremony, Tazanna Worth.
Love,
Your Champions

I drop the note and stare at the fabric, leaning over and fingering it. I can't help but laugh as my heart soars. They want to marry me again? Do it legit this time? And the best bit? They didn't pick a dress.

No, they picked leather. Leather trousers, a corset top with buckles for knives, and a white puffy shirt underneath. There is a black lace cape that looks like it clips onto the shoulders with a pin. I can't help but stare at it—it's our symbol, my symbol...ours.

Tears fill my eyes as I stare. They planned this? They planned a wedding for me? It's never something I thought I needed, but looking at the note, I realise I do. I want to stand before everyone and vow to love them for always. I want to watch them celebrate our love.

The time for pain and hate has passed. Now, it is time for hope and love.

A knock comes at the door, and it swings open. "Okay, hot stuff, let's do this!"

I move to the other room with a bounce to see Piper. She frowns at me. "You're not dressed yet? God, they said you would need help. Don't worry, I won't look much." She winks as I just gape at her.

"What?" I ask, confused.

She props her hands on her hips and grins. "They'd never been to a wedding either. We had them all the time in Paradise, so I helped. I'm here to get you dressed and do your hair. It's a tradition as maid of honour."

"Maid of honour?" I echo, just repeating everything in shock.

She claps with a grin. "I'm so honoured you asked," she squeals, making me grin, and she drops the crazy for a moment. "They are waiting for you, my queen, are you ready to marry them...again?"

"Always." I nod, and she sniffs.

"God, that's beautiful. All right, hottie, let's cover you in leather that they will rip off of you later." She rushes to the bedroom, and I follow after her.

"Piper, what about all my people and the trade route—"

She turns with flare. "No work on your wedding day. Everyone knows, and they are all invited. Don't believe me? Look out of the window. Everyone is here from all four corners of The Wastes to see their queen get married." She steps closer and grasps my hands. "This is about more than just you. This ceremony brings them hope. Hope for a better future where marriages are normal, and so is love. Today is the start of the new beginning, and as you say 'I do,' they will know this world is more than a wasteland. It's a community, a place of happiness, even in the sand and heat."

I'm speechless as she hugs me. "You've done so much for everyone, your men wanted to do this for you. They are also possessive and think it means men and women will stop wanting you, but I've told them I will still have you in my wank bank," she assures me.

I laugh and push her away. "They want this, everyone?" I frown. "Worth, they are used to accusations and death, this? This is

something new, and they are excited to see their badass leader walk down that aisle. So let's make you look like the queen you are."

I lick my lips and nod. "Then let's do this."

"That's the spirit!" She claps. "Oh, talking of spirits, I snuck some in. It's tradition," she informs me, as she pulls a bottle from her bag and takes a swig before passing it to me. Grinning, I take a drink and watch as she starts to get everything ready.

"Piper?" I call, and she hums but carries on.

"Will you ask Nan to walk me down the aisle? And will you be with us?"

She freezes before turning her head to look at me. Her eyes are filled with tears, so I step closer. "You are my family, my sister, and Nan is family too, even if she is cranky... I wish Major was here to give me away, but I can't think of two better people."

"Yes," she whispers, and turns away with a choked laugh. "Fuck, I think it's supposed to be the bride crying on the wedding day, not me. All right, let me get her. You get dressed, and no swords, okay? Just the knives for today."

She spanks me as she passes, and when the door shuts, a wide grin covers my face as I finger the butterfly necklace around my neck. "It got better, Major, like you always said it would. I miss you today, old man, but I know you are with me, walking me down the aisle."

Dropping the necklace, I look at the clothes. "Let's do this. Let's get married," I whisper to no one, but my heart flips at the word, and a happiness like I have never known before fills me.

Last night was dark and bleak, but the sun rose, and with it, the light brought new possibilities and new happiness, if only we are strong enough to take it.

I am, and I always will be.

Because no matter how long or how bad the night seems...that sun will always rise, every day, and you are never alone. Not in this magnificent world filled with such beauty and happiness. If you remember to look for the light, you will always find it.

They are my light, and today, I will stand before my people and declare them mine.

I'm dressed, and Piper is putting on the final touches. She clips on the cape, which flows like water down my back to the floor behind me, and I realise images of crowns, swords, and my symbol are inter-woven into the material again.

They had this made for me.

The corset cinches in my waist, the knives there gleaming, and the trousers look painted on. I am wearing my usual kickass boots. I look regal, like a Viking queen. Piper also managed to tame my hair, and it hangs around my shoulders in waves, some of it plaited with what looks like jewels interwoven so it sparkles. "Kneel," she instructs, so I do, and she places the crown on my head. Standing, I look into the mirror and see me, but a better version.

A true queen ready to marry her kings.

"You were always a queen, Worth. You just look it now," she comments, like she can hear my thoughts.

"She looks too fookin' clean, rub some dirt on 'er." Nan cackles and, with a grin, I turn to her.

"Shut it, old lady, I'm all regal and shit," I retort, then I grab the bottle we are sharing and down some.

"Oh, aye, so queenly." She laughs, even as tears fill her eyes. "Ya look beautiful, lass."

"Are you crying, you old bitch?" I laugh. "No, something flew in my eye," she snaps. "Uh-huh, you're crying, admit it," I tease.

"No am fookin' not," she snarls, yanking out her gun and pointing it at me. "Say it again and I will shoot ya, understood?"

Grinning, I push the gun aside and hug her. She freezes before she melts, both of us unused to showing weakness. "Thank you for walking me down the aisle."

"We are family, kid. It should be Major, but I will do it for him. He would be so happy for you...and so am I, kid. Ya done well, am so fookin' proud," she murmurs as we embrace. "I love ya, kid. I'm honoured ta walk you to your men." She pulls back and points in my face. "Tell anyone I said that, and I will kill ya."

"Got it." I laugh before looking at Piper. "Ready if you guys are." "Then let's get this bang train moving!" she calls.

"Bang train?" I reply.

"Yeah, cho-cho, all aboard the cock train! We all know that's where this will lead to, after all," she jokes.

Rolling my eyes, I follow after her with Nan in tow.

"She ain't wrong. Fuck those boys real good for me, let ma live through ya." Nan offers with a belly laugh.

"You are both weirdos," I mutter.

As we head downstairs and outside, nerves fill me, nerves that won't stop until I see my men. The Ring is quiet and empty, which is strange as Piper leads me around back to the tree, and then she stops me there. "Okay, I go first. Are you ready? It's not too late to run away and elope with me," she teases.

"You couldn't handle me," I fire back, and she sighs.

"I know, but it was worth a shot." She stands taller. "Wedding time, let's do this." She turns and steps out.

Music starts, making my mouth drop out. It's sounds like someone is singing, but there is some form of guitar as well, and I look at Nan to confirm. "It's Jon, seems the young en likes to play."

She steps up next to me, claps my arm, and watches me. "Are you ready for the beginning of the rest of your life?"

The words are loaded, but I know she didn't mean them to be. This is the end of my old life and the start of my new life... Am I ready?

"Yes," I murmur, and together, we step out from behind the building.

Laughter starts up, and when I spot why, I begin to laugh too. Bern is skipping down the aisle in a tiny frilly dress, throwing what looks like leaves down behind him. The gathered warriors howl and shout lewd comments as I stand there with such a wide smile it feels like it might break.

Is this the happiness I deserve for a lifetime of pain? If so, it's worth it. I would take a thousand years at Ivar's hands, a thousand fights to make it to this moment. Happiness always eclipses pain if you let it.

I can't help but watch the warriors. There are so many of them, standing in rows with a gap between the two sections. There must be thousands of them, all waiting for me and my men. The music changes to something rockier, and I step forward, loving that we put our spin on a wedding. They all turn, and when they see me, every single warrior there drops to their knees.

I keep my head held high as my heart soars. We make it to the aisle, and I see my men waiting at the top with Priest behind them. Piper stands opposite them with Jon, Archel, Jago, Clay, and Evan. They are all here for me. My family. My people.

As I walk down the makeshift aisle, I feel the heat on my back as the sun warms it. But it's more than that, I can also feel Major, Vass, and Von there. All three of them are with me as I walk towards my future. They are my past, and as it clashes, I know they are here.

Proud and happy, with me always.

When I take Maxen's hand and turn to face my men with a grin, a breeze blows across my face, bringing me clean air which I take a deep breath of, and my heart settles. They are here, always, because they are in my heart. So even though they aren't here physically like I wish, I know they see me, and they are proud.

"You look beautiful," Maxen whispers. "You make me speechless," Drax murmurs. "Stunning, as always," Thorn remarks. "Like an angel," Jax adds.

"Soulmate, you look like a queen. Our queen," Dray praises.

I stand taller under their praise, as always, with their eyes on me. They surround me, and their love and support fill me until nothing else exists. I stare, unable to speak. They look beautiful, there is no other word for it.

Maxen is in his white trousers, his chest bare and hair back. He looks incredible. Drax and Jax are in matching black jeans and white shirts. Thorn has on a full suit—I honestly don't know where he got it from—but the arms are ripped off, making me grin as I check out his huge biceps. He winks when he catches me ogling him. Dray... Well, what can I say? He's in what looks like a skirt. It has a leather waistband crossing his abs and Adonis belt, with straps of leather hanging down to his knees, covering his cock. I raise my brow, and he winks. "Like it? I stole it from a museum, warriors used to wear it."

Laughing, I turn to Priest as they make a circle behind me, each of them laying a hand on me somewhere. Dray's, of course, ends up on my ass, squeezing. "I can't wait to fuck you later, wife," he murmurs as he leans in.

"Warriors, we are here today to give away our queen, to witness the union of two of our leaders and our queen's men. Today, they become one, they unite The Wastes and our hearts under their marriage. This union represents everything our queen stands for—love, acceptance, and hope for the future," Priest begins, and I smile at him as he carries on.

"Love comes in many forms, and we all know Worth would never be able to settle for just one man—"

"She would probably ride him until he was dead!" someone hollers, making us all laugh.

"Love is about acceptance, it's about patience and understanding, in any shape or form. Between two, three, four, or even ten people. Between men and women, between anyone and anything. Love is love. And today, that is what we rejoice in." He pauses.

"This world stripped us of our love, but here today, we are regaining our chance at love, we are being given an opportunity at a better life, and that all starts here with our queen. Worth, the Champion. The woman who saved The North and created The Nations you see today." He looks at me. "The world is a dark, depraved place, but you managed to find the glimpses of light between those shades of darkness, and in that light, you blossomed from a warrior to a queen, and today, you take your kings."

I swallow as he pauses before he continues. "Do you, Tazanna Worth, Queen of The Wastes, take these men to be yours, in sickness and in health, for richer or poorer, until the fires wipe us clean?"

"I do," I promise, and cheers go up.

"Maxen, Drax, Jax, Thorn, and Dray, do you take this woman to be your wife? In sickness and health, for richer or poorer, until death? Do you promise to worship her, support her, and lessen her burden of leading?"

"I do," they offer in unison.

"You know it, soulmate," Dray adds, making the crowd laugh. "Then by the power given to me by the Almighty, and in front of

the people of our lands, I declare you husbands and wife. You may kiss your men!" he announces.

A huge roar goes up, followed by stomping and yelling, as I turn to my men. I kiss them in the order in which I fell in love with them, starting with Dray. He pinches my nipple through my shirt, making me laugh as I pull away. Next, I kiss my silent demon, gripping his chin until he gasps, and then I move to his brother and kiss him hard as he grinds his cock into my belly. I turn to Thorn next, and he picks me up with his arms under my bum until our heads are level, then he flashes me a wide grin and kisses me softly.

"Forever, my love," he promises, as he sets me down and turns me to Maxen.

I gulp, and we come together, our lips seeking the each other's. Who knew when I saw four men walk into The Rim, this is where I would be today? With their rings on my finger, my brands on their skin, and saying 'I do' in front of everyone in The Wastes.

Not me, but I couldn't be happier if I tried.

Priest is right. Darkness is everywhere, and if you're not careful, it can bury you in its clinging shadows, but there are always shards of light ready to stab through it and bring you back to life, you just have to be strong enough to accept it.

To accept the love you deserve, because everyone deserves love. No matter who you are, or what you have done...or even if you think you don't. And sometimes, that love comes in a form you never knew you needed, but that's okay too.

Love is love, no matter the form, age, gender, or type.

Accept it, embrace it, and that darkness will start to retreat, and even when it tries to grow back through you, your light will be there to protect you and make you stronger when you can't fight against it yourself.

Love is selfless.

Love is strong.

Love is enduring.
Love is forever.
Love is never the end, it's the beginning.
Long live The Nations.
Long live the Berserker Queen and her kings.

Chapter Thirty

What a Queen Wants

We stay for the celebration for a bit. There is booze flowing and plenty of food and fights. I spend the night sitting on my men's laps, watching them battle and move through the crowd like the kings they are, puffed up with pride and happiness, but when Dray's eyes lock on me after a fight, I know it's time.

With a smirk, I slip from Drax's knee and turn to them with a wink. "Time to seal this marriage," I murmur. Grabbing a bottle, I drink it as I stroll towards my room. They quickly follow, making me laugh.

In one stride, I am in someone's arms. I grin as I snuggle against Thorn's chest as they rush inside, followed by catcalls. I don't care. All night, the booze has been heating my belly, but my pussy has been heating for another reason, remembering the other night when I came so close to being with all of them. I want that now. I want them on their knees, worshipping me with more orgasms than I can count.

I want to fuck every single one of my husbands. And what a queen wants, she gets.

Maxen kicks in the room's door, and I slip down Thorn's body once inside. I step back, but they all prowl towards me, their eyes dark with hunger and their hands already going to their clothes as I grin. "Your queen wants orgasms," I demand haughtily, as the door slams shut.

"Then let's not keep our queen waiting." Maxen grins. "Jax, strip our wife," he orders.

He drops to his knees, his grey eyes on mine, as he unlaces my boots. I lift one foot at a time as he yanks them off and tosses them aside. His lips drag up the arch of my foot to my trousers and up my thigh until he's kneeling before me with his mouth at my belly. His deft fingers flick open the leather, and I wiggle as he yanks them down until they, too, are stripped off. His mouth drags back down my bare legs. My head is yanked around and then lips are on me, distracting me from Jax's eyes.

Drax.

Hands join Jax's, Thorn's if I'm right, taking off the cape, my shirt, and then my panties—that was probably Dray, but my eyes are closed, and my lips are being decimated by my teasing husband. His flirting tongue touches mine before retreating, making me chase him as hands cup my heavy breasts and squeeze. Two other hands yank open my thighs for their greedy eyes, and I shiver under the sensation.

Fingers trace along my already wet pussy, and then lips follow. Another set of hands dig into my ass and massage before a spank lands on my cheeks, making me groan into Drax's mouth. He tears away, both of us panting as my body becomes lost under all the sensations. My eyes flick open and clash with Maxen's gaze as he watches me. He's naked now, his cock hard and dripping, but he's observing, waiting, making sure his queen gets what she wants, as always.

Reaching down, I grab Jax's hair and yank it until he groans, those grey eyes closing in bliss as he shivers. "Mouth," I demand.

He whimpers and pulls against my hold, making it hurt more as his lips wrap around my clit. I moan as Drax circles me, his hands squeezing my breasts as Thorn parts my pussy for Jax's hungry mouth. My head falls back to Drax's shoulder as I relinquish myself to their touches, to the sensations they create and the pleasure coursing through me. Two mouths wrap around my nipples—one nipping, one soft. The contrast has me rolling into Jax's mouth as fingers slip into my pussy, two, stretching and stroking.

Fucking me.

All the while, Maxen watches, and I can't drag my eyes away from him, even as pleasure pounds through me, even with all the hands and mouths guiding me towards that edge of my first release.

Jax bites down on my clit softly just as someone pinches my nipple between their teeth, and it sends me over the edge. I jerk and cry out, grinding down onto their tongue and fingers as it surges through me.

When the waves pass, the fingers pull free of my clinging body. "Fuck, you felt so good around them. I can't wait to feel you around my cock," Drax murmurs, making me shiver. Those were his fingers? Fuck.

"Jax," Maxen barks, and like they have planned this—which, fuck, why is that so hot?—he rolls to his back on the carpet, cock hard and standing at attention, with his grey eyes locked on me.

"Ride him, *Mi Alma*," Maxen orders.

Drax pushes me forward, and I fall to my knees and crawl up Jax's body, stopping to lick along his abs. He gasps, and his cock jerks in anticipation. He loves the torture, and so I move up his body, kissing and licking, until I reach his nipple, which I bite down on until he cries out, his hips rising desperately.

"Please!" he pleads, so I release it, happy with the teeth imprint. I sit up and place my hands on his chest. With my hips poised above his cock, I reach down and circle his length, pressing it to my pussy but waiting as I watch him. Only when those grey orbs focus on me again do I slip his cock inside of me, working myself on his length, lifting and dropping as he slides in an inch at a time.

My head falls back and hands tangle in my hair, tugging it farther back as teeth drag along my neck, making me shiver and clamp on

Jax's cock. Hands grab my hips, lifting and dropping me down until he bottoms out inside me and my skin meets his, then I pause, shivering from the full feeling as a moan leaves my lips.

"I want to fuck your ass, baby girl," Thorn growls against my skin as his chest presses to my back, his hard cock nestling between my ass cheeks as I grind and rock on Jax's cock, pushing back into Thorn's with the same movement.

"Fuck yes," I groan, rocking harder, grinding my clit into him. Thorn pushes me forward until my face meets Jax's chest, and then my ass is parted. His fingers glide down between my cheeks to my pussy, dipping inside at the same time as Jax's cock. The feeling has me crying out as I push back fervently.

Jax slips free of my pussy, and suddenly Thorn's cock is there, slamming into me. Jax's arms wrap around me, holding me still as Thorn pummels into my wet pussy, again and again, until I'm almost screaming and pushing back to meet his thrusts. But as suddenly as he started, his cock pulls free, leaving me empty and desperate. Jax kisses me, and then his cock is there again, and we work to get him back inside me.

I rub and grind as he thrusts into me, but he stills a moment later as another wet cock presses against my ass. I relax, used to this by now, and Thorn kisses my back softly.

"That's it, *Mi Alma*, relax for your husbands. Let us take care of you," Maxen calls, and I shiver as Thorn pushes inside me slightly before retreating, pushing back in again past that ring of muscles.

It's slow going. I push back, and he thrusts in until, finally, his giant cock is in my ass. Then we all still, panting as I am held between them, feeling so full I might explode. My ass and pussy are deliciously stretched until I can't take it anymore. I need to move, so I do.

"Fuck, that's so hot," Drax remarks from somewhere next to us.

We start to move in sync, with Thorn pushing into my ass as Jax pulls out, riding the edge of pain. The feel of the friction on my nipples has me helpless between them, letting them fuck me however they want as I chase the pleasure winding through me.

They speed up though, until both are hammering into me so fast, I can barely catch my breath, and each thrust pushes me higher...and higher, until I can barely take it anymore. I need to come so badly. I'm so close, so fucking close.

I turn my head and blindly reach out, seeking, and suddenly, Drax is there with his hand in my hair. "Mouth open, baby girl. Let me fuck that sweet little hole."

My hair is twisted painfully, and tears fill my eyes. "Uh-uh, no crying unless it's from gagging," he teases, as the head of his cock presses against my mouth. I eagerly suck him all the way down until he grunts. I feel so full, it's unreal. I can't think or talk, only feel. Thorn fucks my ass and pushes me onto Jax's cock, and Drax moves in unison as he slams into my mouth hard and fast. All our desires tumble together until we are one big slick, desire-filled mess.

Fingers tweak my clit, and I cry out around Drax's cock. "Come, baby girl, let me feel it around my cock as I fill your ass," Thorn snarls.

Drax bottoms out with a yell, and I plunge over the edge again, coming around their cocks. Jax yells, fighting it, but I feel his release spurt inside me while Thorn fills my ass with a grunt. Drax slams into my mouth once more and unloads down my throat.

Drax pulls free of my mouth as I shiver and shake between them from the force of my ongoing orgasm. I lick away my drool as I try to breathe. When I finally calm down, Thorn kisses my shoulder and slowly pulls from my sore ass. Hands lift me from Jax's cock as I stumble, my legs unable to hold me up.

I am turned to see my other men.

Only two of my husbands are left—Dray and Maxen.

I feel the shared cum dribble from me, but the dirty feeling only makes me grunt in pleasure, knowing it's from my husbands. Maxen grins as Dray prowls around me, and they work together to tease me. Fingers flick, touch, and tease as I stand there.

"I don't know about you, big man, but I want that sweet pussy so I can see her when she drives her knives into my heart," Dray murmurs.

Maxen laughs and runs his eyes down me. "That's fine, I want her tight little ass anyway. I like feeling her fighting beneath me."

Sands below.

"You heard him, soulmate. Are you going to fight for your husbands, or are you tired?" Dray mocks, smacking my ass as he circles me. I grab a knife from the holster at his chest and press it to his throat, making him groan as he stills, those cold eyes melting as I smirk.

"Tired?" I snarl. "You will be when I'm done with you. On your back, husband," I demand.

"Was that an order, soulmate? It felt like a plea," he teases, pressing into the knife until it cuts his throat and blood slowly drips down to his chest. I watch the trail with a moan trapped in my throat. Pulling the knife away, I trace it down the side of the blood trail, dragging it across his skin hard enough to break it. He moans, pressing closer.

"Yes, harder, soulmate, rip me open. Use me, kill me, do whatever the fuck you want to me, just don't stop," he growls.

I sweep my leg out, knocking him back when he's distracted, and he falls to the floor with a thump. I'm on him in a moment, slicing across his chest with shallow cuts as he groans. He slams me down onto his cock and starts to fuck me. Moaning, I use my knees to drop myself down and meet his hard thrusts as I continue to slice and stab, the crimson of his blood decorating his chest. I lose control in a way only Dray can make me.

I feel the others watching me, but everything but Dray fades and the bliss as the knife cuts open his skin. He laughs, urging me on as he fucks me.

I stab and slash like a possessed woman. Blood flies everywhere as Dray laughs and moans beneath me, his cock still filling me, even as I kill him. Our bloodlusts combine until I can't stop, until we are exploding in a deadly mess.

But then Maxen is there to stop me. Fabric wraps around my throat, yanking me back as he slams into my ass. He keeps me there, pulled back as he fucks me, pushing me down onto Dray's cock as he moans beneath me. Blood flows freely from his wounds. Maxen restrains me like a wild animal—the belt, I realise, tightens around my throat like a collar as he owns me.

My air is cut off, and it allows me to relax as they take over. Blood covers my chest and back as we fuck like animals. Dray growls, his fingers cutting into my skin as he drags his own knife down between the valley of my breasts, slicing slightly, spilling my blood until ours is joined.

"Soulmate," he groans. "Fuck, you feel too good—watching you bleed on me, watching you wild."

"Fuck, *Mi Alma*," Maxen breathes.

The belt pulls tighter, keeping me on the edge of too much and just enough as they use my body. As they force pleasure through me and take away the need for blood.

Until it all becomes too much.

With a silent gasping yell, I come and they follow. Dray snarls and writhes like a wild animal as he pumps inside me before stilling. Maxen slams as deep as he can get and fills my ass with his cum as I collapse forward, and he loosens the belt until I can breathe.

"Sands below," I gasp.

We all start to laugh, happy wedding night to me—and this is only just the start.

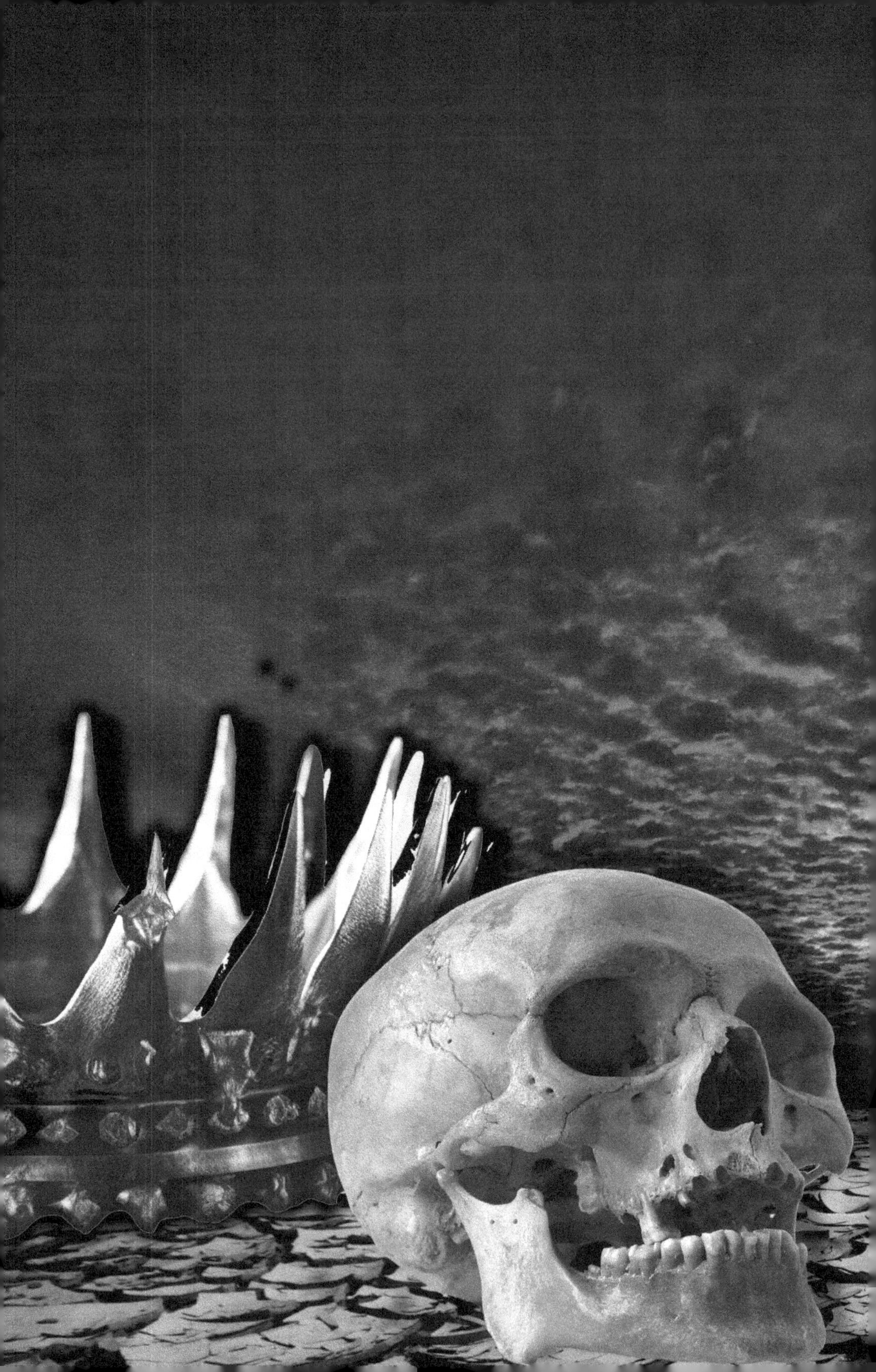

Chapter Thirty-One

The Damned

The next day, my pussy and ass are sore, but in the best way. I have no time to relax as a married woman, however, since I have meetings all day—writing and signing the laws of The Nations, sorting trade routes, and doing everything else that comes with starting from the ground up.

I'm seated in the meeting room the entire day. After signing the laws, Jon shows me the map of trade routes he has worked out, and after a few tweaks, we have something to start with. Obviously, it will get changed as we figure out what works and what does not, but it's all a good beginning. Later that evening, the leaders head back home to tell their people.

Everything is now sorted, and it is time to live in The Nations. Piper is leaving tomorrow, so I have to sort things for that, but I want to check in on Clarissa first. A queen's work is never done. My people have already started to build huts and extra accommodations. I see some of the women helping, and others are around the back of the old ape enclosure, starting to prepare the soil for planting, but I can't find Clarissa.

I search The Ring, and I am just about to give up when I hear a grunt from behind an old food stall. Frowning, I draw my sword and circle around, only for my mouth to drop open as I try to hold back a giggle.

I found Clarissa. She is being fucked against the stall as Bern powers between her legs. Turning away, I hear her yell, and then they fumble while I laugh harder. "Worth," she greets breathlessly.

"Don't mind me, find me when you're finished," I reply and walk away. I hear her mutter something, and he laughs.

Good for them. Glad Bern is finally getting some action.

Not five minutes later, Clarissa turns up, red-faced, and warns me not to say anything. We walk together through The Ring as the sun starts to set. "How are you fitting in?"

"Good. I think they like it here." She turns to me. "Plus, it helps that you are here to keep the men in line. They are all so scared of angering you that they are treating us all like queens."

I laugh. "Good, as they should... So, Bern?" I can't help but ask.

She sighs. "I guess I forgot myself for a moment. He's determined to win me over."

"And he won't?" I question, stopping. "Look, you're older than me. I know that, but I have lived a lot in this life. Let me give you some advice. Don't say no because you are scared of being hurt again, that isn't living, not really. You have a second chance here, embrace it. You might just find the happiness you have been seeking all along. No, that doesn't have to be with a man, but don't run scared...you will regret it in the end. I ran for so long." I look into the distance, where I see Maxen and Thorn teaching some of the women self-defence. I know a soft smile curls my lips. "They chased me, and I am so glad they did. They are my life, Clarissa, but more than that, they are my happiness. When the world gets hard, they are my rocks. For so long I was alone, and until them, I never realised just how hard that was to shoulder."

She nods and looks at them as well. "You are very lucky."

"I am, and I will never forget that for the rest of my life," I vow.

"So, this is it, the beginning of the real North?" she comments, and looks back at me. "I can't wait to see what it becomes."

"Neither can I, but we will do it together. It's a new day, Clarissa, anything is possible." We turn as one and walk.

It's a new day. The sun is shining brightly down on me, and I'm up early. My men at my side as we ready for Piper to leave. She is standing next to her bike with her people, but she sees me waiting and comes over. I step forward, and without a word, I embrace her. She doesn't even grab my ass, which makes me smile as I pull back.

"Be careful out there. Trust no one but your men and come back to us, General. That's an order," I demand.

"Yes, my queen." She grins.

Stepping back, I look to Evan. "Take care of her for me, Doc. I'll try not to hurt myself before you get back."

He grins and hugs me too. "I'll bring back extra supplies just for you," he teases, before walking over to join her other men. My men step back too, giving us queens some space to say goodbye. It's not forever, but a feeling fills me then. Piper will always be a creature of the sand—out in The Wastes, off on adventures.

"I have a present for you," I tell her. "It's a token for my general, wear it with pride."

I grab the jacket from Maxen and hand it to her. She frowns as she shakes it out and then gasps. It's a leather jacket to protect her on the sand, but on the back is her very own symbol and a name for her men.

The Damned.

It's stitched boldly, jaggedly, under a skull with a bolt coming from its mouth and roses for eyes. It's for her, for all of them. "When you get back, we will have one for each of your men."

"Worth," she whispers and looks up at me, swallowing, "this is so much better than pied piper."

I laugh. "You know it. You damn those souls who betray us. Now get going, General. It's time to turn the sands red." She slips on the jacket, and it fits perfectly. Her goggles are pulled down, and she winks at me.

"Thank you, Worth. I will wear it with honour." She turns to leave, both of us not good at goodbyes, even if it's just for now. She will be back, I know that. Piper is a fighter, nothing will kill her.

"Piper?" I call as she turns away, goggles down, jacket in place. "Yeah, hot stuff?" she replies.

"Fight like the champion you are," I tell her.

She nods and turns away, climbing on her bike, and whistles to her men. "Let's go, Damned... How badass does that sound?" She laughs, and their bikes rev as they pull away, sand spraying behind them.

I watch her go with a smile on my face, knowing her story is still not finished yet. She has a whole life in front of her, and with her men at her side, I know it will be a happy one. She doesn't need to find a place like me to be at home, she is at home with them, out there in the sand.

My heart fills with gratitude for the life I have carved from blood and death here in the sand. My childhood was filled with stories of heroes and villains, and I've done things as an adult I didn't know I was capable of as a child. I don't know if I'm a hero, but I'm definitely not a villain. After all, this is real life, not a story, and sometimes it's enough just to survive, and maybe, just maybe on the way, you will meet people who will change your life for bad or good.

Sometimes, the villain is just a bad guy with no reason or depressing background.

Sometimes, the man in the background is the one who truly loves you like a father should.

Sometimes, the old ladies fall in love, and the ones who fight with you teach you lessons of sacrifice and friendship.

Sometimes, the men you meet help put you back together again, and sometimes, they just love all those broken pieces of you.

Out here in The Wastes, survival isn't guaranteed. You have to live everyday like it's your last, and love those who live it with you. I will do that for the rest of my life, because I'm still learning, still growing, and out here in the sand?

This is where I belong, this is where my end will be, and that's okay.

Everything must end eventually, but from these endings come new beginnings, new life.

We will always survive, it is the human condition to persevere. Our world, our Nations are stronger than ever, and as I look upon the horizon with my men at my back, I am home.

I belong.

I am loved.

I am part of a family.

Live or die, we do it together. Whatever the future holds.

Maxen takes my hand, and Dray takes the other. Drax holds onto a shoulder, Jax clutches the opposite one, and Thorn presses to my side. All my men are with me as I watch our future ride out into the sand. They all feel it too—the happiness at finally finishing our mission, our adventure, and our purpose in life.

"I hope she finds her future out there," I murmur. "She will. We did," Thorn offers.

"We found you, soulmate," Dray murmurs, and Drax and Jax squeeze in agreement as Maxen turns to me.

"Who knew when we came to The North we would fall in love with our very own champion?" Maxen murmurs

Their champion. It has a ring to it.

EPILOGUE

Four Months later

Life in The Wastes is good. We have Summits every month with the other leaders, and what started out rough is now a full- fledged nation. The Cities deal with us often, our trade routes are always open to them. We have grown, we have killed, we have healed.

Just like me.

Clarissa and I walk every night, talking over the day's problems and our emotions. She is quickly becoming very dear to me. When Piper is here, she joins us too—three queens ready to face battle every day, who let our guards down around each other.

I strangely miss Piper, but I have never been prouder. She is an incredible general out on the road, damning those souls who try to stop our world.

I have never been so happy, my heart overflows with it. We have had some issues with some not wanting to listen to the laws, but most seem to be embracing them with open arms. It seems everybody was ready for The Nations.

I don't know what the future holds, but I know with my men behind me, I can tackle anything that is to come. A queen is nothing without her kings, after all.

Fingering my butterfly necklace, I stare at the tree as I bid my family there goodbye and go to join my people for tonight's celebration. When I get there, my men are waiting, all laughing and drinking. I slip onto Maxen's lap, and he wraps his arm around me, kissing me solidly in greeting, and it feels like coming home.

"Later, soulmate, I want you to try that new collar out on me," Dray murmurs, making me wiggle with a grin.

"Hey, that's mine," Jax protests, nudging Dray, which ends up with them play fighting.

"Uh-uh, ignore them, sweet cheeks, you can collar me anytime," Drax offers with a kiss.

"You are all animals. She will clearly be with me tonight, won't you, baby girl?" Thorn asks, his teeth shining in a panty wetting smile.

"I think you forget she is on my lap. She's mine, isn't that right, *Mi Alma?*"

"I'm all of yours, and you are mine," I reply, which settles all the arguments and lets us relax and watch the people gathered here.

As I look around at the warriors, warriors from all four corners of The Wastes, I relax with my own smile. We started as enemies, everyone was out for themselves, but now, we are one. A community.

A new world.

A new North.

The Nations

This might be the end of my story, but I will always be here, leading, and ready to protect my lands and people...and my men. Together, we will stand in the sun's rays that shine down on this new world with the sand under our feet, and we will stand tall.

Together.

Berserker, slave, champion, queen, wife. I am all and so much more.

The Nations

I am Tazanna Worth, and this is my story. This is my end.

255

The Nations' Laws

NO EATING PEOPLE
NO RAPING
YOU KEEP WHAT YOU KILL
NO SLAVERY
NO TORTURE
DON'T LIKE IT?
GET THE FUCK OUT OF THE NORTH.

**THE QUEEN OF THE WASTELAND,
TAZANNA WORTH**

About K.A. Knight

K.A Knight is an USA Today bestselling indie author trying to get all of the stories and characters out of her head, writing the monsters that you love to hate. She loves reading and devours every book she can get her hands on, and she also has a worrying caffeine addiction.

She leads her double life in a sleepy English town, where she spends her days writing like a crazy person.

Read more at K.A Knight's website or join her Facebook Reader Group.
Sign up for exclusive content and my newsletter here
http://eepurl.com/drLLoj

Also by K.A. Knight

THEIR CHAMPION SERIES *Dystopian RH*

The Wasteland

The Summit

The Cities

The Nations

Their Champion Coloring Book

Their Champion - the omnibus

The Forgotten

The Lost

The Damned

Their Champion Companion - the omnibus

DAWNBREAKER SERIES *SCI FI RH*

Voyage to Ayama

Dreaming of Ayama

THE LOST COVEN SERIES *PNR RH*

Aurora's Coven

Aurora's Betrayal

HER MONSTERS SERIES *PNR RH*

Rage

Hate

Book 3 *coming soon..*

Monstrous Ends

DEN OF VIPERS UNIVERSE STANDALONES

Scarlett Limerence *CONTEMPORARY*

Nadia's Salvation *CONTEMPORARY*

Alena's Revenge *CONTEMPORARY*

Den of Vipers *CONTEMPORARY RH*

Gangsters and Guns (Co-Write with Loxley Savage) *CONTEMPORARY RH*

STANDALONES

The Standby *CONTEMPORARY*

Diver's Heart *CONTEMPORARY RH*

Crown of Stars *SCI FI RH*

AUDIOBOOKS

The Wasteland

The Summit

Rage

Hate

Den of Vipers (*From Podium Audio*)

Gangsters and Guns (*From Podium Audio*)

Daddy's Angel (*From Podium Audio*)

Stepbrothers' Darling (*From Podium Audio*)

Blade of Iris (*From Podium Audio*)

Deadly Affair (*From Podium Audio*)

Deadly Match (*From Podium Audio*)

Deadly Encounter (*From Podium Audio*)

Stolen Trophy (*From Podium Audio*)

Crown of Stars (*From Podium Audio*)

Monstrous Lies (*From Podium Audio*)

Monstrous Truth (*From Podium Audio*)

Monstrous Ends (*From Podium Audio*)

Court of Nightmares (*From Podium Audio*)

Unstoppable (*From Podium Audio*)

Unbreakable (*From Podium Audio*)

Fractured Shadows (*From Podium Audio*)

SHARED WORLD PROJECTS

Blade of Iris - Mafia Wars *CONTEMPORARY RH*

CO-AUTHOR PROJECTS - *Erin O'Kane*

HER FREAKS SERIES *PNR Dystopian RH*

Circus Save Me

Taming The Ringmaster

Walking the Tightrope

Her Freaks Series - the omnibus

STANDALONES

The Hero Complex *PNR RH*

Dark Temptations *Collection of Short Stories, ft. One Night Only & Circus Saves Christmas*

THE WILD BOYS SERIES *CONTEMPORARY RH*

The Wild Interview

The Wild Tour

The Wild Finale

The Wild Boys - the omnibus

Find an error?

Please email the below information to thenuttyformatter1@gmail.com:

- *the author name*
- *title of the book*
- *screenshot of the error*
- *suggested correction*

www.ingramcontent.com/pod-product-compliance
Lightning Source LLC
Chambersburg PA
CBHW051117300726
48981CB00002B/162